THE COALBEARER'S HOME

ALKA SINGH

Leadstart
INKSTATE

ISBN 978-93-90040-59-9

First published in India 2021 by Leadstart Inkstate
A Division of One Point Six Technologies Pvt Ltd

Sales Office:
Unit No.25/26, Building No.A/1,
Near Wadala RTO,
Wadala (East), Mumbai – 400037 India
Phone: +91 969933000
Email: info@leadstartcorp.com
www.leadstartcorp.com

Disclaimer: The views expressed in this book are those of the Author and do not pertain to be held by the Publisher.

Editor: Mannat Lumba
Cover: Ami Parekh
Layouts: Ashwini Jadhav

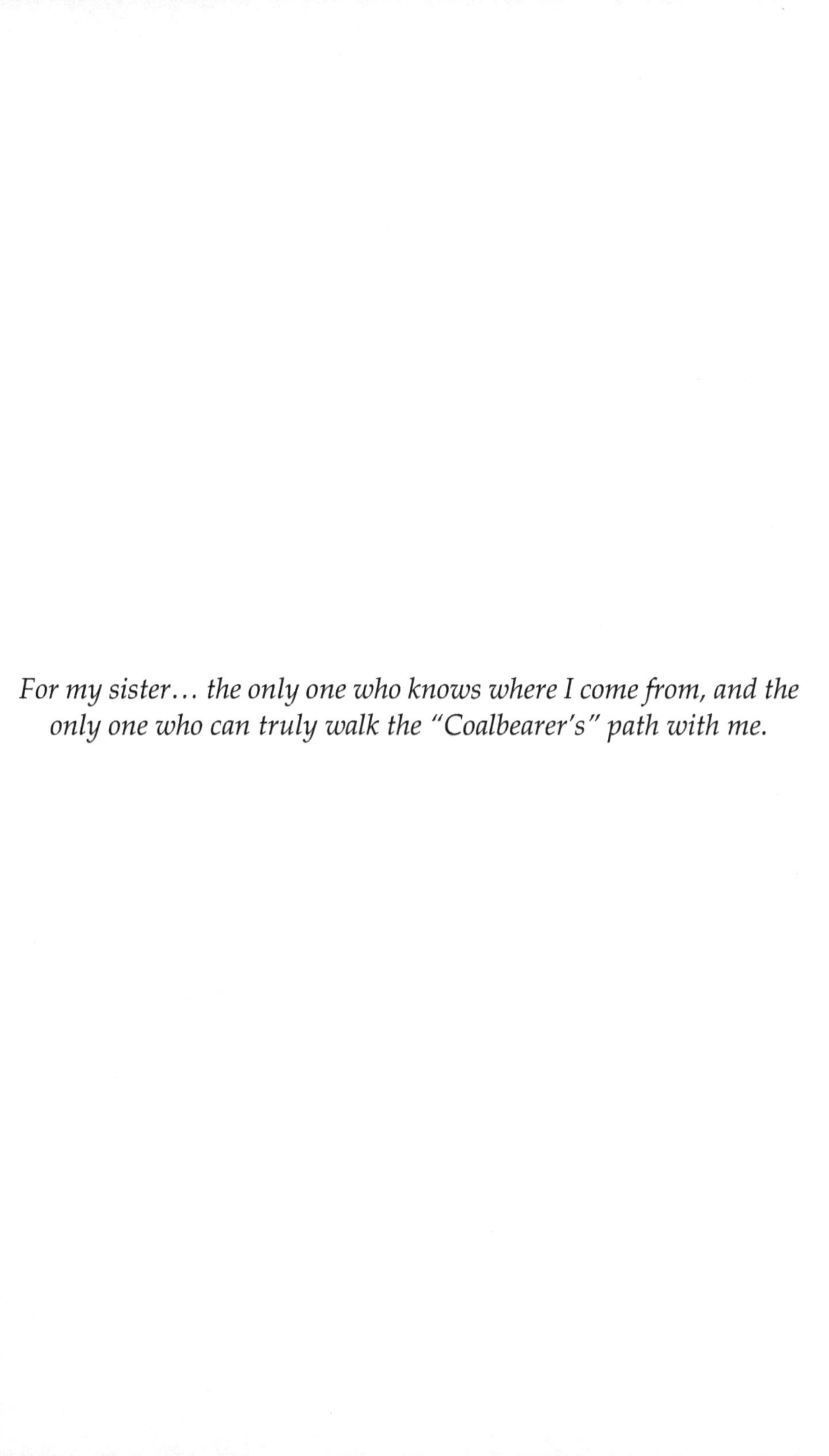

For my sister… the only one who knows where I come from, and the only one who can truly walk the "Coalbearer's" path with me.

About the Author

ALKA SINGH is an aspiring writer. She has penned a collection of poems titled 'Hushed Hues' (Creative Publishers, Mumbai) and a collection of short stories titled 'Beyond Contours' (Notion Press). Alka seeks pleasure in exploring the beauty of quaint, remote and unknown worlds through her writing.

After spending a decade in the corporate world in print and web media, Alka gave it all up to pursue her passion for writing fiction.

Alka is a post graduate in Zoology and has earned an MBA from NMIMS. She lives in Mumbai with her husband and son.

About the Book

I've come to realize that the soil of the place where you grow up runs through your blood. No matter how far you move away and discover beauty in the new, you tend to come back to the soil that nurtured you for nourishment. It's a locus one cannot deny.

I spent all my life in Darjeeling. I say 'all my life' because the years after those first 20 years of my life, post which I moved out, is mere routine. I still go back in time and travel in thoughts to breathe in the mountain air to live. This book is simply proof. The characters are imaginary and so is the story but not a single emotion that runs through it is imaginary, especially the connect with the hill earth and skies. I have witnessed every event marked in history in the book and it never left me. The struggle and turmoil, the desire to belong, the fear, the gloom, the agony, the losses…I have participated in it all. I was a child then, a being without views that I could choose to assert myself. I could not understand political affinities and social stances much but my tender pores allowed the encircling emotions to deeply seep in organically. My heart was shattered when I saw houses burning, when I heard a neighbor crying for her dead or absconding son, when I knew of a friend who could not come to school for the fear of being killed…the list is endless, each still burning in my memory. For me, it is still a human story filled with sorrow carefully wrapped in delicate hope. I could even categorize this book as a memoir…not of facts but of the cumulative emotions of a date in time.

As a storyteller, it has been difficult to be objective about it at times but I hope the story is accepted with warmth and understanding. My sincere intention is to tell it as I have felt it. Years may have passed on but there are many still carrying crater-like voids in their hearts having known nothing but loss all through. This story is a compassionate gesture of standing in solidarity with those unknown souls. I choose to acknowledge them through "The Coalbearer's Home."

Acknowledgements

The coordinates of your life define you in interesting ways. This book wouldn't have been a part of me or the world if I wouldn't have been born in a certain place at a certain time. I wouldn't have felt even half the empathy and compassion if I hadn't witnessed what I did in this span of my life. I wouldn't have written anything if I wouldn't have found joy in storytelling. Therefore, I have much to thank the Universe for placing me where it did.

I extend my deep gratitude to my publisher, the Leadstart team, for having faith in my story and acting as its interface with the world. Thank you so much.

Being a writer is one thing, I was always one. However, becoming a writer is another and I was never ambitious enough. I never thought my habit of scribbling just anything was worthy of print. I will ever remain indebted to my husband for believing in my ink and showing me new horizons.

I feel immense gratitude towards my family and friends who appreciate and encourage all that I write. I count you in my prayers always.

CHAPTER 1

Mani was officially the youngest charcoal porter in the hill-town and hence, had his own share of stardom. At 12 years of age, he was only as tall as the 4.5 ft door frame of the charcoal storage (godown) where he was employed. He was swift in his delivery, no matter how far the destination; his little legs huddling up and down the slopes with the enthusiasm of childhood-almost defying the strength of muscles required for such labour.

Mani, however, was not born with this predicament; although, one look at him and one could be deceived by the notion that he was born breathing coal. He wore an oversized tweed jacket and trousers with hardly any remains of their original colour. His cheeks sometimes showed true colours, given away by sweat on some warm days of the year, but his brows were always loaded with black dust. He grinned while he jabbered and swung his head in gaiety, unperturbed by the jute support of the cane carrier, which remained hanging on his head all day long.

The charcoal dealer paid him a paltry amount but made it up with a meal and shelter, allowing him to sleep inside the storage on the coal dumps. Every night, when Mani spread his bedding, he missed home terribly in spite of his tired limbs. His thoughts wandered away to a pretty yellow cottage where he lived with his parents and a baby sister…the chrysanthemums his mother tended to, the butterflies, beetles and ladybirds that kept vying for his attention, the black Tibetian terrier they had for a pet…it all seemed like a far-away dream. Refusing to let in any other thought, he consciously reminisced lying beside his mother, his face huddled between her neck and her bosom, the warmth of her red knit blouse lulling him to sleep…and he felt he was home, peacefully asleep.

It was a Thursday morning. Kishan, the errand boy at the tea and snacks stall opposite the storage had kicked Mani's door once. It was an arrangement…Kishan would slip in a cup of tea every morning through the ventilator. Mani would pay him Rs. 5 a month in return. Another bang on the ventilator window and Mani was wide-awake. A second chance lost and he would miss his tea. As Mani came closer, Kishan jutted his face inside.

"Here you are, you sack of coal…why can't you just get up in one knock…," Kishan muttered in disgust. After all, it was a secret practice…and he would lose his job the day it would come out in the open.

"Hmm…" Mani grunted.

After the tea, Mani went back to sleep again as his employer would not turn up before 9. It was a Thursday and shops remained closed. The dealer came only to release Mani from the den…and lock him in at night.

It was yet to be 9, and Mani marched up and down the small space to control his bursting bladder. He cursed the dealer with clenched teeth, muttered expletives that he had recently learnt from Kishan.

"*Sala…harami…*" Mani muttered hesitantly at first…but with greater aplomb after every round. It somehow distracted him from his bladder for some time.

Just then, he heard a lock being keyed in and sighed with relief…

feeling suddenly guilty about the cussing. The door opened and out rushed Mani to relieve himself, not even acknowledging the dealer or bothering to say a word.

The dealer always wore a bewildered look. Dark and thin, he was shrewd as a Fox; a canine out to accentuate his character…the Fox 's accessory.

"*Ae* Mani…*ae* Mani…" he screamed, but his shrill effeminate voice did not carry him too far, so he shook his head in surrender and sat down to work at the desk placed near the small entrance.

The dealer, Ram Sahay Jaiswal, was what the locals referred to as one of the '*Madhesiyas*'. The name, originally used as a reference for traders coming in from Central India, now bore a derogatory tone… such that even *Madhesiyas* took it as a personal attack if used aloud. As happens with the organic growth of civilization and communities, there is always a territorial instinct where the original community creates a hostile barrier for other communities trickling in. Dogs exhibit this tendency explicitly whereas human tendencies emerge more complex and subtle…the perils of human beings ascending to the summit of being human. Knowingness is always more twisted. And the irony of survival was such that *Madhesiyas,* so plagued by the taint, absorbed all local mannerisms and tried their best to blend in, the only giveaway being their dark skin and at times, the sharpness of their features. Some even felt pride in remaining rootless, basking in the fragile breeziness of rootless leaves…realizing little that you had to have your own roots even to borrow nourishment from other soils… or a small tear was enough to wipe you out. Ram Sahay was one such being.

Nevertheless, his Fox like features, his wheatish complexion, his appallingly "*Madhesiya*" accent, nothing dissuaded him from portraying himself as a local. He was probably under the impression that he gained customers in this pretext, but the truth was in the charcoal; his horrendous accent did account for some flocking, for it was more often free entertainment. At times, he stooped to so much muttering '*hajur…hajur*' that some customers felt they had been paid obeisance, and hence bought the charcoal in self-pride. In the most hideous ways, the Fox 's strategies worked and he was unassumingly one of the most successful in the row of charcoal dealers along the street.

In a while, Mani came back, fresh-faced, ready to be ordered around.

"*Hajur*…?" he whispered.

"Go get me some tea from Phulchand," Ram Sahay said.

Mani gleefully ran across and shouted out to Kishan, "Kishan, one tea for *Kaka*."

He loitered around the shop, especially around the huge oil pan in which gram-flour onion fritters were being fried.

"Here you are," screamed Kishan from one corner of the shop, holding out the tea in a medium-sized glass. Mani rushed to get it from him and Kishan shoved in two *pakodas* in Mani's tweed jacket as soon as he stood close enough. Mani chuckled with delight. Thursday could never get any better and Mani felt joyful.

Kishan always felt protective about Mani. He was a typical case showing unreasonable contempt for Ram Sahay because of the familiarity they shared, which transformed into pity for Mani. Kishan was also a *Madhesiya* from Ram Sahay's remote village from Bihar. He could interpret the Fox 's moves better, and almost detested Ram Sahay and his family of traders back home. Kishan's father was a landless farmer, oppressed and pushed around by the haughty Sahays, scheming for the pettiest of gains. Kishan, having seen the plight of his father, drew parallels and imagined Ram Sahay tearing off Mani's flesh bit by bit…and hence had grown protective about Mani.

CHAPTER 2

Thursday was an eventful day for both Mani and Kishan. It meant casting off coal and oil, respectively, to recognize their true selves again. It was the day of bath for both. Both had an unspoken hurriedness in the way they went about their work. They kept glancing at each other across the street as they went about running errands for their respective employers. The excitement kept building up till noon… and the adrenaline rush in the last hour was inexplicable. It meant the release of chains and the revival of childhood…even if just for a few hours. Ram Sahay locked his godown at noon and instructed Mani to be back in time. Mani paced up and down the slope, sat against the door of the godown and exchanged pleasantries with people walking past.

At around quarter to one, Mani could barely contain the uncontrollable uprising within him and shouted out in a voice, unusually shrill with excitement.

"*Aaaeee* Kishan…are you done??"

Kishan's employer, a man barely into his thirties, looked up from the counter and then smiled to himself. He probably understood childhood. He looked at Kishan and jerked his head, gesturing at him to leave.

In barely two minutes, Kishan and Mani scampered up the slope, held their hands up and laughed loudly…as if embracing the blue skies above. The sweet and lingering taste of freedom, and the amazing rush of blood it brings to all the cells of one's being in the form of joy, is probably felt the most after a spell of confinement. Light definitely shines brighter after running through darkness, and is irrelevant without the other.

Kishan and Mani indulged in the leisure of strolling, hands across each other's backs, headed to the backyard of an old bungalow at the other end of the market, away from the hustle of downtown crowded with coal godowns, sooty eateries, swampy smelly vegetable and fish markets, meat stands soaked in blood, granaries monopolized by the *Madhesiyas*…all things that appeared submerged in a layer of muck and dust but essential…like the spokes of a wheel in the cycle of life. Survival was not necessarily inviting, one needed to feel the vibrance of life beyond this muck. And to add to the wonder of this chaos…an old ropeway built by the British hung across like a colossal landmark as the clumsiest yet the most efficient mode of transportation to the Jail. Well! Perhaps it was the most important structure after roads and rails on which dreams of colonization were established.

The boys wandered through the colour burst of the market place. The clothes on display distracted them…Kishan especially, a conscious teenager, swallowed desires and drooling temptations, imagining himself in various outfits. He suddenly broke free of Mani and jumped over to a stall selling shorts for boys…probably to be worn for a game of football, for most of them displayed a screaming slash of fluorescent delight, ranging from neon, orange, to an atrocious pink, the kind a man required real galls to wear, and here was one…a wannabe… mesmerized by it all. The haggling began, as was the tradition of the flea market.

"No, 150…"

"75…that's the actual cost."

The spectrum was set.

"Not a penny less."

"But you can get it for half anywhere!"

"Please get for me too, sir, if you find it."

"Ok…but why can't you come down a bit…I wonder if you want to sell it at all."

Finally, the negotiation came to a halt…and Kishan became the proud possessor of the coveted fluorescence. His excitement doubled at the thought of wearing it.

There at last…the bungalow stood. They walked towards the backyard fence…their Thursday ground of bath and celebration. There was no stone laid down for this ritual…but yes, necessity, and of course, serendipity by the name of Bansi, the link to this bungalow. Bansi was Kishan's cousin who worked as a gardener at the bungalow… and therefore, coincidently, also had access to a continuous supply of water.

On reaching, Kishan and Mani hissed and whistled a familiar tune, probably the gate code, but no one arrived to take them in. Mani then softly called out "*Ae* Bansi…"

Kishan too cupped his mouth with his hands and called out softly, "Bansi…*oye* Bansi…"

Bansi came running, his wide grin displaying the most disorganized set of teeth one can ever imagine. A lanky fellow, Bansi was just a year older than, Kishan but far taller.

Kishan and Bansi had been perched upon this far-away hill-town in an exodus that took place two years back. Stormed by the flood-fury of the Kosi River originating from Nepal during the monsoons, their sinking village in North Bihar had brought them so far. The will to survive combined with the fear of the flood, was such that they took to fleeing to a height where no water would reach. But life follows its own route impervious to the need of human insurance…so they remained stuck up in various landslides till they finally reached the top of the hill.

Many a time, when Kishan and Bansi bragged about the stretch of water they swam through…the nights in water, their churning stomachs and muscles, the snakes and floating bodies, the undying hopes…and the great escape, Mani maintained a stoic silence for he had encountered it all too fast. The fire of his misfortune still burnt insidiously, for he somehow never escaped it with the ashes. The loss remained in him like a dull un-subsiding pain.

Two years back, some *Madhesiyas* had got together to help some of their brethren, the flood refugees, and hence Kishan and Bansi had found places of shelter in the sweet shop and bungalow, respectively.

The bungalow was a double-storeyed house with large windows all around it. Wild grass grew all over the place except the entrance, which had a small stretch developed into a garden by Bansi. Bansi was in love with the Orchids, which he had not seen back home, and thus tended to passionately. He had grown exotic ones- pale white and indigo- and considered them his pride.

Located in a secluded corner at the end of the market place, the bungalow, like all deserted lonely bungalows, also had a story engraved in its walls. The owner, a recluse, had nothing more to him than his inheritance. Khagendra Bahadur Pradhan was the sole inheritor of a business of sal and pinewood, which he had done nothing to further. There was a time when his grandfather and father monopolized the market, but that was then. In the present times, the market was littered with wood smugglers, most of them once employees of the Pradhans, small-time sellers and opportunists who wanted to encash on this prime business at the bleeding feet of the crestfallen giants of the business, the Pradhans. The grandeur of the Pradhans was like the kind of wood sold nowadays…polished on the outside but termite-stricken and hollow inside. There were times when one saw a sane KP (as Khagendra was referred to in town) walking down the streets. People left way for him, and remained stilled by the aura of mystery he carried with him. Other days he remained drowned in alcohol, living unperturbed by the circadian rhythm. Bansi had even spotted him brushing his teeth at 10 in the night, a ruckus following thereafter. Reportedly, he was disgusted with the kind of breakfast served to him. The three boys had had a good laugh when Bansi related this incident to Kishan and Mani.

The midday sun was soothing. Mani and Kishan peeled off their layers of clothing and hugged each other in reflex as the chill touched their bare bodies.

"*Aaachoochoo*," Mani screamed in excitement.

The backyard had a tap to which a long rubber pipe was attached to water the plants. Kishan took the pipe off, unwrapped a bar of detergent soap and got down to washing his clothes. Mani took the cue and sat down to do the same. Both sang together as they washed off stubborn dirt from their clothes. After some time, they finished scrubbing and bathing and wore fresh crisp clothes that they had washed last Thursday. Kishan wore his fluorescent glory and both felt as if they were given a new life.

Mani was standing in the sun, basking in its warmth. The entire view of the bungalow was visible from there. He glanced all around and lost himself in thought. However, he started feeling uneasy and looked all around…he somehow felt he was being watched and his stomach churned…for far beyond, at the window at the right end of the bungalow, a pair of eyes were set on him…those eyes that he had avoided sometimes in the market…bloodshot, intense with loose skin-bags around…KP's eyes.

Mani looked away instantly in nervousness and a strange fear overtook him, for this was not the first time he had caught KP staring at him in this peculiar manner from the window. Frozen with fear, he dug his eyes in the ground below. Bansi and Kishan had been talking beyond and he hoped they would come and release him from the swamp of KP's stare. Mani had, however, not shared this happening with the boys, probably because it was something that his juvenile thinking could not comprehend. It was an unreasonable fear that awashed him since the last few Thursdays, and it stabbed him like hell…his words were looking for reason but he found none, and hence, remained speechless.

Bansi and Kishan brought some leftover food from the kitchen to exactly where Mani stood motionless. They squatted on the grass, spread some newspaper, and ate to their heart's content…Mani tried to nibble but he still felt the gaze…an unspoken pain in it weighed Mani down. Mani remained mellow for the rest of the day, much to Kishan's surprise. Little did he know that the charm of the Thursday was slowly being replaced by a creeping dread in Mani's untrampled mind. How threatened could childhood be if the one overpowering emotion became fear to darken one's heart forever? Mani's heart now found comfort in the wretched coal, a sense of oneness…black, dark and unsolved.

CHAPTER 3

Friday came as a comfort; the comfort of Kishan's call early in the morning and the thought that those red unsettling eyes could be averted…at least till next Thursday. Mani jumped to a single call that morning.

Ram Sahay came in early at eight. He had this absurd habit of sniffing, and twisting his mouth every time he sniffed. It somehow annoyed Mani and he imitated the act for the pleasure of benign vengeance…many a times Mani glanced across at Kishan, whistled at him to draw attention and sniffed like his master. The boys giggled to themselves as they went about their work. It eased their monotony.

Mani rushed out to wash as soon as Ram Sahay opened the door and returned within minutes at the latter's disposal. The Fox hardly looked up from the money he was counting and said, "*Ae* Mani…Go, take 10 for *Badi…Chiple Jhora.*"

"*Hajur,*" said Mani and headed towards the coal mound. *Badi* was a regular and it was the way of the Fox to address customers in the mould of a personal relationship…it was the bait. So Ram Sahay was everyone's maternal or paternal uncle, brother, or had a foster one tucked away in every corner of the town.

Mani disengaged his basket from the wall, filled it with coal and put it on the enormous weighing scale. He had mastered the art of weighing, and more often than not, he matched the exact measure in a single attempt of filling his basket. Ram Sahay secretly delighted in the little boy's adeptness.

Delivering coal during early mornings was a trip Mani loved. His journey through town usually turned out to be very interesting. The streets were mostly dotted with school children rushing to school, the whites in their uniform sparkling in the morning light. This pulsating rush built up a strange excitement in Mani, may be of a possibility that he could be one of them too. It planted a dream in his heart.

When children saw him with the basket full of coal, they ran towards him…usually the girls…to touch his basket as they screamed "Good luck…good luck." How he loved this celebrity moment. He immediately transformed into a little monk handing out his blessings with the broadest smile. In fact, the small town loved his smile and all the women stopped by to smile at him, some charmed by him, some feeling so much warmth towards him that his heart felt a gush of love more soothing than the winter sun. After delivering the coal, he waited to return till all the children had reached school for he could not bear to pass on 'bad luck' with his empty basket. He hardly cared about the already wrinkled adults going to work…they were usually joyless and empty themselves, so it hardly made a difference anyway, the bad luck.

As Mani was walking down the slope to the godown, he spotted the Fox talking to a man with a Gurkha cap from a distance. He noticed that the cap rested slightly asymmetrically and Ram Sahay was grinning from ear to ear, hunching atrociously to appease. Mani collected himself and hid behind the gunny bag-laden truck parked in front the grocery store at the beginning of the slope. It was KP, not a doubt about it. But why would he come for coal himself when he had a battery of servants to do it? And why at Ram Sahay's particularly? At this hour? His head reeled with questions and he kept hiding as he did not want to look into those eyes…rather feel them on himself. He waited for the storm to pass as his heart beat hard fearing being seen. Was it possible and could it happen that he had taken all the bad luck upon himself today, the little monk?

Ram Sahay looked unusually pleased and Mani struggled with his irritation at that.

"*Kya re Keta…*" Ram Sahay said in his obnoxiously *Madhesiya* tone. He usually spoke like this when unguarded and probably on a day he had earned well. It was too early to decide that and Mani wondered what was up with the Fox.

"Delivered?" Ram Sahay asked. Mani simply nodded in affirmation.

"Here…take this. Go, have something," Ram Sahay said handing out a two rupee note.

Mani took it for his stomach was churning with a mix of hunger and apprehension and he really needed to wash down the nausea with food.

As he headed towards Kishan's shop, deep down his gut, a feeling was hovering…even the child in Mani knew that the Fox was happy only when he had laid a trap…and the two rupee note somehow felt like feed for the bait.

Kishan on the other hand was ruminating on his own woes. His neon shorts had made him so visible that all others had become invisible to his employer. So while he slogged everywhere, the others shirked…and so easily. Already bitter, Kishan saw a grumpy Mani standing outside and whispered in an irritated tone in Mani ears.

"Now…whatever happened to you? Why are you going around with that mashed potato face of yours?"

"Nothing," said Mani wryly. "Here…two rupees…give me something to eat. Anything!"

Kishan was perplexed but had no time to breathe also, so he thrust a newspaper filled with savouries in Mani's hands. Mani sat outside and started munching on them, barely giving a thought to what he was putting in his mouth. He threw half of it to the stray dogs that had crowded around him.

Later in the day, Ram Sahay sent Mani to deliver coal a number of times…but still the day did not seem to ease out. It was gripped with a strange heaviness. Mani wasn't himself that day…he chased the dogs away…he did not charm the grocery store 'Bada' for a packet of biscuits in the evening…he hardly sniffed to imitate the Fox even when Kishan had whistled out twice…and he hardly looked up to return greetings to passers-by who usually smiled, winked or said a pleasant word to earn the good-luck smile of the little monk. Mani felt lonely… he could not see a friend in anyone. He needed to be understood that day.

Dusk came and Mani longed to be locked inside, for only darkness could provide solace to the hollows of his heart. Strangely, the Fox remained glued to his desk even as night crawled in. A dim yellow bulb hung over Ram Sahay's desk and Mani sat staring at it. Large wooden gates of the neighbouring shops were being drawn and chained with chunky locks. Kishan's shop shone the brightest, as all the others had closed down. Mani intently studied all the sounds as if it were his last chance to do it.

At eight in the night, the Fox finally got up. He stretched his neck and looked up and down the slope, the hollows of his cheeks resembling accentuated pits like that of an animal's…a swine's precisely. Mani dug his head in his palms, waiting for him to leave so that he could go home in his sleep. He longed to be home tonight.

"*Kya re keta*…you'll not have dinner?" The Fox 's shrill voice surprised Mani. Moreover, the sudden concern was even more confounding. It had been Kishan's lookout so far.

"Come, let's go home." Ram Sahay called out to Mani. "Your *Kaki* has cooked mutton for dinner."

Mani was too young to understand mistrust in the entirety of its form, capacity and consequence, but he was experiencing a hunch in the form of an undeciphered emotion laced with fear and abandonment.

His mouth was watering but not at the thought of meat swimming in the hot spicy gravy, but owing to a nausea originating in his gut.

"Come…come fast." Ram Sahay said firmly, his tone suddenly changing, bearing urgency in it.

Mani knew he was choiceless so he dragged himself and helped the Fox lock up the godown. There had been instances when Mani had been offered dinner and was made to sleep with tired greasy labourers in a dingy room below the Fox's house…it seemed it was one of those nights.

The Fox looked around like a squirrel and hurried up the slope. Mani followed wondering why his mannerisms were so compulsively sly. "Oh… Fox Fox Fox!!" He said to himself. They walked past Kishan's shop but Kishan was nowhere to be seen.

Ram Sahay lived in a congested locality, a block behind the clothes market or 'chowk,' as it was called. One had to play 'hop-skip-jump' to cross intersecting open drains to reach the stairway leading to his house. The area was filled with a stench no mutton curry aroma could abolish. Ram Sahay called out to his son from the staircase itself.

"Dharmesh *beta*, take out the stool in the verandah…we have come."

Ram Sahay was terrified of his wife, a short, big-busted woman with ochre vermillion applied on the middle parting of her hair. She despised having Mani over and even more when she had to give him to eat.

Dharmesh, a seven-year-old boy obeyed his father and brought a low stool for Mani to sit. He kept looking at Mani curiously as he fidgeted with a toy. The Fox 's wife also came and peeped at Mani making her disgust felt. In a while, Suman, Ram Sahay's 16-year-old daughter came with a plate of rice topped with gravy and two pieces of mutton. She smiled and said softly, "Take…eat your food."

She was the most human face Mani had seen in the entire day and he smiled back at her. She was an ordinary looking girl but displayed warmth in her eyes and smile that made her endearing. Many Thursdays, Mani had caught Bansi teasing Kishan taking Suman's name and he wondered if it was her they were talking about. Kishan usually blushed and chased Bansi. Mani laughed along then, although he wasn't part of that particular conversation between Kishan and Bansi.

The food warmed up Mani and his tired eyes were drooping with sleep. But the day was yet to end. Ram Sahay came out and said, "Come Mani, come fast."

Mani got up and shook himself out of sleepiness. He was longing to sleep and hence hurried so that he could stretch. But Ram Sahay turned neither towards the dingy room downstairs nor the slope leading to the godown. He started walking hurriedly in the opposite direction, looking back only to confirm if Mani was following him. The Fox climbed up the market lanes, a bewildered Mani following him until he stopped. He stopped at the gates of KP's bungalow.

A sharp spear of fear struck Mani's spine as he thought, "WHY HERE?"

CHAPTER 4

Bansi was already at the gate and his jaw dropped when he saw Mani. He even gestured questioningly as Ram Sahay walked past them, but Mani, in inexplicable trepidation, wished he knew better. He averted Bansi's gaze and walked past, touching the little daisies, which shone prettily in the moonlight. He went and sat in one corner on the steps of the porch leading to the entrance of the house. Bansi's inquisitiveness followed Ram Sahay inside the house while Mani sat outside, alone, and in the solace of darkness…short-lived as it was…

For a moment, the blanket of the night felt soothing. The moon spread its white light uniformly, but only those with light within, reflected it…some of Bansi's orchids, a few daisies fluttering in the soft night breeze and the white china roses on the fencing. Fireflies danced around and bats screeched…a lone cuckoo was hiding somewhere… it was calling out in pain, unable to sing that night. Mani recalled the stories his mother had told him about a cuckoo bird who had left her young one in a pigeon's nest and would cry every night…

Just when he was letting the night carry him home, the fox came out hunching and baring his cavernous teeth and sunken cheeks.

"*Aei* Mani!" He called out. "Didn't you hate sleeping in the godown? Now you will get a bed to sleep and good food to eat. See what I did for you, your *Kaka*...I got you a home...heeheehee...." He laughed hideously and then suddenly stated in a firm tone. "You will be staying here tonight onwards."

Mani stood numb, thunderstruck. He felt as if he was reeling in a trap, a merry-go-round circumscribed by a pair of piercing red eyes. The only thing Mani wanted to do at that moment was flee, but life had not allowed the liberty of choice to emerge in Mani's existence, so every emotion had but one expression – silence – which was usually interpreted as willingness and sometimes misread as happiness. Bansi fidgeted behind the fox in excitement as if Mani had struck gold...or maybe he was happy he had a companion now.

Mani's arrival at the bungalow was, however, still a question swimming in a well of ambiguity. For what would a coalbearer carry indoors other than his dark fears? But time never stands still and so it ticked by...the Fox left and the night came down darker and heavier. Mani slept with Bansi that night, in the small room next to the kitchen extending into the backyard. It was almost two years since Mani had felt human contact and the warmth put him to sleep right away.

"Mani...*aei* Mani," Bansi called out. Mani rubbed his eyes to see...today it was Bansi, not Kishan and a pang of pain hit him in the chest. He missed Kishan, his only friend, like never before. And today was just Friday...almost a week to go.

"*Ooai* Mani." Bansi called out again. "Go, wash yourself at the tap...and come with me." Mani followed Bansi into the kitchen. Bansi handed out a small wooden stool for Mani to sit. A fat chubby woman was busy doing something but turned around as soon as Mani came and squealed as if a new pet had been brought to the house.

"Ahhhh!! This is him!! Oh my God!!"

Then she brought two mugs of tea and handed it out to both of them. Mani hesitated but took it after Bansi signaled him to. The fat lady turned around to look at him a number of times and she grinned every time she looked…she was certainly amazed for some reason as made obvious by her dilated pupils.

Mani suddenly became aware of the sheer comforts of staying in a house, but still he felt something missing, an undecipherable emptiness. The child in him could not exercise discrimination to understand his yearning…for sometimes, one misses home more in an alien house…sometimes even more than in the darkness of coal shacks. The domesticities of a house reminded him of his own and he drowned in an unresolved sadness.

"Come Mani…come with me," it was Bansi again. "I'll teach you how to plant Orchids." Bansi was in high spirits this morning… he had found a new focus in this camaraderie and his excitement was obvious. On hearing him, the fat woman suddenly turned around and blurted out, "No…you go alone…leave the boy here."

"Why, Sushma *Kaki?*" Bansi could not understand the reason Mani was here in the first place…and then this coverture…he sarcastically thought if Mani had been brought to peel potatoes for *Kaki* and grimaced.

"Do I have to tell you everything? Go…do what you do, leave the boy alone." *Kaki* said firmly.

"Go now…run, will you?" She seemed to be losing her patience.

Bansi left, scratching his head over all this fuss around Mani, while Mani sat fidgeting with a small piece of straw he had picked up.

As soon as Bansi left, Sushma *Kaki* left her chores and said, "Come *baba*…what's your name? I'll show you your room and help you change into new clothes."

Startled by her affectionate tone, he muttered in a cracked voice, "Mani."

"Ok Mani, come." Sushma *Kaki* brightened up as if she liked the name.

Mani walked in a daze, following *Kaki* through a huge living room. His eyes widened on seeing the grandeur around. Beautifully carved ornamental teakwood furniture, exquisite lamps, bronze and marble statues and adornments, soft carpets and rugs, huge chandeliers… Mani was walking through the palaces he'd imagined in the stories his mother narrated…it was like a dream but without the joy. Instead, he felt a strange hollowness and even the multitude of lights could not erase the stagnant dullness the house bore. He wondered if even the inanimate objects needed human contact to exude warmth and comfort. At the end of the living room, there was a staircase that led upstairs. Sushma *Kaki* turned to take the staircase but Mani stood still. He shook his head vehemently. He could not go up. How could he? He had seen those pair of eyes there on many a Thursdays…staring at him from one of the windows on the first floor.

Mani blurted out instantly with joined hands. "No *Kaki*, I'll not stay upstairs. I'll stay here, downstairs with Bansi. Please *Kaki*…please.

Sushma *Kaki*, unable to read the fear behind the lines, misunderstood his pleading for hesitation and shyness. She laughed, as if amused, caught Mani's hand tenderly and led him upstairs. Mani was on the verge of tears, feeling totally helpless and clueless as to what was happening.

There was pin-drop silence on the first floor. Mani did not dare to lift his head and look around. He was blinded with fear. The staircase opened into a corridor. They walked through an open space, a living area with repetitive exquisiteness and dullness as Mani had absorbed downstairs. He held on to Sushma *Kaki*'s hand tightly and she led him to a room on the right-hand corner of the bungalow. She opened it with a key and led him inside. "Come *baba*…this is your room now."

Mani's confoundedness kept getting entangled and knotty with every passing hour. After all, he thought to himself, why was he given a separate room…that too upstairs, where no servant came? In fact, why was he being treated differently, unlike Bansi?

The room had large windows with curtains. The windows looked out into the backyard, just like KP's room. There was a cozy bed, so puffed up that Mani stealthily poked his finger to see how deep it was.

There was a chair and a table in one corner and a dressing area at the other. A chandelier hung from the ceiling, and it somehow irritated Mani, for it eradicated the simplicity of the room. It was meant for the exquisite, the room. He felt slightly at ease locked inside the room though. Sushma *Kaki* opened the wardrobe and took out some neatly ironed clothes.

"Come Mani, clean yourself up," *Kaki* said.

Mani thought to himself, "but today's just Saturday…and I took a bath just the other day."

Sushma *Kaki*, pressed with the urgency of the chores to be completed for the day, did not waste time and pulled a dazed Mani into the bathroom and started undressing him. Since the last two years, ever since he had escaped the fire back home…he had lived like an adult. To be suddenly treated like a child again felt extremely strange…and embarrassing. So he shook himself off and started undoing the buttons of his loyal tweed coat himself. This changing seemed no less than a ritual…a baptism…to mark the event in which he was discarding his old life and entering a new one, however uncertain. Letting go of the tweed coat brought a mist to his eyes.

When Mani came out of the bathroom, wearing beige cargo pants and a bottle-green pullover, Sushma *Kaki* looked at him stunned. The look in her eyes was that of amazement but unusual, as if her eyes were travelling beyond…to a different story. She composed herself, came closer to Mani, cupped his face in her hands and kissed him on his forehead. She suddenly became pensive thereafter.

"Come down for breakfast," she said before leaving.

Terrified of being left alone upstairs, he came running after her and said, "I'll come right away." Unknowingly, he had caught hold of one end of the shawl she had wrapped around herself. Sushma *Kaki* smiled tenderly and thought the child was overwhelmed by the unfamiliarity of the place. She put her hand around him and started walking down the steps. Very softly she whispered in his ears, "This is your house, *baba*…do as you wish."

"My house? NO!!" Mani was as startled as ever, losing his grip and tripping on the soft slippers he had been given to wear.

"Hmm! Don't you know?" Sushma *Kaki* said reassuringly. "*Dada* has taken you as his son."

"*Dada*…meaning KP?" Mani wondered. "*Dada*? Why?" Mani, the little coalbearer, remained lost in the hurdle of new identities being hurled at him one after the other.

"Why?" *Kaki* became grave again. "Sometime later dear. Come, have your breakfast first."

Sushma *Kaki* probably had the answers. She seemed to be witness to all that was happening…and probably also why it was happening at all. She was the witness and the narrator, who saw so much more than the screenplay, the only person to see beyond the garb of the characters. It reflected in the smoothness in the way she went about her chores, her blending in with the dullness of the bungalow, her knowingness of the house and the pensiveness on her face at times. It was *Kaki* alone who 'held' this house together, probably the last remains of the proof that this used to be a house, a home to some.

CHAPTER 5

Mani held on to Sushma *Kaki's* shawl till they both reached the kitchen, the warmest place in the house. Mani noticed a gunny bag filled with charcoal lying in one corner of the huge kitchen and suddenly felt instant joy, the kind of exhilaration one feels on meeting an old cherished friend. He took a wooden stool and sat close to it, feeling safe…a little like home. *Kaki* got busy with her chores. In a while, she kept another stool in front of Mani and placed a bowl of porridge and an omelette for him to eat.

"Here you are…isn't it your favourite?" she asked, rather in confirmation.

Mani nodded indifferently. It was tough to explain that he had long forgotten the luxury of favourites, for he couldn't afford them. It was the aroma of food that was his favourite, and a meal, a luxury. He ate the food quietly, relishing every morsel. After finishing, Mani got up to wash his hands, and the bowl and the plate.

Suddenly, *Kaki* rushed towards him and said, "Leave it *Nanu*…" She snatched the utensils from his hand and he wondered why, because that's what he did whenever he ate at the Fox's house. "*Nanu*…" the name kept ringing in his ears, too. His mother used to address him by that name when she felt a gush of affection for him. Moreover, *Kaki* had awkwardly looked away when he expressed surprise on being addressed as '*Nanu*.'

When the Fox brought Mani home, it was assumed by one and all that the bungalow was to have one more servant, but this special status, this fuss over him seemed misplaced. Moreover, Mani felt suffocated being this child '*Nanu*.' He had been on his own for a long time now and he felt stifled. Mani sat quietly in the kitchen corner and reminisced about his freedom to hop around the entire town, talk to all and sundry…and above everything else, his dear friend Kishan. Mani wondered how worried Kishan must have been on not finding him sleeping in the godown this morning. A night changes everything, he thought to himself and he sighed as he missed Kishan terribly.

Kaki snapped the rhythm of his thoughts. She said, "If you want, go and play outside…your tutor will be coming at 11. Next year onward, you can go to a school."

Mani did not know whether he felt happy or sad. He always dreamt of going to school…how he envied the bright and gay children marching to school in the mornings. But something was amiss… probably the home he dreamt of returning to after school. This felt like confinement, the bungalow.

Kaki interrupted again. "Wear your shoes when you go out… here they are." She brought a pair of sneakers in a red and grey pattern. "Try them," she said as she waited with her hands on her hips. Mani wore them…they fit him perfectly. A satisfied *Kaki* bent down to tie his laces when she saw him fiddling with them. A memory flashed across Mani's mind and he felt a surge of affection for *Kaki*. He placed his hand softly on her shoulder and she looked up and smiled. It is amazing how thoughtfulness travels through the smallest of gestures and touches the innermost corners of one's heart. You can either be receptive to the joy, or the moment is lost altogether in the sands of time. The shoelace had certainly tied a bond here.

Mani went out, shy and awkward in his gait. He was yet to accept his clothes as his own. He walked out into the porch…his eyes actually hovering around looking for Bansi. The garden was a pretty sight. The pansies, poppies and roses fought for attention, but such was the beauty in each that all stood out and none overshadowed the other. It was probably this harmony that enraptured one's senses.

In the far corner, he spotted Bansi, huddled and engrossed in removing weeds with a weed scrapper. Mani came up from behind and pounced on him. Bansi jumped with fright, letting out a small cry and Mani laughed for the first time in two days. Bansi turned around, regained his composure, but when he looked to see who it was, his jaw dropped. He studied Mani from head to toe, not bothering to close his mouth, and then averted his eyes, as if Mani were a stranger. The new clothes stood like a wall between them, dividing them into categories where the osmosis of friendship could not happen. Mani sensed it, pulled Bansi's arm and said, "They gave me. *Kaki* says KP has taken me as his son…she says I have to sleep upstairs but I don't want to stay here." His blurting out had a subtext of fear to it, which of course no one knew…or would know.

Bansi was relieved. Mani's clothes had not changed the insides of him after all. "Son!?" Bansi exclaimed, coming closer. His face was a wonderful sight of befuddlement. The boys failed to understand why KP would randomly pick a coalbearer and make him his son! Mani, although, had seen a secret in those eyes…he knew it was not random.

"Ok, go now," Bansi said. "Sushma *Kaki* has asked me to stay away from you," he said as he sulked. He had been so excited when Mani came. Little did he know that barriers would be laid between them.

Mani felt a bit light after speaking to Bansi but was lost as ever. He went back to the kitchen to sit next to the coal sack. The tutor would be coming any time soon, too.

She came in at dot eleven, a young lady in her 20s. She was wearing a suede brown jacket and her long ponytail swung around as she moved. She broke into a broad smile on seeing Sushma *Kaki*.

"Come Shahana," *Kaki* said. They appeared to be familiar with each other. Mani walked around like a shadow behind *Kaki*.

"Is he the one?" Shahana asked enthusiastically…as if she were excited to teach.

"Yes, yes," *Kaki* said. "He's your lad now…all yours." They both laughed cheerfully. Mani did not look up even once all this while. Sushma *Kaki* walked them to a small parlour separated from the living area by heavy curtains. The large windows looked out onto the green expanse of the garden. Mani instantly liked the place, and knew this was where he would spend his days…if he had to. The only furniture kept there was a round table with two ornately cushioned chairs. All looked perfect till Mani's eyes reached the ceiling and he dropped them in disgust. The chandelier! "Couldn't they just do without one?" He wondered in disgust. It's amazing how humans connect and disconnect with inanimate objects too. It probably reminded him that he did not belong here…just as how the coal sack made him feel at home.

As they settled down, a whiff of Shahana's perfume crossed the room and Mani felt invaded - differently, pleasantly. It made him feel good to be there, near Shahana.

"I'll get some stationery and tea for you," *Kaki* rushed out leaving them alone.

"So, what's your name?" Shahana asked.

"Mani…" Mani barely whispered.

"Uhhh…No!" she said. "Your name is Mani Pradhan."

Mani felt repulsed. He hated it, this name. He didn't want it at all. He shifted in his place in unease. He felt like an animal tied down with chains. "NO!" he said emphatically in desperation.

Shahana was taken aback, but before she could say anything, *Kaki* entered with a tray in one hand and stationery in the other. Shahana leaned across to take the stationery from her while *Kaki* placed the tea and cookies on the table. Mani was yet to recover from this imposed identity and he looked away sullenly.

Kaki placed her hand affectionately on Mani's head and said,

"Learn well from Shahana…you'll not find a better teacher." She left thereafter.

As soon as she left, without even lifting his head Mani blurted out, "I am NOT Mani Pradhan…I am Maniraj Khaling. I have a name. My parents gave me one." His voice was broken and enraged and his eyes had welled up. Even Mani was surprised by his own display of emotions. He had no clue how he had brought himself to tell Shahana what he did. He had not disclosed his identity even to the Fox. Somehow, Shahana made him vulnerable with her presence; she made him lose his dehiscence completely.

Shahana stared at Mani for a good two minutes, her brows arched and hands clasped under her chin. Then she got up slowly, came closer and put her arm around him. She kneeled down in front of him, took his hands in hers and said, "You know what…I'll tell you a secret."

Mani looked up at once and looked at Shahana for the first time. He was struck by her beauty. She reminded him of a Goddess, the one in the garden grotto of a school he passed through a number of times when he used to deliver coal.

She continued. "You know what…I don't even know where I was born. The orphanage sisters told me they found me as a baby, left outside the gate. They took me in, gave me a home. And that's reason enough to thank God, isn't it?"

Mani looked at her in surprise. Moreover, he felt deeply connected in a way he felt with no other human. This was a guarded space with Kishan too. He felt a faith in Shahana…and she became that only someone for him who made him feel like staying back.

"So let us start…did you ever go to school?" A conversation started and so did a relationship, a journey. Mani talked his heart out to Shahana, telling her every detail of how he lived coiled up quietly in the darkness of nights so far. The flames within his little heart were doused a little by the soothing presence of Shahana. He had found someone whom he could call his own.

CHAPTER 6

As dusk fell and night approached, the bungalow stood solitary encased in a dim yellow light. Mani felt a strange restlessness enveloping him. A conflict troubled him, that between him, his new name and the bungalow. He detested both, the name and the bungalow, yet felt heavily chained by both. He felt disgustingly imprisoned by his new name the more he thought about it. Somewhere at the back of his mind, he was also aware he would have to climb those stairs to go to sleep. A strange fear came over him.

He whiled away time listening to Samsher *Bada's* stories of old days when he was in the Army, his lost stories of pre-Independence. Samsher *Bada* was a distant cousin of the Pradhans, and the caretaker of the bungalow now. His moustache, nicely tended tufts of white feather brush, sat neatly under his rather round nose. His eyes sparkled when he told and retold his stories, even though the puffs around his eyes had reduced them to mere slits. *Bada's* pride was his black headgear with the metallic Gurkha brooch, the symbol of the spirit he so identified with. Mani, a shy boy, smiled as *Bada* spoke, and that was response enough for *Bada* to regale in his stories.

"…there they were, ripe like tomatoes in the heat…the Britishers,"

Bada described the war as he gesticulated. "We, all village lampoons… we were the first of the 2nd Battalion, 10th Gurkha Regiment in the East India Company. Ten of us, the *Kiranti* (East Nepal) Gurkhas. We stayed at the Takdah base."

Mani struggled with his limited exposure to Army vocabulary but this is what made the story even more mesmerizing for him. It took him to another world and he listened in wonder, the most beauteous element of childhood. Once the sense of wonder is lost, one becomes an adult. *Bada*, meanwhile, was transported to another world and time, a time in which he had found himself in his highest glory.

He resumed with all elan, "It was 1915. We were sent to Turkey… what did we not endure? Rain, blizzards, frostbites, you name it. Ahhh! I lost so many of my friends…so many…. Dilip, that *Limbu* fellow, Birkhey, Keshav…" He sighed in remorse and remembrance and then sprang back again. "But see…I came back!! I came back whole." He laughed aloud, his laughter echoing in the night sky.

It was indeed a feat, the Gurkha led battles of World War 1. They assisted the British across the trenches of France to Persia. Gurkha Battalions had received some 2000 gallantry awards for their valour. *Bada*, however, described the Gallipoli campaign in 1915 when they became heroes after capturing a heavily guarded Turkish position, so much so that it came to be referred to as the "Gurkha Bluff" in history.

Bada spoke of these in monosyllables…probably mindful of Mani's limited knowledge but he was so happy with the latter's listening that he perceived it as zeal. *Bada* almost made up his mind that he would continue this glorious tradition through Mani. He would train Mani to join the Indian Army. What a proud moment it would be…he dreamed away.

"You should, you should," *Bada* thought aloud. "No place like the Army if you want to become a man. And now we fight for our country, our pride…no more outsiders." *Bada's* patriotism was oozing through.

It was pitch dark now and cold too. Mani wanted to go inside but he did not know how…and where. Just then, a heavy slurry voice roared, "Sushma…Sushma…"

Mani trembled and instinctively caught hold of *Bada's* hand. *Bada* pressed Mani's hand in his own and said comfortingly, "It's OK. It's Khagendra, down for breakfast." *Bada* chuckled first, probably to ease Mani but his face turned to dismay soon. He shook his head…in disgust and surrender.

"*Hajur Dada,*" Sushma Kaki's voice almost went unheard.

"Get me my breakfast," the man thundered.

Mani, wondering as much as why KP was asking for breakfast at this hour, was struggling with his own reflexes, his urge to run away…for those eyes he feared to look at, they were hovering around searchingly. Mani kept hiding behind *Bada*. *Bada*, although unaware of the reason, could sense the child's fright and held him closer behind.

The voice reverberated again. "Is this breakfast Sushma… breakfast? This is a meal. Who eats a meal early morning? Haven't you ever served breakfast?" The house echoed with the shattering of ceramic plates and bowls, which he probably flung in a fit of rage.

Mani shivered but *Bada* assured him. "Don't worry child, it's his habit…the drunkard." He spat sideways in disgust. "Loser!!" *Bada* muttered again. "It's an everyday affair. You don't worry. He's harmless…this is all he can do." *Bada's* pent up anger at his cousin surfaced even though he said it to pacify Mani.

Mani just hoped KP was what he had been told…harmless!

Then in a surprisingly sane timid voice, KP enquired, "The boy… has he come home?"

"*Hajur Dada,*" Sushma Kaki replied. "He's fast asleep," she added. Why…no one knew.

"Hmmm," KP grunted. "The boy…look after him well, Sushma." He staggered away upstairs again.

Mani's legs were shaking through it all. If only he found strength in them, he would run out through the gates to freedom.

Bada turned to Mani and stroked his head affectionately. Mani's forehead was moist with sweat and wet *Bada's* palms. *Bada*, alarmed initially, pulled Mani closer to him.

"Why are you frightened child?" He asked. "This fellow, he's harmless. The bloke! He blew up everything in the bottle. Ahh! Those were the days in this bungalow, when Dhirendra was alive." *Bada* mused away. "The entire place used to bloom in ebullience."

Mani rightly guessed Dhirendra to be the man whose portrait hung in the living room. *Bada* had more to tell…about the grandeur of those days.

Mani listened, intently initially…but slowly, *Bada's* voice started fading away…as if in a dream.

Mani had fallen fast asleep, his head neatly placed in *Bada's* lap. The coal-shacks had perhaps found a warmer replacement.

CHAPTER 7

A week passed by at the bungalow and Mani was gradually blending into the ambience. His life was no longer his alone. It was suddenly tied to Sushma *Kaki's* responsibilities, *Bada's* affection and dreams of seeing him as an Army officer, Shahana's laughter and the bungalow's breath. The entire fuss and flurry around him made the bungalow come alive.

Mani waited every day at 11at the gate to hold Shahana's hand to bring her in after showing her Bansi's Orchids in bloom. He felt he had held it all along, and every night when he went to sleep, he thought he'd hold it forever. This feeling of attachment was strange and new to him. It made him feel shy and his cheeks felt hot whenever he thought about it but nevertheless, it was extremely special and he cherished it like nothing else.

Just yesterday, *Bada* saw them coming in and jested. "There there…come all…our son is bringing in his bride."

Shahana burst into laughter, her head back, sun rays dancing on her porcelain face. She found it so endearing, she pulled Mani closer to her. As for Mani, he couldn't take his eyes off her…and an unusual dream took residence in his smitten eyes."

Mani was smart with his studies. He had learnt a lot in a short span of time, that's what he had heard Shahana tell Sushma *Kaki* the other day. The only point of disagreement was his name. Mani insisted on writing it as 'Maniraj Khaling' and Shahana fidgeted in helplessness. After all, she had been appointed priest for this baptism.

It was Mani's 15th day at the bungalow. It was past eleven and Mani was becoming restless as it meant less time to spend with Shahana. He was pacing up and down the porch when he heard an unusual voice from behind…someone clearing his throat. The voice, how could he not recognize it? It produced an instant reflex in him for he scurried down the front garden to hide behind the China Rose shrub where Bansi was cleaning a few pots.

KP emerged from the entrance, his eyes gently covering the entire place with their gaze, the thirst in it felt only by his object of search. It is amazing how thoughts never go unnoticed in spite of all shielding. Its energy just cannot be contained; it travels to communicate. Mani did not have to look up to know he was being searched for.

"Samsher *Da*," KP called out in a loud booming voice. *Bada* was yet to come but the house came to a halt. It appeared as if a wave passed through the entire place turning it to stone. Not even a bird chirped. Mani dug the earth with his eyes…terrified to look up, and well…meet those eyes.

"O Samsher *Da*," KP called out again. His tone was unusually benign today. *Bada* came in waddling through the gate. After all, who expects the sun to rise from the west? It was only 11 in the morning. No one was prepared for this contingency. *Bada* thought some cloud was about to burst. He was panting, half in amazement and half in apprehension.

"Hey…what happened?" *Bada* asked, hardly able to conceal his surprise. It had been months since he had seen a sane KP wearing ironed clothes, with eyes not drooped in intoxication. He did go out at odd hours, no one knew where…but one could be sure he'd be back in an hour barely able to walk.

KP laughed out loud, although the outro of it held a little pain. He was aware of the grief and helplessness he caused. He also knew it was only because of these people, *Bada, Kaki*…that he was possibly surviving. They stood by him and did not desert him in spite of all his unruliness.

"Get the Land Rover, *Dada*…I've got to go for work," KP said matter-of-factly.

Bada's organs started dancing inside him on hearing this. He was oozing with excitement and rushed to do the needful without a thought, as if a moment of delay would betray the moment altogether. It felt too good to witness this change in KP…just too good to be true, but today it was happening. In barely five minutes, the vehicle was parked in front of the porch. Bada was beaming with joy and as he got out of the car, he called out to Bansi.

"Bansi…hurry child…get the hose. The car needs a good wash." Mani peeped at the unfolding of events at the bungalow from behind the China Rose. His thoughts were stuck on Shahana too…and he felt gloomy without her.

KP left the bungalow in the sparkling vehicle…leaving behind brimming a new hope. Was spring around the corner?

CHAPTER 8

The exaggerated attention around KP had stripped the day of its significance, although Mani felt less weight on his head, as he knew the bungalow was empty without KP. He walked around the bungalow in freedom. Shahana did not come and the day was approaching noon. But yes! There was much to be happy about. Today was a Thursday. Mani would meet Kishan today. Mani rushed to the backyard hoping to find him there.

Kishan was very much there, washing his wrath out of his clothes.

Mani called out, "Kishan, Kishan." The eagerness in his voice was apparent. Kishan turned at once for he was desperate to see Mani…but he looked away instantly, his eyes expressing betrayal.

Mani walked up to him and stood by the tap, the same one that had made so many Thursdays memorable for them. Kishan refused to look at him. Running out of patience, Mani turned off the tap. Kishan looked up and said, "You did not tell me." The hurt in his voice was explicit.

Mani said, "As if I knew… the Fox dumped me here."

"Oh really!" Kishan retorted. "But you're living a royal life here. Why should you complain?"

Kishan surrendered to silence thereafter, leaving Mani confused if he was hurt because Mani did not tell him or if he was jealous of Mani's life. The hurt was certainly misdirected. They both knew that it wasn't because of a betrayal contrived by either of them, but one laid down by the barriers that stood in the way of the bond they shared. It is strange how externalities cage the insides of a person. A Mani in expensive clothes could no longer spontaneously reach out to Kishan in his pink shorts. Mani's friendliness somehow looked like a distasteful ornamented obligation bestowed upon Kishan.

Kishan went back to washing his clothes saying, "I need to wash my clothes," probably emphasizing the distance between their present lives and also the absence of the thread of solidarity that held them together. They led lives unrelatable to the other now. Mani obviously did not have to wash clothes now, and what did Kishan care about rotation and revolution, which Mani was learning from Shahana!

Mani felt torn and lonely, for he was yet to belong here or anywhere else. He knew he would never want to go back to the Fox's coal shacks even though he missed little fragments of his life back then...and he knew how he hated going upstairs to sleep. Kishan's behavior only accentuated the gnawing misery in him, which had started after having to come to terms with Shahana's 'betrayal'-as he thought so- today. Mani was longing to belong somewhere in his heart, he longed for a home...and this, Kishan would also not understand for he had one, even if far away.

Two more Thursdays came and went. Mani no longer tried reaching out to Kishan but watched Kishan and Bansi from his room quietly. A dagger pierced through him on seeing the camaraderie between Kishan and Bansi, but he tried distracting himself with books that Shahana brought him to read. His thoughts philandered and his ears strained to hear what Kishan and Bansi chatted about but he pulled back, sometimes with his contemptuous thoughts.

"Oh! Silly people…they must be talking about Suman, the Fox's daughter. I was anyway not in it even then…so why should I feel left out?" He reasoned. Last Thursday, out of sheer spite, he laughed exaggeratedly while reading by the window, ensuring the boys noticed him. Such is the web of human emotions! It usually entraps you in a spot you hate the most. Mani, trying to seek attention from his friends he missed so much, unknowingly displayed a haughtiness that only deepened the divide.

As if this poisonous jealousy wasn't enough, Mani was slowly being displaced from his childhood by another adult anomaly slithering up his back slowly, that of becoming a naïve sexual being. At nights, when Mani struggled to sleep fearing the door would open any time, he tried distracting himself with thoughts of his home but at times, they appeared faded and too far away. Instead, his head brimmed with his new object of wonder and fascination…these days his thoughts involuntarily drifted towards Shahana. And the more he thought about her, his heart tightened when their eyes met. He longed for her to take hold of his hand, stroke his hair…or display some affection physically. Her touch made him feel alive in a way he had never experienced before…and he wondered why. He dreamt of a space where all he saw was Shahana, laughing and looking dreamily at him…and in all ways, existing just for him. He was indeed struck by a blind emotion for the first time.

Chapter 9

The bungalow had put on a different hue since KP had started eating his breakfast on time. There was a pleasant hum in the way *Kaki, Bada* and the rest of the servants went about their work. The bungalow's circulation seemed to have been rejuvenated. Every individual seemed to be driven by a sense of purpose in his or her activity.

KP had been going to the timber depot regularly, much to *Bada's* joy. He was the only one who had witnessed the rise and fall of the Pradhans in every perspective, and he was filled with hope. He got up early morning to see if the car was washed and ready. The nights were quiet now, the crockery spared.

Mani no longer held Shahana's hand when she came. He hid behind the parlour curtain as he watched her arrive. His heart pounded too much and he literally had to hold it back with his fisted hands. He averted her gaze and centered his entire focus on following her instructions. He somehow felt let down by Shahana...since the day she had been absent. Moreover, his thoughts about her at night made him feel conscious and guilty. He was afraid she would find out and leave him. Insecurity is a diminishing emotion...one risks staying in separation to avoid separation, making it inevitable.

However, Shahana's fondness for Mani grew everyday…she had not met a brighter child. She beamed at his dedication to learn, and only the other day was so delighted, she gave her 'Maniraj' a warm kiss on his forehead. Mani spent the entire day like a ripe tomato, unable to recover from the dizziness brought about by the fluttering of butterflies in his heart and mind. He now liked to spend his days in solitude…reading, thinking about all the conversations he had with Shahana and dreaming about her. Being with Bansi or Kishan no longer excited him, although Thursdays always came with a little pain when he saw them together.

Sushma *Kaki* fussed over Mani all the time. She called out obnoxious baby names, which drove him up the wall. He simply hated the '*Nanus*' and '*Kichus*' she indulged in a singsong voice, while following him around. He blatantly expressed his indignation when she mindlessly thought he needed to be dressed and undressed. She would laugh aloud at his irritation. At times he wondered, would his mother have been this way too?

It was a Saturday. Two months had slipped by since the bungalow had been resuscitated by Mani Pradhan. Mani woke up to the sound of incessant honking. He rubbed his eyes and walked down the stairs to the kitchen for his milk. Yes! Sushma *Kaki* had replaced his commoner's tea with the bourgeois' milk. On hearing clanking sounds, he rushed to the entrance. *Bada* was screaming out at labourers while they unloaded bamboo poles from a van.

On seeing Mani, he gleefully smiled and said, "Today is your 'badday'…what do you want from *Bada*?"

The Birthday! This was a whole new concept for Mani… something he had just started to become aware of from the books he was reading. He could hardly reminisce any such day of celebration from his own small life of reference back home. Faded memories took him to a day when once a year his mother took him to a temple and cooked his favorite sweet bread *(selroti)* for him. Shahana had, in fact, asked him a number of times about when he was born. On receiving no answer, a formal rebirth had been planned probably. It was yet to be ascertained if the chosen date was random or significant. The date was a certainty, the 14th of June.

Sushma *Kaki* was even more indulgent in her baby talk today. "Ahhh!! My *baba*…" she squealed as she reached out to Mani to embrace him.

"What's happening outside?" Mani asked, unable to contain his curiosity any longer.

"Eee…don't you know?" She trailed off again. "*Dada* has organized a birthday party for you."

She was beaming with excitement and joy but Mani failed to share *Kaki's* joy. The entire bungalow seemed swept away by gaiety, but Mani could not relate to it in any way except that it was a different day. It was nice to watch the hustle and bustle around but that was it. Personal happiness was still an empty space for Mani and everyone seemed to be blind to it. Mani sat down on the porch steps, exactly where he had sat the night he came to the bungalow, and watched the vibrant flow of activities that had infused the bungalow with life.

He watched in wonder. Tall bamboo poles were dug into the ground at regular intervals. Intersecting poles were tied with jute ropes and a rectangular structure was hence constructed in the space between the entrance of the bungalow and the garden. A red tarpaulin was spread across to cover it all. A lanky fellow worked swiftly and Mani remained mesmerized by his adeptness. Samsher *Bada* limped vigorously all around supervising every knot and dimension.

As he crossed by, the thin fellow called out. "Oh *Kaka*, no tobacco?" He grinned to show his stained teeth. The crow's feet at the end of his eyes were unusually distinct, noticeable from a distance too. Samsher *Bada* took out a tiny plastic container from his pocket and offered it to him. Sweat trickled down from the sides of his forehead staining the bandana he had tied around with a faded piece of cloth. Mani watched in wonder at the little container for it opened from both sides. The fellow took out some brown dust from one end and then a whitish paste like substance from the other on one of his palms, and then continued to rub it with his thumb in leisure. He then took a pinch and thrust it inside his lower lip, which stood out like a lump. He then looked around and his eyes rested on Mani. Mani quickly looked away becoming conscious.

"Oh *Kaka*...the son?" The fellow asked staring at Mani.

Samsher *Bada* nodded with a smile. His eyes were filled with pride and a delight...something so pure that Mani felt drawn and protected by it. They both smiled at each other in knowing. But Mani could not conceal his awkwardness today. He felt uneasy with all the attention that was being showered on him today. He had become comfortable being irrelevant and inconspicuous. This life was becoming a tad difficult to handle because around this façade of attention and importance was a fence of expectations that was tightening every day. He was realizing every minute that he was no longer perceived as his own person any more. He was the bungalow's pride, someone's son, *Bada's* dream, *Kaki's* purpose, Kishan's enemy, Bansi's master...no longer Mani. He was becoming Mani Pradhan. The only place he felt like being tied down to was being Shahana's favourite student, for she did not stifle Mani. Mani could hardly put into words the emotions that rose in him these days, but all he could make out was that today his boundaries felt even tighter. Was Mani losing his freedom forever?

Mani started walking around to evade the strange feelings he was facing today, and tried to distract himself among the women who were making garlands out of marigold. He offered to collect the flowers of a similar size in baskets, so that their garlands would turn out symmetrical. They giggled, all amused and grateful. In a while, the porch pillars and the bamboo poles were all adorned with marigold garlands wrapped around them. Two chandeliers, although less elaborate, hung from two sides of the tarpaulin ceiling, much to Mani's disdain. "Ugh!! Here too?" He thought to himself.

In some time, Mani heard a very distinct clearing of the throat in the lobby. The voice was approaching the entrance. Mani's restlessness became involuntary and he started looking around in anxiety without lifting his head, probably for a place to hide. He went and sat down on the porch steps, at the farthest corner, hoping he would be less visible there. But then, he heard it again…loud and clear, at arm's length. Mani froze. He shut his eyes in reflex wishing unreasonably that the earth would split open and he could jump in, vanishing forever.

KP marched out into the yard. He had probably come to inspect the decorations.

"*Dada…*" his voice boomed.

"*Ho…*" *Bada* responded as he waddled hurriedly towards KP.

Mani could not lift his eyes. He had blinded himself but all his other senses were working overtime. He almost mimicked a bat, echo-locating KP while the latter walked around. Triggered by fright, his entire mental space involuntarily concentrated on KP. Such was the power of alertness. He could somehow feel KP's eyes resting upon him, he could feel the heavy silence in the air in KP's presence and he could sense a similar alertness in KP's mind too, although it appeared better concealed. The only bottleneck was the communication. Both did not know what one was trying to tell the other, although they were dealing with an unspoken intensity whenever they happened to be in the same energy field. Thanks to the direction of sound waves, Mani sensed by KP's voice that he was looking away and not at him anymore. He dared to open the corner of his eyes without lifting his head. His eyes travelled slowly and then remain arrested by another 'unusualness' apart from those bloodshot eyes. KP's feet! Apart from the unusual but typical redness they bore, they had six fingers each. A tiny appendage jutted out from each tiny toe. For a few seconds, this fascinated Mani so much, he forgot his fright and stared with eyes wide open, but looked away again when he noticed the feet curling, as if they had sensed what was happening behind them. After Mani's harrowing 15 minutes, KP left in his car allowing the former to breathe in temporary peace.

Mani's entire day was spent watching the preparations. The backyard was busy too. A whiff of aroma invaded the entire bungalow as delicacies were being prepared near the tap. The only person who was entitled to time and hence laze around was Mani, so he loitered around watching everyone. He noticed Kishan amongst the battery of cooks in the backyard. He felt a strange mix of emotions. Half of him felt happy that his friend was part of this celebration and half of him felt a little haughty, as if Kishan deserved to know his rightful place by serving Mani. This second emotion felt a bit alien. So, was he really getting behind the mask of Mani Pradhan or was he simply hurt by Kishan's rejection of his friendship? Well, not all answers are found. Some questions you simply have to let go.

At around three in the afternoon, Sushma *Kaki* pulled Mani aside and took him to the kitchen.

"Where the hell have you been all day? You haven't even had a morsel of food. Come now, come…hurry! Eat your food fast, we've got to get ready fast. They'll be coming any time…all the guests." She said in one breath. One could sense her haste and anxiety.

Mani ate his food, a plate of rice with black lentil curry *(kalo dal)* and a tangy tomato and fresh cottage cheese preparation *(chhurpi ko achar)* that he loved. He smiled at *Kaki* as he ate and that was the appreciation that lifted her spirits. She grinned from cheek to cheek as she vigorously cleaned the kitchen table while he ate. Then they went up to his room where a surprise was awaiting Mani. A pile of new clothes was heaped on the bed. Mani pulled a chair near the window from where he could watch Kishan going about his work. Sushma *Kaki* began unpacking all the clothes one by one. She stared at each one of them with her index finger on her cheek…then shook her head or screwed up her nose. Her eyes dilated when she came across something she liked. She put them aside. The rest, she meticulously folded and packed again and put them in one corner of Mani's wardrobe.

She then called out to Mani. "Come Mani, try these." He walked up to her reluctantly, almost tired of the hullabaloo now. What was aroma in the morning became nausea now, as Mani's room was filled with all the smoke and smell of food being cooked in the backyard.

She took the clothes and measured them on Mani's back one by one. She finally selected one.

"Come, let me wash your face properly. It looks dirty." Sushma *Kaki* started pulling him towards the bathroom. Mani, however, shook himself off and went straight to the basin. Sushma *Kaki* laughed and resigningly said, "Ok *baba*…you do it yourself." She had got used to his 'acting-big ways' as she called them.

The outfit was a traditional one, the '*daura sural*' – a wrap-around shirt with criss-cross knots paired with fitted pyjamas, usually worn during weddings and festivities. It was not in the usual beige and creamish shades but was made out of a beautiful maroon silk fabric. A fitting beige corduroy waistcoat completed the outfit. A headgear, a black cap with a golden accessory (that of two khukris facing each other in a diagonal cross), further enhanced its entirety. But the real beauty of the outfit was revealed when Mani wore it. His apple cheeks bloomed with the reflection of the maroon outfit and his eyes shone like pearls. Sushma *Kaki* stared at him mesmerized with tearful eyes… that of sheer joy. She thought, "Could any child be dearer than her '*Nanu*'?" She rushed and planted her affection on his cheeks even before he could react. She hugged him an endless number of times, squealing in delight. She pulled him towards the mirror asking him to take a look at himself. He suddenly became shy and conscious and looked away. He felt alien…as if disowning his reflection. It just wasn't him… the boy in the mirror. Ah! The rush of incomprehensible emotions! He fidgeted in his room uncomfortably…glancing at the reflection once in a while…probably to become accustomed to it. It was a strange mix of excitement and melancholy. The outfit felt like a foreign costume. It looked attractive but was not one that was temporary, and therefore could be discarded after the show. It bore a permanence that made Mani feel extremely binding in its identity, one which he felt repulsed to accept and it made him feel all the more claustrophobic.

Guests started pouring in at around five in the evening. Chairs and benches had been arranged in the yard. A gaudily decorated couch and a table were kept in the porch. Mani was made to sit on the couch. When he entered the porch, there wasn't a soul who did not gush about how charming Mani looked. *Kaki's* eyes were almost untraceable, her face stretched with pride and glee. Mani's first guest was an old lady wearing a gold ornament around the ridge between her nostrils. Frail and wrinkled, her body could hardly hold the enormous necklace made of green shimmering bead bunches interspersed with chunky gold beads. She was made to sit beside him and Mani was asked to seek her blessings by bowing down to her with folded hands. She peered through her eyes to look at him and kept her shivering hands on his head and he felt a rush of pure affection. She was KP's mother, Mani's grandmother as he learnt, who stayed in a farmhouse a few kilometers away from the city.

As people started filling in the space, Mani could sense those eyes again. He did not have the courage to lift his head and trace them in the crowd but he felt them on himself for a long time, his face reddening and giving away his fear. There were people who came with gifts, some who came and blessed him and some who headed straight to where the food had been laid out at the back of the shelter. But among them all, it was Mani who felt like a stranger all the while. Standing out in the crowd, his isolation carried a new colour today, that of privilege. The most interesting guest, however, was the Fox. Appearing even more shriveled after the long hiatus and hunching ridiculously, he could not believe his eyes when he saw Mani. He grinned with all his teeth out and exclaimed, "*Arre* Mani! You look so handsome, just like a prince." Mani felt awkward for he was not used to such sweet words from the Fox. However, he felt a sinful pleasure secretly, that of getting even. He didn't know if he were ought to be feeling grateful but getting even, yes! For, in spite of all the comforts, the Fox had burdened him with an identity his soul was unable to carry. The Fox had sold him for money and not done some noble service as he claimed…if he were to believe the deal Kishan had come to know of and related to Bansi who informed Mani. Twenty thousand rupees, that was the amount the Fox asked for and got. When Bansi told Mani, Mani put two and two together…and figured out what had transpired that morning when he saw KP at the godown early in the morning.

It was dark outside and people were still around. Mani, however, felt a sense of incompleteness. The only guest he was personally waiting for had still not arrived. He talked to himself. "I'm sure she must have been invited…wonder what's taking her so long." He quickly looked all around and there she was…entering like an angel in a white sequined sari with a silver belt delicately worn around her waist. Her beautiful long hair fell across her face as she walked, and she delicately held them behind her ear. Mani was so mesmerized that he felt the crowd had disappeared and all he saw was Shahana, like in his dreams. Their eyes met as she came closer and she smiled the sweetest smile on earth. Mani smiled for the first time in the entire day. She put her arms around Mani and gave him a warm hug. Totally blown away, Mani stood, still scintillated by her beauty, fragrance and warmth. He must have been looking at her without blinking for she laughed as she waved her hands in front of his face jokingly. He was happy and felt good about the celebration for the first time. Shahana had brought him a gift, probably books wrapped up in a golden paper with a red satin ribbon. Someone from the crowd called her out for dinner and as she turned to leave, Mani realized she wasn't alone. A tall bulky man, rather stylish, wearing a blue blazer held her hand as she walked down the porch steps. Mani's heart started beating fast and he could not keep his eyes off her. His curiosity about the man was inexplicable. Shahana meanwhile seemed extremely comfortable and happy as she laughed and slid her hand around his arm. Mani felt somewhat sick inside, his stomach churning as if he had lost his favorite possession. He felt annoyed that she appeared to be happier with someone else than she was usually with *him*. He was stung with loneliness, and dullness pervaded the air after that. Welcome jealousy! Today he was also standing on the threshold of adulthood and he probably encountered these farcical emotions that comprise it all too soon. Losing childhood is the sad part, gaining adulthood a trap forever. Did it even deserve a celebration?

Finally, the crowd thinned out and the day ended. Mani did not care to notice if angels still existed in white gowns or had left, leaving him feeling empty. Sushma *Kaki* came rushing twice with food for Mani but he refused to swallow a morsel. Assuming the event had tired Mani, *Kaki* took him to his room and tucked him in bed. Even Mani felt a blanket of sleep would comfort him out of his uneasiness; the night would wipe out the darkness inside him…so he wished as he looked out to see the shimmering moon in the night sky from his window. The moon…it looked bright and beautiful like Shahana in the crowd. A lump formed in his throat and he turned over to evade the thought, closing his eyes to lose himself in sleep.

CHAPTER 10

Sleep is a mirage on some nights. It vanishes when one desires it the most. Like all else, it establishes its significance through elusion. Probably, this is the universe's only way to teach value to humans. Mani's mind was a restless animal tonight. It simply refused to obey. He tossed and turned but sleep evaded him. He wanted to be with the soothing moonlight…but turned away when it reminded him of Shahana. The moonlight was his escape…the moonlight his imprisonment.

Two hours had passed. Mani was wondering if he should put on the lights and read one of his books, but he didn't want to get out of the quilt either. At least it was warm inside. He just let all thoughts circle in his head in submission. The bungalow was cast in stillness and silence. But no…not yet! Mani thought he heard a door creak. His ears stood up to catch any sound…and just when his body started relaxing…it creaked again and closer by. Horrified, he remembered that he had forgotten to latch his door from inside last night. In a reflex, he jumped out of bed to lock himself as soon as possible. No! He was not afraid of ghosts, jackals, banshees and the like. He had conquered them all long ago in the pitch darkness of coal shacks and deserted streets in the night sky, where he had spent many a nights in solitude…only a pair of eyes blacked the senses out of him, and how!

The moonlight made the white door even more visible, and just when Mani reached out for the door knob, the door opened a little… and there he was, standing there reeking of alcohol, and his blood-shot eyes bearing an amplified intensity even in the darkness. Mani stood motionless…his insides screaming out but his voice betraying him. Only a whimper escaped his mouth and instantly KP's hands covered his mouth. Mani felt dizzy with fear and his legs trembled so much, he could no longer stand. He lost control and sat on the floor. He simply had no clue what was happening and why. The door was ajar now and KP had almost crossed the threshold…ironically, invading the only place where Mani thought he could not be followed by those eyes. Inebriated, KP could hardly hold himself. He screwed up his face in disgust when Mani fell. He was trying to come closer and Mani was trying to stay as far as possible. He slid into the corner and huddled near the bed. The more he slid back, the closer KP came. He was reaching out his hands as if he wanted to touch Mani's head but his face carried an intense pain, which confused a terrified Mani all the more. Tears started streaming down Mani's face in helplessness and he started sobbing. KP took a step back, probably not knowing what to do. Then he stepped back and thumped the wall with his fist in frustration. He staggered away thereafter, slamming the door as he left. Like a frightened deer who had found some respite from its predator, Mani ran and locked himself inside, and hid under his quilt, covering his face. He had faced his biggest fear today and now was certain that it wasn't without reason. The vibes were not baseless. But it is a horrendous state to be in…being gripped by fear without understanding the intention or reason behind it. Mani sobbed, longing for the coal shacks, totally shaken by all that had happened tonight. His racing breath was just not coming into its own and he did not even have the courage to drink water to soothe his parched throat from sobbing with fear. The night was long and endless and he was witnessing the entirety of it with eyes wide open for the first time.

Whenever his eyelids felt slightly heavy, images of KP cascaded and he shuddered. When he tried too hard not to think and tried to focus elsewhere, Shahana too did not comfort him tonight.

This was it. His thirteenth birthday perhaps, but he had definitely boarded the ship journeying into adult emotions, for he had started oscillating between fear and heartbreak, and so soon. Ah! What a beginning. Now his entire life would be spent learning to overcome each of them as one raced against the other.

Mani heard incessant banging on his door and he jumped with fright. His room was invaded with sunlight and he could barely open his eyes properly. He had probably fallen asleep at dawn for it was very bright outside.

Kaki was anxiously calling out to him and frantically banging his door. "*Baba*…wake up *Baba*…why do you latch your room? Are you OK…are you in there…wake up *Baba*!"

Her face was red with anxiety when Mani opened the door. He himself could barely walk. He felt a strange numbness in his head and went back to bed. *Kaki* ran up to him and touched his forehead. It was burning; he was running a temperature. She rushed down in panic and returned with Samsher *Bada*. *Bada* also touched Mani's forehead and nodded. Mani felt at peace to have them both at his side, but he had no heart to smile. *Bada* turned to go but Mani's limp hand caught *Bada's* finger and he refused to leave it. Tears trickled down the corners of Mani's eyes and *Bada* was at a loss for words for the first time. He sat on Mani's bed and ran his hands through the boy's hair.

"Go Sushma," he instructed. "Get the boy some milk and call for the doctor."

"Don't you worry, child." He assured Mani. "I'm sitting here right beside you."

As Mani sat up to drink his milk, he sensed a flurry of chaotic activity downstairs. The shelter constructed yesterday was probably being deconstructed, for one could hear the sounds of metal clanking and poles being thrown on the ground. In some time, a stout man-supposedly the doctor-came to see Mani. Bansi was accompanying him and he stood at the door with bewildered eyes. Falling sick was a new phenomenon in Pradhan Niwas, and all the more significant as the most important member of the family had fallen ill. The house seemed to be caught in frenzy today.

The doctor carried out all the usual examinations. Mani, meanwhile, started feeling queasy inside again, as if a strange heaviness in the air was getting closer to him. KP was standing outside the door, hands crossed and looking down at the floor. He was probably suffering a terrible hangover for he looked totally worn out, or maybe he was paranoid for he was the only one who did not need an explanation regarding Mani's illness. However, the doctor spoke to him before leaving and handed over a prescription. Samsher *Bada* hurriedly took it from him and left with the doctor. In between, Bansi took a chance and sneaked into the room. Although clumsy in his expression of concern, he stood beside Mani, wondering how he could cheer him up.

"Shall I call Shahana *Didi*?" Bansi blurted out.

Mani could not contain his resentment and said emphatically, "No!"

Bansi then asked again, "Do you want to meet Kishan?" Mani looked away.

Torn between being a friend and an uneasy servant, Bansi was recalling the people who he had seen Mani laugh with, but somehow he was hitting the wrong notes today. Much water had passed below the bridge.

Bansi was at a loss for ideas and words, and stood beside Mani's bed quietly. Little did he know it was his presence that was soothing Mani's wounded heart today; his silent concern, the ointment.

CHAPTER 11

A week of sickness came as a blessing for Mani, for apart from the fever, he also needed time to recuperate from the disastrous episode of having come face to face with KP, and of course, the 'betrayal' by Shahana. He was hardly left alone and that was the precise remedy for him. *Kaki* and *Bada* would divide their time to be with Mani during the daytime and Bansi slept on the floor in his room at night.

Bansi revived Mani's old days as he related all that had happened in the marketplace after the latter came to the bungalow. One of the most interesting stories was about the Fox. Bansi told him he managed to get a replacement for Mani very soon, and how it became the talk of the town after the new lad fled with his day's earnings last month. And yet another story when he almost beat up Kishan because the latter had started following his daughter to school on a regular basis. Mani ached to ask him why Kishan was not coming on Thursdays so often now, but he did want to appear interested so he kept quiet. But Bansi was on a gabbling fit in his excitement to become Mani's friend again, so Mani hardly had to ask him anything. Bansi told him how the Fox provoked Kishan's employer to kick the latter out of his job. Mani felt a rush of sympathy for Kishan and he was confused by his own oscillating feelings. "Ah!! The Fox…how apt the name," he thought to himself.

With labored reluctance to avoid any expression of concern, Mani asked, "So where is Kishan now? Has he got a job?"

Bansi rattled off again. "He went back to our native place. He had come before he left. He said he did not feel like staying back any more."

Mani wondered if any of this had to do with him leaving the godown. Maybe Kishan missed him too much. He was too young to be able to discriminate the irony of human attachment. Like a dragonfly, drawn by the flame that burns it down, humans also insist on finding love where there's none, and that's a deathtrap indeed.

Shahana had started coming for classes in the mornings again… Mani did look forward to her coming, but their camaraderie had lost its flavour. He appeared more bottled up most of the time and she, somewhat less interested in trying too hard to help him open up. Her indifference disturbed Mani even more, but he had no choice. In fact, he could barely understand why he felt annoyed with her most of the time these days. He glanced at her in between his study at times and would find her lost…drifting away to some other land, and he felt sort of insulted. Nowadays, he noticed she would also be in a hurry to leave and never forgot to look at the mirror, powder her face and apply lipstick before she left. This would irritate him no bounds and he hardly said goodbye to her with a smile when she left. Interestingly, he purposely did something to annoy her these days. Just the other day, he wrote 'Maniraj Khaling' on all his books with a black marker. Such is human behaviour; there is no addiction like the attention of another human being. Her attention…and sole attention was what he had tasted, loved and was seeking all the time.

Fifteen days had passed. Sushma *Kaki* informed Mani that KP was not very pleased about Bansi sleeping in Mani's room and that Bansi would not be allowed upstairs any more.

"Please...please...please...*Kaki*..," Mani pleaded with her. A torrent of fear rose in him as he knew twisted intentions existed...for why should it matter to KP at all?

Kaki laughed for she thought Mani had started enjoying Bansi's company and therefore was not agreeable. "Oh ho!! What are you boys up to? I'm sure you both stay up giggling at night...disturbing *Dada*. You two have had it now!" She chuckled as she said this.

Mani's face was drenched with apprehension but all *Kaki* could interpret was a brooding child. "Come here you...stop sulking now. I've made yum chicken soup for you, it will change your mood right away." *Kaki* said lovingly as she took his hand and guided him to the kitchen.

Mani ate his food but his mind circled around what *Kaki* had told him...looking desperately for a way he could avoid the nights alone upstairs.

"*Kaki*...," he blurted out suddenly. "I don't like my room upstairs. I want to stay here...downstairs." His eyes were wide with expectation.

"Now now!! Look at this one. These boys are definitely up to something or why would *Dada* warn me?" *Kaki* said sternly. "It is so quiet and comfortable upstairs *baba*. Moreover, all the rooms are occupied downstairs...where will Bada go...where will I sleep, we can't sleep upstairs." *Kaki* made it look like a dead end.

On reading the dismay on Mani's face, she said, of course with a clause. "Ok dear, you come to my room when you don't like it upstairs...but don't make it a habit." Then she came closer, cupped her hands around Mani's ears and said, "Don't tell anyone...*Dada* will get angry."

Mani smiled a little...for any escape was tremendous relief. He went out looking for Bansi instantly, but found him with his head buried in his garden. Without lifting his head at all, he said. "They told me to stay away from you. Please go."

Mani, disheartened with the bungalow interfering and causing so much waxing and waning in his friendship with Bansi, left for his room. It was midday and night was far away so he could have some peace. He walked up the stairs slowly, the discomfort in his heart increasing with every step. He slowly opened his room and went and lay down on his bed. He tossed and turned in anxiety, wondering why KP had not allowed Bansi to sleep. He thought of all the nights he slept under the stars with the mongrels on the streets, sometimes even cozying up between them. He never knew fear then...and here in this mansion...overly protected by humans, he was struggling with an unknown fear. Uncertainty is indeed killing, more so when laced with fear. Mani decided on what he would do tonight. He would act sick again and insist on sleeping in *Kaki's* room downstairs. With some consolation in this idea, he drifted off to sleep.

It is a meadow...a seamless vast meadow. Mani, Kishan, Bansi...and Bablu, Kishan's far-off cousin who works as an errand boy for a jeweller, are playing a game of hide and seek. They are all laughing and having fun. At one end of the meadow is a pond, but they have been warned not to drink water from it for a beast lives in it. Kishan, however, wants to try some daredevilry and says he will drink the water and run away from the pond, but as soon as he goes near the pond, a hand grabs his neck...it is the beast and his face has an uncanny resemblance to that of the Fox. Kishan screams out to Mani to save him. Mani runs towards the pond but another hand grabs his neck...

Feeling extremely suffocated, Mani woke up with a start from his dream...only to find KP holding him by his arm. Mani sat up startled and terrified, half recovering from his crazy dream and half in shock on seeing his living nightmare right in front of him. Mani closed his eyes and started trembling in fright...and this probably irritated KP even more for he started losing his temper. KP appeared in a disturbed state of mind, looking here and there and shaking his head.

"*Chhora...,*" KP said, and started howling and crying. This behavior was so unusual, it made Mani's stomach churn and retch, and he felt he would throw up any moment now. He refused to open his eyes though, his heartbeat racing as if motored by an insanely powerful engine. KP got up and thumped his fists on the wall again, all the while sobbing profusely. He suddenly ran back to Mani, kneeled down by his bed and started pleading.

"Give me one chance, *Chhora*...one chance. I didn't do it...believe me, I didn't do it. Oh Brinda...why don't you forgive me...why don't you?" KP pulled at his hair and cried as he said all this.

Mani could not make out any meaning behind his words and the abominable fear rising up in him came out as green vomit, spreading all over the bed and some of it on KP. He even choked on some of it and was coughing incessantly.

KP suddenly came back to his senses and rushed out insensitively. Mani felt he had annoyed KP even more and would have to face worse consequences. He was now in a pitiable state. Crying more out of fear than anything else, he ran downstairs to look for *Kaki*. *Kaki* heard him rushing down and panicked on seeing him. In her innocence, she blamed herself for feeding him the chicken soup. Mani's tears had layers to them but *Kaki* could not think beyond an upset stomach. She, however, helped him change and made him comfortable in her bed. Mani's head reeled with what he had witnessed and he could not bear the thought of facing KP again. The word '*Chhora*' echoed in his head... it felt like someone else that KP talked to...someone else, not Mani. KP was filled with pain whenever he talked to '*Chhora*' but expressed no feeling for a frightened Mani. In fact, it irritated him no end. Night was approaching, but Mani's sobs were refusing to die down. Mani was hiccupping every half an hour...as if a reminder had been set in him.

Sushma *Kaki* had resumed fussing around him and Samsher *Bada* also came to see him twice, looking a bit harrowed...as if he knew there was more to this sickness than simply chicken soup. He did not try to cheer Mani up. He just ran his hand through Mani's head and went away. *Kaki* made a light lentil soup for Mani at night. Mani stayed back in *Kaki's* room that night. He finally drifted off to sleep as *Kaki* softly caressed his head.

Mani did not know how long he had slept as yet, but his eyes suddenly opened wide…it was still dark outside and he heard *Kaki* breathing heavily right next to him. He tried to turn and go off to sleep but the shadows in his mind started lurking around. Stillness is a balm, but only until it makes you face the noises in your head in their loudest form. One by one, thoughts about the night's fiasco started sliding in his head. KP's undecipherable anger and pain made no meaning to him but instilled a greater fear…for he knew now that it was about an opportunity to be caught alone, any time…any day. Mani's heart started racing again as shadows of a hundred KPs with mad red eyes, clenched teeth and clenched fists started dancing around him…some laughing and mocking…some bawling…but all following him like zombies. He sat up panting and parched and thought he would feel better after drinking water. He gathered all his guts to walk through the living area to the kitchen across and get himself water. He tiptoed out of *Kaki's* room and looked around. The night was still and chilly… not even an insect buzzed. He stood there at the entrance of the living area for a few seconds, only to accustom his eyes to the darkness. He knew the house well by now, so he quietly walked across, reaching for the right things at the right time. But as soon as Mani started pouring the water in his glass from the steel jug, the water made a sound on hitting the surface of the glass and he became conscious. He poured it drop by drop and drank to his heart's content. He could hear a cock crow far away and thought it was probably dawn.

He decided to go back to *Kaki's* room but suddenly he felt the wooden flooring creak somewhere. He stood still in the corner outside Bansi's room near the kitchen and strained his ears. After about five minutes he heard a door bang…upstairs. His eyes dilated and a shiver ran up his spine. Reflexively, he slipped inside Bansi's room and realized there was no latch on the door when he tried to bolt it from inside. Bansi was sleeping soundly like a log of wood with his mouth wide open, his bucktooth shining in the night light. Mani panicked again when he heard a far-off sound…that of someone clearing his throat. He knew for sure who the other night owl was and was terrified to the core of his heart. Then a question struck him like lightning. What if KP was checking on him? What if he guessed he was in Bansi's room? He remembered *Kaki's* cautioning and imagined he would come down any moment now, wild with fury to check Bansi's room. Not able to figure out what to do…he looked around and his eyes rested on the door leading to the backyard. He slowly walked up to it and stretched hard to unlatch the door. Toiling and perspiring profusely, he finally opened it and slipped outside into the cold dark night. He sat outside it, tired with fear, and thought of what he would do next to reach *Kaki's* room. But a voice in his head was prodding him continuously to run…just run. The voice was getting louder and louder in the quiet of the night…and apparently so loud that Mani got up and started to run across the backyard till he met the wall. He looked back at the bungalow, especially the window upstairs on the right side and looked away instantly as he saw yellow lights on. He hid behind the Rhododendron tree and was pretty sure KP had seen him running. He imagined numerous consequences and he felt shadows creeping up his back. He peeped once again and saw the curtains were drawn…but his palpitations refused to die down and the voice did not stop hooting *run, run, run*. Mani strained his eyes thinking in which direction he would run…and noticed bricks jutting out from the wall in the corner behind the tree. Without giving it a second thought, Mani started climbing impulsively. When he climbed over to the other side, his hands hanging from the edge of the wall, he realized the wall was pretty high on the other side as it was facing a slope. He knew, however, that he had no choice left now. He clenched his eyes and teeth, curled his legs a little for control and jumped with all his might. Fortunately, the slope saved him from the impact on his bones, making him tumble instead because of the imbalanced fall. Mani tumbled a few times and regained his balance as the momentum decreased.

Here, sitting on the slope in the early dawn of June, Mani realized he was no longer a prisoner of those walls after three long months of fear. However, the voice was yet to die down in his head and so he got up and began to run…directionless…but hopefully away from KP's shadow. Birds had begun chirping and there was a typical freshness in the air, and Mani knew it was dawn. A new day was breaking and with it a new life…yet again…hopefully. Mani had visited every nook and corner of the town as the coalbearer, but he seemed to have missed the slope. He did not know where he was heading…whether he needed to go uphill or run downhill. Following his instinct, however, he ran downhill and after running about 50 metres, he could see the town market. He felt relief and took the road parallel to that of the main road through the market. He did not want to go back to being the coalbearer again…and the Fox, never again…so he took a new route today…an alternate road that led him out of this town altogether.

He had run quite a long way and the colour of the sky was slowly changing. He saw many women washing the front of their houses, ready to begin a new day. Panting hard, he stopped running now and walked slowly…and leisurely. He was thirsty and his legs were giving away. Luckily, he noticed a woman filling a can of water around the bend of the road. He stopped there and saw that it was a natural spring. Even in the faint daylight, he noticed a slightly suspicious expression on the woman's face. She must have been in her forties and was wearing a wrap-around with a tunic and had also tied her head with a cloth. She looked at him from top to toe and asked, "Where are you headed to so early? Whose son are you?"

Mani suddenly became conscious and realized the fault was with the night suit…the clean satin blue night suit, his clean skin and new slippers, for he had never invoked suspicion in anyone as a coalbearer with the dirty tweed coat at any time of the day or the night.

Becoming conscious he mumbled, "No one's…."

Whether this was the harsh truth or an expression of freedom, but this was certainly not an answer that would nullify the lady's growing suspicion. Realizing this quickly, and taking a chance, Mani made up a story instantly.

"Oh *Kaki*…don't you recognize me…the little monk? I bought coal so many times to your house and still you don't recognize me?" The tone was such as if he were offended on not being recognized, the celebrity. He continued with an explanation, "My '*mahajan*' asked me to collect some due amount from a *Kaka* who stays around that bend, near the 'Durpin point'…you know business starts early and I have to go back to deliver coal…can I have some water *Kaki*?"

Not really able to swallow what she heard, the lady just moved away with her can with a "Hmmm…"

Mani drank as much water as he could with his cupped hands and thought he should move faster lest he raise even more suspicion. He wished he could discard his clothes…they were such a nuisance, but he didn't have a choice. So he walked away quickly but only after waving out to the lady who was still staring questioningly, standing at her doorstep across the road.

He walked till he reached the stretch where there were hardly any houses or shops. Darkness had totally gone and the morning was bright and clear, the dew drops on the grass below wetting his satin pyjamas as he walked. Far below, down the slope, he could see an unusually long concrete structure. He took the lane going downhill and saw a wide road with metal tracks criss-crossing and a few vehicles plying. He guessed it was probably the main road. On coming closer, he could read the hoarding on the long structure. It was written, 'GHUM RAILWAY STATION.' Yes! Mani could read and write now.

On reaching the end of the lane going downhill, Mani noticed a train was chugging…creating huge clouds of smoke. He ran across in an impulse and got on to the train, on to a new journey.

Chapter 12

Mani had jumped on to the train just in time, for as soon as he got in, it started moving. Although there were just three people in the compartment, Mani chose to sit on the floor near the door. This was the same train that he used to love peeping inside, and would hop on and off, playfully on his return, whenever he had to deliver coal to the railway station side of the town. Many a time, tourists waiting to take a ride would want to take a picture with him…the dirty little monk with the coal carrier. He would oblige them with his most charming smile. Never had he thought he would be travelling in the train…but when had he thought he'd be a coalbearer…or for that matter, KP's son…or prisoner?

The train took many bends and slowly came away from the wooden cottages, hutments and roadside shops under the azure skies and vast frills of green hills, layer beyond layer. The majestic Kanchenjunga shone in all its glory as the golden morning sun emblazed the entire range. The view was so elevating that Mani was totally absorbed…his heart feeling a joy so pure…the kind that did not need a reason to be, and its extent, inexplicable. It filled him with hope. Such is the divinity of nature…it gives you back to yourself…washed with purity, joy and hope. He felt free like the eagles soaring in the sky.

As the morning progressed, school-going children started hopping on to the train at approaching stations. They giggled and chattered in excitement, and for once he could relate to many things they talked about because he had learnt about them from Shahana... and there, a chord was struck by memory...Shahana. He suddenly realized he would never see her...or Sushma *Kaki*...or Samsher *Bada*... and he suddenly missed them intensely. He felt as if someone had slashed his heart with a sword...how worried they must be! He imagined *Kaki* crying helplessly and started feeling the impact of what he had done for the first time. Questions started rising up in him like worms crawling out of a can...and the loudest one was, where was he going after all? He started feeling nervous and wondering what he would do if he were found.... He imagined a merciless KP thrashing him with his fists and himself curled up in fright. Couldn't human beings ever stay in one place in their minds? The ecstasy of freedom was slowly dying down and clouds of uncertainty slowly rising around Mani. Having lived a protected life had probably made him insecure, for never as a coalbearer had Mani worried how his next hour would be...it would come as it would and Mani would just be in it. But not anymore...for everything got worse with the hunger pangs in his stomach. *Kaki's* pampering and care and the thought of warm delicious food she cooked for him made him feel miserable and his eyes filled with tears...for he had certainly found a home in *Kaki* and *Bada*...if not in the bungalow. And Shahana...well...He missed her even if he refused to.

It was midday now and Mani was tired of sitting in the train. Moreover, he could no longer tolerate his hunger. He made up his mind to get off on the next station. The train passed through steep gradients and at times he felt as if it were hanging on the track, for all he could see was a fathomless gorge before him. At one such steep gradient, he noticed the passengers all excitedly peeping out. A man with a typical Gurkha cap, a local probably, took the opportunity to play guide to the others and declared with deep pride.

"This is Agony point, the most important gradient on this route."

Mani, the child, could barely make out of the greatest metaphor of his life in this statement so he joined the swooning tourists who responded with an "Ahhh!!" They were anyway speechless, totally enraptured by the beauty of the landscape. There below them lay the vast expanse of a deep gorge; surrounded by green pine, chestnut and magnolia trees, sun-kissed with the diamond-studded Kanchenjunga sitting prim on top of it all like a tiara. "The queen of the hills"… one would know why in this very moment. The dainty train looked incapable of taking the sharp cuts and bends but amazed everyone with its adeptness. A passenger, with typical Caucasian looks, looked on serenely satisfied as if he were witnessing Mark Twain's journey on this steam-engine toy train when the latter described it as "most enjoyable day on earth."

In about half an hour, a station arrived and the train slowed down to a halt. Mani got off without a thought just as he had got in. He did not have an address to reach today; the entire world was his home. He got off at a small, inconspicuous place that read "Gayabari." The train took off after halting barely for a minute after its significant chugging, and puffed away making smoke clouds in the air. Suddenly, Mani felt anxious once the train went out of sight. Should he have alighted here? He felt confused and the fact that there was not a soul around made it worse. The tiny railway station, which was barely as big as a cowshed, looked abandoned, as if mirroring Mani's present situation. Mani walked around a bit as his legs were stiff sitting for over seven hours. He realized the weather was humid and hot…and the satin bed-suit he was wearing had grown limp with perspiration and dust. Unaccustomed to the heat, he opened the front buttons of his shirt right up to his navel for aeration. Mani went around the back of the station shed and relieved himself in the thickets there. He looked around and saw a monkey *(langur)* hanging from one of the branches by one of his arms, a few feet away, looking as surprised as Mani. Mani quickly came away and sat down near the stationmaster's door…hoping some human would come soon. Vehicles zoomed by on the highway but not a soul was in sight. Probably tired with waiting and hunger…and lethargic from the humid weather, Mani lay down there and fell off to sleep.

"Oye keta…oye kancha!!"

Mani woke up with a start…it felt as if the Fox was trying to wake him up…on days he came early to the godown. He rubbed his eyes but there was no coal around…the light was bright and piercing. An old man wearing a grey shirt and khaki trousers was trying to wake him up. He had a green flag tucked under his left armpit.

Mani looked at him and smiled. Sometimes, a human can elate you too.

"Who are you? Where have you come from?" The man questioned.

Without even blinking, Mani said. "I'm hungry and very thirsty *Kaka*. Please give me water."

The old man got up and opened the office. "Come inside," he called out to Mani. He handed a jug of water and a steel glass to Mani. Mani drank like never before, never having known thirst like he did today.

"Don't go anywhere, I'm coming," the man said as he walked out of the door. He went out to one end of the platform and held the green flag. A train puffed by, filling the whole place with smoke. Mani did not know about guards and was amused.

As soon as the man returned, he asked inquisitively. "Do you do this for all the trains all the time?"

The man simply smiled at the boy's innocence, ignored his question and asked again.

"What are you up to? How did you come here?"

"Give me something to eat *Kaka*…I'll die of hunger." Mani said unhesitatingly as he dodged the man's questions. He was definitely not in favour of revealing the truth and was looking for a way out of it all.

The man took out a packet of 'Parle G' biscuits and gave it to Mani, and waited patiently till he voraciously ate it all up. Mani never felt so satiated before. He was just savouring the last piece when the man threw his question again.

"Ok now. Enough dilly-dallying. Tell me, where have you come from and who are your parents?" He asked in a go, his elbows on the table he was sitting across, palms locked supporting his chin. He had smelled something fishy and was out to know the truth.

"Ugh!!" thought Mani to himself. "Parents? Got to be this satin nuisance."

Before the man got more suspicious, Mani said, "I ran away."

"Ah! I knew it." The man slapped the table as if he had unlocked a mystery. Feeling confident, he got up and walked around like a detective. "Where from?" He asked again.

Mani was sure about one thing. He would not bring the bungalow back in his life ever. He made up quick story or rather borrowed Kishan's.

"I used to work in a sweet shop. They used to beat me there. I ran away." Mani uttered in a small voice.

The man was hardly convinced. "Do they give out such clothes to errand boys these days in sweet shops?" He asked, sarcastically with his brows arched.

"No no…these I took from the owner's son. I used to sleep at their place. They used to make me do the household chores too." Mani was soon concocting a story and thought this would certainly invoke some sympathy but the man was unrelenting.

"Chores eh!! With those soft clean hands…indeed!!" The man was slowly losing patience with Mani's lies…and Mani realized he couldn't goof up now. He had forgotten that the bungalow had made him look like 'Mani Pradhan' and he could no longer borrow Mani, the coalbearer's identity. The bungalow was like a vulture for it was just not releasing him from its claws and this worried Mani. He could not bear to go back now.

"Let me work here, *Kaka*. Anything. I'll do anything." Mani began pleading. "Please *Kaka*...please."

It must have been around four then, for suddenly children started running across the platform like a swarm of bees. There was probably a school nearby and it was over for the day. Mani wondered where they were going and where they had come from, for he had seen no human habitation in the vicinity. However, he was acquainted with the nature of habitation in the hills so he knew there were pockets of communities or bastis around, hidden away in bends and valleys. This thought gave him a glimmer of hope. Suddenly, a female voice interrupted his stream of thoughts.

"*Namaskar* Guard Babu. Who's this? When did railways start employing kids?" She laughed as she said this, a fat woman in her forties. She stood at the doorway breathing heavily.

"*Namaskar Guru Aama*." The man replied to her greeting. "Looks like a rich boy run away from home...but won't speak. Stubborn creature." He looked at Mani as if offended by him. Mani dug his face in the ground.

"Oh! Is it?" The lady suddenly became interested. "Where to, young lad?" She asked.

Mani said nothing.

They both went a few feet away and engaged in an elaborate conversation. Mani was dying of apprehension and his biggest fear was that of going back. At no cost, he thought to himself. He was wondering if he needed to escape from this place too as the guard had taken it upon himself to get this 'rich boy' home. He stood at the door watching the kids go with backpacks when he noticed the guard and the lady walk towards him.

The guard spoke first. "Listen young boy...here *Guru Aama* is going to keep you at the school as an errand boy till we find out about you so that we can send you back. Do you get it? We will file a report about you in the nearest police station so don't think you'll get away. And don't you act smart, or you've had it. We have our eyes on you."

The lady nodded in agreement throughout with a stern face.

"Come with me now," she said. "You'll stay with me till we find out about you."

Mani was relieved he had found a place to stay...but his fear did not leave him. The clause about the police was snatching away his peace, but he could hardly do anything about it...at least for today as evening was approaching fast. Moreover, he did not want to run away from a meal...no, not today. He was fatigued and was craving for food and a place to sleep.

He followed *Guru Aama* across the road to a small man-made lane, and walked along the grass and ferns through turns and bends till he could spot ten to twelve small cottages in a terraced pattern. Smoke was coming out of some of them and he felt a strange warmth in his heart, for the small basti reminded him of his home...the one he had lost to a fire, the one which had made him a wanderer. He hoped *Guru Aama* lived there too.

On reaching the first house, he knew she did from the familiar smiles the people flashed on seeing her. A granny sitting outside one of it said, "You're late today, Bimala."

"Yes, *Chhema*." *Guru Aama* replied. "Bought a boy for the school today." She stood away from Mani so that the old lady could see.

"Aha! What a plump one you've found." Granny seemed to take an instant liking for Mani and Mani smiled shyly.

Guru Aama laughed and walked on. She stopped at the fifth house, a small wooden cottage with flower pots arranged neatly outside. She unlocked the house and asked Mani to come in. There was a cozy kitchen and a wash area in one corner and a room with two small beds, an almirah and a table in the middle. The entire upholstery was done up with colourful crochet mats and covers...even the window pelmets.

Guru Aama realized she hadn't even asked the fellow's name. "Hey, what's your name? You have to tell me about yourself...I need to tell the police, too. He just lives next door, Rubin *Bhai*. He'll come in the evening."

Whether she was speaking the truth or staging it all, no one would know, and Mani, not yet.

"In fact, I'll just talk to him. I'll come in a moment, don't leave the house," she said and left with the door ajar. Mani wouldn't have anyway…not today. She came back after around 10 minutes. "He'll see you tomorrow. Here, take these clothes and change." She had brought shirts and shorts…the same ones the children were wearing as uniform. Mani took them willingly for anything was better than what he was wearing. He was in a hurry to discard that identity anyway…that of the rich boy. She showed him the tap that was outside the house. The water was therapeutic and Mani leisurely washed himself. He went inside the wash area and changed. *Guru Aama* had begun preparing dinner.

"Come here…what's your name? Help me with the dinner." *Guru Aama* called out in a placid tone.

Mani suddenly missed Sushma *Kaki* immensely. It hit him that he was no longer anyone's '*baba*' and baby. He was slapped with a change of identity again. He would not be served food for free here.

"Mani…Maniraj Khaling," Mani muttered. He was not sure if this name was safe here and he did not know of any other name. He had discarded 'Mani Pradhan' with the satin clothes.

"Okay," *Guru Aama* said without much interest. She was more interested in getting the dinner done. "Here, chop these vegetables," she said.

Mani managed somehow, although he knew what a mess he had made when *Guru Aama* gave him a rather disgusted look.

However, the day did end and what a day it had been. A meal and a warm blanket with a roof on top was heaven on earth today. Mani closed his eyes and descended into a sweet slumber as the first rains of the season came pouring down dancing on the asbestos roof.

And so began a new life for Maniraj Khaling…in the custody of

Guru Aama. His entire life revolved around her from wake to sleep. He followed her to school and back, and his dream of going to a school was fulfilled. He sat at the back of any class that interested him any time, got up to ring the bell, make tea for the staff, helped with the totaling of bills, ran every errand and practically became the circulation of the school in no time. *Guru Aama* paid him Rs. 50 a month for it all. He came home with *Guru Aama,* helped her with all the chores, and then came the best part of the day - study time when he learnt the lessons she taught him. Observing his interest, she promised she would allow him to appear for the school-leaving certificate exams if he learnt well, and he learnt with tremendous zeal.

No police came for an enquiry ever. No one on this earth was looking for Maniraj Khaling and he slowly realized *Guru Aama* had no other person in her life other than Mani. Thoughts of his old life came before he drifted off to sleep on most nights but he knew they were as far as a dream now. He liked his old name clubbed with his new life, gracefully laced in simplicity, and most importantly, fearlessness.

CHAPTER 13

Four years had passed by. Mani's life had taken a different route altogether and nothing was the same, not even Mani. Naya Basti, Gayabari was his address…whether his permanent one, only time would tell. The basti, where every other house was a family extension, where every person was a relative, not only in the way someone was addressed, but in spirit too. Mani had not experienced a single day when he was not absorbed in the course of life of some Granny, Grandpa, Uncle, Aunt, sister, brother, baby…you name it. Someday he would be tending to someone ailing, someday he would be busy with someone's spring cleaning, gardening, cooking for a feast…someday someone's marriage, death or birth…someday running errands, getting a grandpa's pension from the bank, running to the post office, or going to the market, even if it meant a 10-km trip and back. Mani had no family bringing him up…but an entire community, yes. It had its perks too…for he had indeed become the apple of everyone's eyes. God's grace came down upon him through everyone's true affection for him.

Although not sure of his birth year…and if Mani were to consider a certain birthday in his life as true, he was seventeen now…a youth with eyes full of dreams of manhood, a greater life, an identity. Mani hadn't grown very tall, only up to five feet, four inches to be precise, but a light moustache, a sparse beard and of course the rush of hormones in his blood made him look different. His red cheeks had freckles and he had learnt to do his hair in a way that it looked as if he had a middle parting.

Guru Aama's house had been a good refuge, for although he was not sure if he had found a home but he had definitely given her a home. She had grown fatter, unhealthy and careless whereas Mani, strong and mature. Mani managed most of the non-academic affairs of the school. Mani managed the entire house from chores to every decision. Mani managed *Guru Aama's* health and stoic disposition.

In short, Mani managed her entire life and everything had happened so organically, it looked as if things were meant to be this way since forever.

Mani had developed a keen interest in music, for since he landed in *Guru Aama's* house, his closest companion was the radio, which he repaired as soon as he earned some money. The entire neighbourhood was treated to his soulful singing as he went around with his chores and no one complained about it. In fact, the charmer that he was, helping one and all, big or small, whenever he got the opportunity, he was adored by most people and most of all by Guard *Kaka*. Guard *Kaka* reminded Mani of Samsher *Bada* and Mani liked being with him. He compensated for the lack of a father figure in Mani's life. In fact, he did tell *Kaka* his story one evening but concealed the names claiming ignorance, for who would not know the Pradhan business family and their legacy. Mani also asked him if he had really informed the police or if it was just a threat. Guard *Kaka* had laughed out loud to that and said, "Do you think a rich spoilt brat would survive more than two days here? He would be bawling to go back home once the thrill of his adventure was over. Ten days on with you, we knew you did not have anywhere to go back to…and *Guru Aama* needed a boy anyway. We didn't need to."

Mani had completed his school-leaving certificate exams this year and was now planning to join a college 15 km away from Gayabari, the only college in that area. He had asked *Guru Aama* once but she said nothing.

Two days later, she said indifferently, "I won't pay you the monthly Rs. 50 once you join college."

Mani knew he would be needing the money if he went to college and understood her apprehension too…for her asthma and obesity had made her so dependent on him that she knew it would be tough for her if the bird left the cage.

He replied instantly. "No *Guru Aama*…I'll manage everything, the files and bills at school, the food, washing…everything. I'll make sure I finish everything. You will only need someone for the tea…and the bell. If you want, I can arrange that too…in fact Jyoti *Bhauju* would gladly do it. She gets bored at home as Tilak *Daju* is away or drunk most of the time." It was no secret that Mani was also everyone's best friend, the kind compassionate listener…and, therefore, a witness to everyone's life in the neighbourhood.

Guru Aama said nothing as usual. She was probably simply relieved Mani would not be leaving the house.

At night before going to sleep she said, "I'll pay your fees for the college."

Mani was overjoyed. He knew *Guru Aama* was not a heartless being…it was just that she did not know her way through emotions. She avoided them…or rather, did not know how to use them. The only role she excelled at was that of a strict schoolteacher and most of her interactions were one-way and instructional. Mani wondered and chuckled a bit at times, thinking if she was born in the school itself…a fat, short-haired baby wearing a sari with a big mole near her left ear. He had asked her often where her family was and she had remained silent. She did not care to ask Mani where he came from too. She had this peculiar habit of behaving as if Mani did not exist when he asked something she did not want to respond to. The neighbours told him she came to work in this school since it had been established and had lived alone. No one came to visit her and never had they seen her leave the place. She carried a heavy past no doubt...and probably it had converted into her weight and asthma now. Mani wondered if she too had escaped a life like him...or maybe had faced worse, and it was this thought that maintained his compassion towards her in spite of her stoicism. It made him stay with her against all odds.

Chapter 14

July came and it was a significant one. It was 15th July, 1985 and the first day of college for Mani. Firsts are always precious…they stay with you forever. The first butterfly you run after, the first sunrise and sunset you consciously gaze at, the first time you watch the waves of the sea coming closer to engulf you, the first time you travel alone, the first human you cherish…College had many such firsts in store for Mani. Strangely enough, this was also the first time he would be part of the process of formal education, for even after having practically lived in the school, his name was entered into the register as a student only six months ago to appear for the matriculation exams. But here, registered as Maniraj Khaling for Higher Secondary-Arts, he walked shoulder to shoulder with his generation, undivided by destiny yet, all carrying hope like the bright morning sun.

Kurseong College had the apt motto that said;"*Akash tira pakheta chalon, prithvi basera.*"

It verbalized the eagle soaring in Mani's heart, looking up to the beauty of the blue sky, his feet firmly grounded as he walked uphill towards the college by the slopes, neatly lined by white parapet. The hope was that he too would own a little of the blue sky, his name too would bear an address that time would not dare dismiss.

Mani had another boy, Norbu Lama, accompanying him from Gayabari. The latter stayed in the locality on the main road, about 2 km from the railway station. Although they weren't thick pals yet, college had brought them together in purpose. Both the boys, carrying the humble simplicity of the place where they came from, realized the very first day that college was a foreign land. All kinds assembled here. They nervously followed the others around for the induction lectures on the first day and could barely utter their names when asked for an introduction. The town boys and girls grabbed all the attention, some with their confidence, some with their attitude, and some with their fashion sense that bordered on the weird in Mani and Norbu's minds. An entire generation seemed to be coloured in a rage of punk...the influence that was yet to touch these simple homebodies. The leather jackets, the strange hairdos, boys with shoulder-length wavy hair and rugged stoned looks...girls with permed-up hair and short skirts with puffed up blouses...and the conversations that hardly involved anyone but a 'Madonna' or a 'Michael Jackson' or worse, hard rock... it was overwhelming, extremely overwhelming.

As the first day was closing in, Mani and Norbu were walking down with a feeling of alienation, doubting if they would fit in this strange world. They felt as if they had been swimming in unknown waters all day long and felt tired and lost.

On the way back home, Norbu innocently asked Mani, "What about the studies? Where and when do they do that?"

Mani, equally confused, weighed down a heavier question. "Norbu, do you think we did the right thing by going there? What will I tell *Guru Aama*?"

No, not one human being had braced them for college. Little did they know that this in itself was a bracing for life, and not without the clause that life...wayward, unstoppable as it is...never meets you prepared. One prepares for it and then again - every time with bits and pieces of what one has learnt last.

As they hopped on to a bus that would take them home, they looked pensive, unsure if they wanted to even attend a second day.

Norbu got off first. "Tomorrow, at eight," he called out. The enthusiasm that was there the evening before when they had met to plan for college had waned. Mani simply nodded his head in response.

Days turned to weeks and then to months. Mani and Norbu, soul brothers now, gradually realized that the college was not foreign shores where they had mistakenly landed, but very much the oyster, and it was up to each one climbing up its slope to make what he or she wanted to make out of it. So, many conversations about Bollywood and Sri Devi too crawled out of the layers slowly. In fact, the wooly perm on top of female heads…it wasn't inspired by Brooke Shields but Meenakshi Seshadri back home. And well!! There were talents that couldn't go unnoticed and Mani very soon emerged as the 'Kishore Kumar' of Kurseong College with scores of female admirers dreaming about him singing romantic numbers only for them. As soon as the layers came off little by little, Mani realized the College was the place that made them feel they were a part of this huge world… an eye-opener where there was so much to discover and learn and above all, become. Mani and Norbu no longer hid in corners to eat their humble lunch that they carried from home, shying away from the hip crowd splurging treat-outs and bars, which they thought was the norm initially. Like conscious and shy caterpillars, they crawled in but discovered a humungous truth about trendsetting. They learnt that one need not blindly follow the crowd. Struggling as each one was to build an image, and therefore, desperately searching for latches to hold on to, they realized that you could be the one to set your own trend, be it inspired by ideology or taste. They learnt to spread their wings and fly. So, soon there was a place to hang out for the 'Bollywood types' (sic-'Hindis') as much as the 'Guns and Roses' (Hollywood) types. Apart from this cinematic divide, there was as much freedom of expression for the Communists (which came as a natural advantage in Bengal) as the new Congress era under Rajiv Gandhi. Yes! College was definitely the place where it seeped in that it was every individual's contribution that made Governments, superpowers, and created this massive political energy that had the world in constant drive. The birth of the citizen and the adrenaline rush of power, it took birth in College. Education was not only about the written word here, and as far as the written word was concerned, there was a place for one who couldn't take his eyes off books, as well as a place for many who didn't care to touch books in years. It was indeed a wonderful place, the open sky embracing all dreamers and gifting a paintbrush in each hand to draw their own path to cross life.

And then of course, there was Neetu, the girl who openly admired Mani but Norbu secretly had a crush on. So soon enough, all memories of college were built around these three- Mani, Norbu and now Neetu. They ate together, sang songs together and went hiking and exploring hillsides together. Neetu was a tall slim girl, with hair flowing down to her hips. She dressed casually…never too elaborately… and was in jeans and sneakers most of the time. She had soft dimples when she smiled and pretty features. Though she came across as a plain Jane, there were many who were interested in her. Mani too thought about her sometimes…and smiled when sunlight hit her sparkling brown eyes, for she reminded him of Shahana. He avoided thinking of any possibility beyond that for he knew his life was still at *Guru Aama's* mercy and his heart could not afford the vulnerability of ecstasies and aches that came with love. He loved Neetu's company though and cherished her as a friend.

Being constantly occupied, Mani felt as if the days of this year were rushing by. The daily rut of getting up at dawn, doing the household chores, rushing to college and then to the school, spending some time with Guard *Kaka* (as he now looked out for Mani more than the trains)…and then again back to the basti and cooking dinner hardly left any time for himself. When the 10-day break for 'Dashain' was announced in college, Mani felt the chill in the October air for the first time. The change in weather at this time of the year affected Mani in a strange way. The rest of the world seemed overjoyed to welcome this festive period while Mani felt hollow and lonely inside. He missed having a family most at this time of the year, when he saw scores of relatives joyously arriving and leaving his neighbours' houses with the significant mark of blessing on their foreheads illustrated by a generous mix of raw rice and red vermilion, the "Tika." He hardly remembered any such celebration from his early life as a reference, but when he missed, he missed Sushma *Kaki's* and Samsher *Bada's* enthusiasm and the efforts they made to see him happy. He remembered how their faces lit up when they were around him…family had to be that way in his imagination, and *Guru Aama's* stoic ways depressed him all the more. *Guru Aama* and his foreheads appeared untouched and forlorn throughout the season and the former appeared least affected by it, whereas the latter secretly pined to feel joy in the scarlet symbol. Moreover, the basti which seemed to be one big family all year through, felt somehow divided by the thickness of blood during this season. All houses were occupied with their 'own people' and such was the tacit assertion that Mani felt left out everywhere. So he made up his mind to do something different this year…on his own.

He noticed most of his neighbours were on a cleaning spree, painting up their houses, polishing their brass, putting up new curtains and doing up their houses to the best of their affordability. Mani set out to do the same. He sun-dried the mattresses, put up new glaze paper on the shelves, rearranged everything, washed the crochet curtains and bought some blue paint to do up the entrance porch. *Guru Aama* just lay down and watched him do what he was doing. The fact that she did not disapprove could be taken for granted that she'd approved. Lately, she had bloated up excessively and had even stopped going to school. She blamed the incessant coughing as her excuse to stay back home although there was more to her illness. And how would Mani know…for wasn't he still a teenager…how much more burdens of life could he carry at eighteen? Knowing and premonition was in itself the highest perfection one could achieve in this sea of uncertainties that one called life, and Mani had just begun living it…there were smaller illusions to trap him at first, like this festival season. His own want for affection stroked some expectations from *Guru Aama* in him that made him brood about her lack of any emotion, and thus, he was blind to the blood she had been spitting out these days while coughing. She wouldn't tell anyone anyway. So she lay on her bed all the while and Mani kept misreading it as disinterest, and in his resulting irritation, avoided even looking at her. Contempt, as Mani was experiencing these days for *Guru Aama,* is the first struggle one faces before coming to the realization that family…and a happy one…is more about acceptance than anything else, and how would he find joy in being one if he kept looking for Sushma *Kaki* in *Guru Aama*? Some lessons are definitely learnt the hard way. Caught in this whirlpool of conflicting emotions, the only event that he could actually look forward to this holiday period was the 'Fulpati,' the carnival and bull fight that thousands collected to watch on the seventh day of the sacred nine-day long festival dedicated to Goddess Durga. Early morning he left with Norbu for Kurseong to be a part of this celebration. He rejoiced in the traditional songs and dances, the dance of the masked demons, and dissolved his loneliness in this collective celebration. He noticed that Norbu was somewhat distracted, as if searching for something or someone but shook his head when Mani looked at him questioningly with raised eyebrows. Norbu left Mani to watch the bull fight, cock fight, etc. alone in the latter part of the day, saying he had some work and needed to leave. Mani found it a bit strange and wasn't really convinced by his excuse but did not ask much for he wasn't disposed to ask too many questions. Norbu left and Mani found himself company in a bunch of excited children hooting and whistling while they watched the bloody games of animals killing each other.

The last day of the break and the first day of 'Tika' arrived, the day when the house entrances were decorated with marigold garlands, meat delicacies were prepared and the Gods were worshipped at home as the first visitor. Ironically, one can assume him to be the most loyal relative and hence is consecrated first in every house. Mani too had spent the last evening making garlands, and he decorated the door and the small deck railing that demarcated the porch from the lane passing by *Guru Aama's* house. Yes, he still couldn't call it his too…even if he had brought it to life. The externalities were managed so far but what next? Mani was wondering what to do when *Guru Aama* spoke for the first time in all these days and in a tone that had mellowed and become pliable like soft dough.

She constantly had a cloth on her mouth these days as she coughed so often, so she muttered through.

"Won't you do the *puja* Mani? And how will I put Tika on your forehead if you don't make the arrangements? When will you get the sweets? Hurry…go."

An ecstatic current of happiness ran through Mani's heart. Just these words made him feel so energized, he felt as if he could shift mountains. He experienced the elation he had been longing for since the last few days as he trudged through compulsively with the cleaning. In this one moment he felt that he had been doing all that just to avoid being miserable, but what he would do now was for the joyof having *Guru Aama* with him, of belonging somewhere, of making a difference to someone… just these few words made him realize that she was there throughout, involved in spirit, appreciating silently.

Without wasting a second, Mani ran up the slope to buy some sweets from the only sweet shop in Gayabari. He returned in an hour to find another surprise waiting for him. Sitting primly on the bamboo stools beside *Guru Aama's* bed were a young couple with their backs to the door. Mani was flummoxed. He thought to himself, "Did *GuruAama* have her 'own people' after all?" On hearing the door open, they turned and Mani was all smiles to see Neetu and Norbu. Neetu looked ravishing in the traditional attire and Mani could not take his eyes off her.

"Stop staring you bloke, you're making me conscious," she said as she approached to give him a sheepish hug.

Mani suddenly had so many reasons to celebrate today. He felt rich today, rich with family and friends and beamed with joy. *Guru Aama's* little cottage looked so bright and hustled with so much activity that it made the neighbours curious in spite of their own engagements. Their celebrations had grown stale over the years but the one at *Guru Aama's* house had a novelty, freshness to it...amplified multiple times by Neetu, who shone like a Goddess in a red sari and hair flowing down to her waist. Suddenly, a question flashed across the eyes of all women in the basti. "Who is she?" And that would be the most interesting conversation for the next few days, Mani laughed to himself as he thought so.

Neetu had thoughtfully brought mutton for Mani. Meat was the sacred offering to the Goddess and was cooked in every house. Many animals were sacrificed at her feet on the eighth and ninth day of the festival, which was distributed as Prasad. Soon enough, Neetu helped Mani with all the arrangements and they cooked a simple meal together. Mani felt a kind of warmth only a female presence can bring into a house and found so much joy in doing things together with Neetu. He smiled thinking if this could be forever but brushed aside his musings quickly. When everything was readied, Neetu asked *Guru Aama* to put 'Tika' for them. Mani helped her get up slowly and they sat down in a row on the floor. She kneeled in front of each of them and coloured their foreheads with the auspicious 'Tika.' They sought her blessings by joining their hands and bowing down to her and she placed her right hand on their heads. She gave them sweets, flowers, the *'Jawara'* that Mani brought from the neighbours and some money as a token of her blessings. Mani had never felt so overwhelmed. He was washed with emotion as he went through this ritual and his eyes welled up throughout. After they received their blessings, Mani applied 'Tika' on *Guru Aama's* forehead and bowed down with joined hands to express respect. *Guru Aama* kept her eyes closed all through the ritual, her hands joined and close to her chest. Neetu nudged him later, saying usually only the elders gave their blessings to younger ones. He smiled at that knowing some rules needed to be flouted if it involved a loved one's happiness. He knew in his heart what meaning this little act had for *Guru Aama*.

Neetu and Norbu left in the afternoon after having lunch with Mani. Mani went to see them off till the main road. Norbu walked ahead of them, somewhat distant. Thinking it was just his way to be, slightly quiet and distant, Neetu and Mani started singing songs to attract his attention. He remained unaffected and dismissed them with an "Aech…what rubbish!"

On reaching the road, he suddenly became grave and said, "Mani, since when is all this happening?"

Totally surprised by the question, Mani said, "What…what happened?"

"Don't tell me you don't know," Norbu said somewhat disgusted.

Mani and Neetu looked at each other dazed.

Norbu looked at the ground for some time and then said calmly. "When you people were helping *Guru Aama* to kneel down on the floor for the 'Tika', the pillow fell. And I saw…I saw a whole lot of bloodstained cloth, a whole lot. Mani, I think she is very ill."

Norbu's words struck like lightning. Mani recalled *Guru Aama's* coughing bouts and the permanent cloth at her mouth these days. A spear of guilt ran through him for not having been able to see her suffering. He looked at Norbu and ran up to him and hugged him.

"What should I do now?" Mani asked Norbu innocently.

Neetu pitched in instantly. "One of my cousins is a nurse at Kurseong Hospital. I'll ask her."

Neetu and Norbu left while Mani walked down the slope pensively, wondering what he would do now. When he reached halfway, he noticed Gurung Sir's door slightly open and decorated by a marigold garland barely covering the sides of the door. He thought of going ahead and meeting him today. He could be counted on for sound advice regarding anything. He'd definitely know what Mani ought to do.

CHAPTER 15

In spite of his hesitation, Mani took the diversion and hurried down the lane that led to Gurung Sir's house. The thought that *Guru Aama's* health needed immediate attention rattled in his head and his heart paced a little faster than usual.

Gurung Sir's house was in the course of construction and was a confusing dump of bamboo poles, iron rods, bricks and mortar. Only one end of the house on the first floor was complete, although it was still drab and grey, as it was yet to be painted. A stingy garland was the only dash of colour in the entire scheme of dreariness. Mani could hear voices as he approached the door that was left ajar, and wondered what to do…for Gurung Sir's perennially grave expression was difficult to read…Mani would never know if he was disgusted with Mani for coming at the wrong time or something else was lurking in his head.

'But when was the right time anyway? And *Guru Aama?* No no… this is serious,' he thought to himself. He would not allow the world's idiosyncrasies to get in the way of his pressing task, so he went ahead and knocked without a second thought.

"Who's that?" Gurung Sir asked from inside.

"Sir…it's me," Mani answered rather shyly.

"Oh…come in," Sir said.

Mani walked in with his head bent down and stood aside. Neither was he asked to take a seat, nor was there a place where he could. He noticed two other people sitting in the living room. They were dressed in trousers and jackets, and wore black caps with metallic badges showing two khukris in a cross, the Gorkha pride, on one side.

One of them was speaking with great emotion. Pointing to his cap and bordering on rage, he remained unfazed by Mani's presence and spoke, probably in continuation of a conversation they were already having.

"Gurung *Daju*, this badge…this cross has a somewhat elitist effect on those who do not wear it. People wearing it command an unspoken respect from those not wearing it…as if they were doing a favour on the latter for upholding the Gorkha pride, and therefore, are entitled to be looked up to. When academicians like him wear it, they burden it more with a kind of farcical intellectualism that only complicate its ownership. The irony is that, the pride matters, and upholding it is a greater virtue these days than those who actually made the weapon a symbol of virtue. The Gorkha soldiers remain unacknowledged and also the many who actually know the art of wielding the khukri, but perhaps, not the depth of its purpose. This is where he is playing, *Daju*…the naivety of this population, this is what this man is converting into his opportunity."

He seemed to be fuming whereas the other two listened intently. Mani could barely make sense of the conversation except the wrath that this person had against a certain 'him.'

The other person nodded vigorously to prove his agreement and then spoke, in a comparatively composed and softer voice. "Yes yes, Sarat *Bhai*…we have toiled all these years for a place in history…a place to call our own, and the opportunist that he is, he makes it look like there never was a voice. Krishna Subba, Deoraj Sharma…were their sacrifices empty? Are they not '*shaheeds*'? Statehood was our demand. He jumped on to the bandwagon and is talking violence now to gain popularity amongst the masses, threatening our very ideology of non-violence. Can you beat that? He has simply snatched the '*Pranta Parishad*' off our plates! And I'll tell you what he's planning now…"

Gurung Sir interrupted with a cough…probably a signal that plans were definitely not to be discussed in volatile environments. He retorted in a light tone. "And when was politics about ideology, Nar Bahadur? If not about opportunities, would Jyoti Babu be ruling over us for his second term, too? And will do so for the third time too… especially after last year's maths after Indira *Ji's* assassination. Do you think the center will take up anything against Jyoti Babu? Never!!"

Sarat *Bhai* and Nar Bahadur, brothers in arms against a suspicious 'he', could make little out of Gurung Sir's misplaced reflection. In fact, they were rather confused for nothing of it was about Jyoti Babu. And did he not believe in the goal at all; was he expressing dissent? Why was he sounding so discouraging? And was he actually supporting the 'he'? Mani wanted to giggle looking at their puzzled expressions for this was so typical of Gurung Sir. His Political Science classes always went off into a tangent of unexplored areas in a discussion, and he invariably came up with a philosophical observation that no one could get a hand on. But well, he was a genius after all…that's what the college history said through corridor gossip.

"What happened, Mani? Some book you want?" Gurung Sir asked, for this is how he had become acquainted and familiar with Mani after he'd arrived to the neighbourhood two months back. Mani, of course, helped him with errands, and hence had privileged access to him, which was impossible otherwise, considering how reticent he was.

"No Sir," Mani replied. "Actually…I wanted to ask…No, actually *Guru Aama* is very sick." Mani blurted out before he could get confounded framing proper sentences. "I don't know what to do Sir, she's coughing blood all the time." The urgency on his face was apparent.

"Hmmm," Gurung Sir grunted.

"Ok brothers." He suddenly got up extending his hand towards the two gentlemen. They were taken aback but had no option but to take the cue. This is what made Gurung Sir so unusual. One could never predict his next move, one would never know the way with him. And yet, no one could mistrust him for he was a man of principles. Mani had been told about how he'd refused a number of awards by local and state authorities for his insightful research on the political evolution in the hill region. He'd dismissed all saying they were political gimmicks. Mani recalled how he had laughed in class one day saying that all they wanted was him to stop thinking and speaking. "They want to maim me," were his exact words. As much as his thoughts and philosophies were publically revered, he detested publicity all the more. Perhaps this was the reason why he had decided to settle down in this inconspicuous Naya Basti of Gayabari in the eve of his retirement. In this new uprising for 'Gorkhaland,' political turmoil was increasing day by day, and the demand for statehood was also fuelling individual aspirations of leadership, and all found their roots extending to Gurung Sir. So, ironically, the very reason why he'd decided to settle down in Gayabari was defeated, for not a day went by when some aspiring politician did not arrive at his door. The satire was that each thought their meeting with him was clandestine. Gorkhaland was a completely new platform inviting the best players to exhibit their prowess, as to establish leadership so pockets of population were being brought to boiling point through the best of a budding leader's words. Strangely, no player in this intra-war could claim to have an original voice. All their public speeches and evocations were inspired by Gurung Sir's philosophies and studies, and yet, one could never be sure if he was in it at all. In fact, at times one doubted if he were even supporting the cause at all.

The two men put their hands together to greet Sir and got ready to leave. Just as Mani was wondering if he should leave too, for he had hardly got an answer, and still not sure if the cue included him too, Gurung Sir said, "Nar Bahadur…do me a favour." The gentleman came forward eagerly for every favour for Gurung Sir was also an opportunity to earn his guidance. "Arrange for a stretcher and a vehicle as soon as possible. A patient needs to be taken to Eden Hospital."

"Ok Sir," the man said with folded hands.

Mani felt great relief and a rush of gratitude for Gurung Sir. He fidgeted with his hands not knowing how to express it. Dialogue was anyway more difficult with Gurung Sir.

"Mani, stay at home tomorrow…they might come any time to pick *Guru Aama*." Gurung Sir stood by the door ready to close it after them. This was a blatant cue, and Mani too left with the men after bowing with folded hands.

Climbing up the hill, Nar Bahadur asked Mani, "You're his student? Who's sick?"

Mani nodded and said, "*Aama*." He felt goosebumps all over… this was the first time he had acknowledged *Guru Aama* as '*Aama*,' even though the reason to do it was to simply avoid an explanation. Before the man enquired further, Mani pointed out towards the basti. "I live there Sir, the fifth house going down the slope. Sir, what time will you send the stretcher?"

"Let's see…depends on availability…stay at home tomorrow." He assured Mani and walked on with the other man while Mani followed them.

"Do you think he supports us, *Daju*? Was he trying to say it is right to use violence? I'm sure the fellow is trying to sway him in his support. I heard he had come to Gayabari last week, the scoundrel." Sarat *Bhai* was yet to get over his asperity and it seemed Gurung Sir had only intensified it with his tangential observation.

Nar Bahadur, the elder among them, laughed loudly. He probably knew Gurung Sir better and perhaps also understood Sarat's state of mind. "You're young, Sarat…and one is usually too certain about things when young. It's where confidence and sometimes arrogance comes from. But it's also the blinding factor. If you want to go far, you will have to learn how to look through disagreements. And Gurung Sir…well…if you don't know how to read between his lines, it's no use coming to him. You don't come to him to ask him to join the gang…you simply don't. He doesn't belong anywhere…he belongs only to humanity (maybe). For him, the rest, i.e., this unrest, this cause, parties, ideologies, etc., are merely subjects of study. Don't misunderstand him, simply learn from him."

"Hmmm…I guess so," Sarat *Bhai* replied pondering on Nar Bahadur's suggestion. "I was wondering why you were not inviting him to Ladenla Road for the meeting tomorrow. I get it now."

Mani was an involuntary witness to this conversation but it had stirred something inside him, a strange curiosity arose in him about the subject they were talking about. He felt as if he had accidentally been granted secret access to information about the discovery of another world. Yes, he now understood there were bigger worlds, other than his own small one and great things were happening out there…although all beyond his comprehension at the moment.

The gentlemen took the lane towards the main road while Mani walked down towards his house. He was suddenly hit with the realization that he'd forgotten to ask who he would ask for after reaching Eden Hospital. There was another thought that was creeping up slowly, that of going to Darjeeling…the place he had run away from five years back. He brushed aside the memories…he had after all nothing to do with that life now. Who would recognize him now? The Fox? (He found it funny to think about the fox and giggled to himself.) Not even *Kaki* or *Bada* even if they stood face to face…but how he would contain his urge to acknowledge them was the pain point. He wished he would never have to face them. He consciously shifted his thoughts to *Guru Aama* and thought he would ask Norbu to stay with him tomorrow.

Norbu came in early that morning, looking paranoid. Mani had sent him a message through his neighbour going to town. Norbu was probably imagining the worst for he rushed in without knocking. His stretched face relaxed a bit when he saw *Guru Aama* sitting on her bed drinking tea. Mani was collecting things and stuffing them into a cloth bag.

Mani instantly smiled on seeing Norbu, as if half his worries were already taken care of by the latter's presence.

"What…?" Norbu questioned Mani. He was careful about not mentioning any subject to avoid awkwardness for Mani.

"Mani says I need to go to the hospital," *Guru Aama* answered for Mani. "I don't think I need to though." It seemed as if Mani and *Guru Aama* had been waiting for Norbu for ages, to initiate this communication for them with a 'what.'

"Oh yes!! She doesn't need to…she was shivering with fever all night, coughing continuously, but she doesn't need to. And Norbu, you've already seen what all she keeps under her pillow…but she doesn't need to." Anger and sarcasm are the best shields for concern and worry, especially when one does not want to display one's own fragile state of mind. Mani, already mounted with *Guru Aama's* serious condition, and with little experience of the ways of the world, and more precisely, the medical world, did not know what to expect or how to go about it. He was actually hoping for clear instructions where there weren't any, and yet he had to lead. Uncertainty was already baffling and he definitely couldn't take *Guru Aama's* tantrums to add to it. Besides, what would he tell Gurung Sir? After all, it was sheer luck that things had fallen in place, or simply getting her to the hospital would have been a Herculean task. 'Wish she would understand…,' Mani thought to himself.

Guru Aama looked at him totally surprised. Her condition was no longer a secret. And her life, not only hers, like she'd always thought. She suddenly felt as if Mani was more in charge of it now…the way he went about deciding things for her, taking care of her needs and looking after everything that she thought was her extension - the house, the school, her health, even her food. She felt like a small child once again and her heart turned to pulp. Silent tears streamed down her cheeks like never before. She was wondering what had come over her.

She was definitely not this person she was behaving like. This image she lived with all her life, that of 'Guru Aama,' the strict teacher, the strong woman who took no nonsense…somehow it was all slipping away from her own hands and it seemed so trivial now…so small. She realized that unknowingly she had built a small world with Mani's nurturing…and had never known that it was the most beautiful part of her life. She was suddenly longing to be a mother to Mani, fill that emptiness in her heart where the blood seemed to have clotted and turned to pain, but had no clue how. The tears were probably that of helplessness. But as it is with the immense complexity of being human, the biggest wall is between what one feels and what one expresses. So in spite of her maternal instinct wreaking havoc inside her, all she said was, "I don't need to go to the doctor, I'm fine." She lay down and turned her back to them.

Mani, bewildered to see her tears for the first time, felt he had deeply offended her in some way and felt like banging his head for taking the liberty to speak like that. Norbu looked equally dazed and the two went outside the house to clear their heads. It definitely wasn't functioning right, they thought.

As soon as they were outside, Norbu asked, "Why did you call for me?"

Mani said, "Gurung Sir has arranged for a stretcher and vehicle. We're going to the hospital. Have you ever been to one?" Ignorance always comes wrapped in sweet innocence first, before it blows up in your face to reveal its ugliness.

"Hmm…once when my brother had had an accident. He lost balance and fell from the terrace. He hurt his head. I was twelve then. I simply went to enjoy the ride on the Land Rover. I had never set foot on any vehicle before. That was my first travel experience." Norbu was like that, crystal clear in his thinking and precise with words. One hardly saw him caught up in intersecting lines of thought and hence he came across as extremely clear and reliable. It gave one the impression of rare maturity in youth, and was hence noticeable. Thus, Norbu's presence felt reassuring to many, even when he least intended it.

At around 11 a.m., two men came with a stretcher followed by half the neighbourhood. A stretcher spiked the amygdala in every person's head in the hills. One could not view it logically as a 'mode of transport.' A stretcher was not an everyday affair. A person saw it only once or twice in one's lifetime. It was a harbinger, a symbol of something grave and unpleasant…like the rising gloom before death. In this instance, however, it was the case of the stretcher not knowing its address, so it was as if a bad omen was travelling. The medical attendants were none other than '*Yamduts*' in the basti people's imagination. The people sending it had not asked for Mani's name and it hadn't occurred to Mani too, so the stretcher had been going from door to door asking, 'Have you asked for one?' Apprehensive neighbours spoke in hushed tones, wondering on whom the omen would befall.

Mani put out his hand as soon as he made sense of the commotion. "Here, here…" he shouted out. "Bring it here."

Everyone's eyes popped out. "Mani?!" The exclamation had a hundred questions in it. Soon, light dawned on everyone and the entire neighborhood came together to get *Guru Aama* to the hospital. The closest neighbor, Rubin Uncle as Mani addressed him, offered to come along with Mani in spite of his relatives having arrived for Tika, and Mani felt humbled with gratitude yet again. He smiled, for he felt the Goddess had answered his prayers. He had found the hand he was looking for. He would not be swimming in unknown waters. *Guru Aama* would be fine soon.

Guru Aama had covered her face as she was laid on the stretcher to avoid the daylight, and of course the sympathetic faces that were staring at her as she was carried uphill, to be taken to the hospital. She had considered sympathy an insult all these years, and had never indulged in it, give or take. This bloody illness was attacking everything she identified herself with. Rubin Uncle had taken charge now and reprimanded everyone for creating unnecessary chaos. People went back to their homes and festivities.

CHAPTER 16

*G*uru *Aama* was kept in quarantine as the prognosis said tuberculosis. Diagnostic confirmation would take some time. The day they arrived at the hospital was chaotic, as Mani and Norbu followed Rubin Uncle through a maze of wards, corridors, dull yellow bulbs hardly making anything visible, and cubicles filled with the stench of phenyl, medicines and dirty loos. The nurses scooting about in their white dresses were the only relief in the intensified moroseness of the place.

"There you are…let's go home boys," Rubin Uncle said as he rubbed his face with a handkerchief in the evening. Sweat or no sweat, this was an unconscious action people resorted to after a grueling day. It gave a sense of completion, the ritualistic initiation of rest after much exertion. "The last bus leaves at 5:30…we'd better hurry now."

"*Guru Aama?*" Mani questioned innocently. It felt strange going back without her. He had never gone back to an empty house.

"She's ill Mani…it may take weeks till she is fit to go home," Rubin Uncle sounded very grim. "Ok, hurry now…you have a lot to do. Tomorrow early morning we need to come back with food for her and some money. You need to go to the bank too."

Money? This was something Mani had hardly given thought to. He had some remaining from the monthly amount *Guru Aama* gave him for household expenses, but thereafter?

"How much money do we need, Uncle?" Mani asked nervously.

"Oh! Don't worry about that…just bring *Guru Aama's* passbook tomorrow. She has probably enough in her account. Come boys, we need to run down to the bus terminus."

As soon as they got on to the bus, Mani sat near the window as they passed through familiar and unfamiliar roads, reliving his small but tumultuous life through these lanes. His silence was heavy, not relaxed like Norbu's.

Mani got up early the next day, cooked and packed all that he thought *Guru Aama* would need with Sheila Aunty's (Rubin Uncle's sister) help, and was ready to leave with Rubin Uncle by eight. He would be on his own today as Uncle had to go for work after seeing to the money at the bank, and Norbu had to go to college. In all likelihood, this would be the pattern of Mani's life for many weeks to come.

Guru Aama was under intensive care and no one was allowed to see her. All requirements were mediated through a nurse. Mani, therefore, had no option but to loiter the entire day. So he began exploring the hospital that was spread out on an elevated surface in the middle of the market place, as if a hill had been flattened out to build this structure. It stood out like a plateau in the middle of the town, and was considered a significant landmark with respect to its history and location. The town owed its significance to the British for what had it been without them? Simply home to a countable population of Lepchas. The British came and developed the town by building the roads, the heritage railway, the tea gardens and sanatoriums, creating easy passages for refugees, and bribed and bought labour from neighbouring Nepal and Bhutan. It was a different matter though that they would scream, 'My Land- etc. Land' the loudest later on. Of course, one would have to credit them, for they used their sweat to build what was established as 'the queen of hills.' Eden Hospital, one of the many symbols of the British legacy, was one of the first hill sanatoriums built by the British, mainly for the recuperation of British soldiers. In fact, it was somewhat like an observatory from where you could study the town, at least the part that spread across one side of the hill constituting the main town.

Mani walked across the front yard where vehicles were parked and placed his leg on the parapet bordering the plateau to take an eagle's eye view of the town, all of which was once his own for he belonged nowhere and thus everywhere. His eyes took an involuntary route and rested on a point that, in his mapping, could be the bungalow, the lost lad 'Mani Pradhan's' bungalow…a tiny speck of yellow and red in a thicket of green. He shuddered when he realized how close he was to it. The psychology of time is such that it stores the memories that are best forgotten. So, blurred images of the warm times with *Kaki* and *Bada* crossed his mind, but vivid pictures of KP…his bloodshot eyes… his rage…his ruthlessness…the eerie silence enveloping him…and his reddish skin with a sixth toe jutting out…were inerasable. It seemed Mani was still living the fear. The past never leaves you until you decide not to look back. It is like the ghost in folklore that you heard about from your grandparents. As per the rulebook, the ghost would follow you no doubt. But once you left it, in spite of all distractions and attention-drawing conspiracies plotted by the ghost, you were not supposed to look back. 'NEVER' they said with the sternest of expressions, because ghosts were real and they sucked you back into a vortex from which release was impossible.

Mani regained the present as vehicles behind him and those in and around the terminus on the main road below honked incessantly.

'This town has changed…changed in so many ways. To start with, it was never so loud.' He thought to himself in disgust as he walked away from the emission-filled enclosure. He walked to the quieter side of the campus and discovered that it included a few doctor residences, classrooms, and hostels for nursing students. He felt at peace there and sat down under a tree, a place that would be his hub till he was around. Pretty girls in white smiled and giggled amongst themselves while a few shied away when Mani smiled back. They probably thought he was there to watch them…and not because he had nowhere to go. Mani grew conscious initially, but then turned away and ate the peanuts and *churan* he had brought from the only shop in the vicinity. After some time, tired of sitting, he went in to check with the nurse if the reports had arrived.

"Oh, there you are…where did you disappear?" The nurse asked, almost scolding him. The senior nurses had developed a rather distinct tone…to the point, and overly strict. They even looked at everyone in a distinct manner, for thanks to the yellow bulbs, almost all wore bifocal glasses as if to compensate for the dimness. The smiles and cajoling could only be heard from the new nurses, who were probably unaware of the hell they would be spending their entire lives in.

"Ok listen…you need to get these injections immediately." The nurse instructed. Seeing him still standing with the prescription she had handed out to him, she said in an irritated tone, "Uff…hurry up, will you? The pharmacy is upstairs…go ask someone."

Mani darted off. He had seen the wooden stairs going up and ran upstairs. It creaked and he wondered how it was still there in spite of the flights throughout the day. The pharmacy, rather a storehouse, was like a dungeon, which you reached only after crossing a tunnel-like dark corridor. Mani wondered yet again why the beautiful structure with symmetrical rows of green and yellow wooden arches neatly stacked one after the other, had so much darkness inside. Is it true then…that whatever humans construct is a reflection of them?

Guru Aama was struggling to breathe when Mani came back with the injections. The senior nurse just grabbed them from his hands and a few younger ones huddled over her to put on the oxygen mask. All of them were wearing masks and spoke to each other in monosyllables. Mani stood bewildered, nervously watching the alien world of the white nurses. Half an hour later, a nurse called out to him.

"These are her reports. The doctor will come in the evening. Don't go anywhere." She said, emphasizing on the last phrase.

Mani nodded his head and asked hesitatingly, "What's wrong with her?"

"Chronic tuberculosis...and she is asthmatic too. She's quite serious...let's see what the doctor says." The nurse walked away quickly, may be to avoid Mani's expression, but it hardly changed because he could barely make out the meaning of 'serious.' That it deserved an impact as the nurse probably expected was known only through experience, and this was Mani's first. He had not been introduced to the equation that 'serious' in hospital parlance equaled 'cannot be saved.'

Three days went by. Mani usually ate what he brought for *Guru Aama* because she was hardly eating. The doctor was yet to come and all Mani did was sit under the tree with an hourly visit to the cabin where *Guru Aama* was kept. At times, out of sheer curiosity, he felt the urge to walk down old lanes just to see how things had changed, but changed his mind when he thought it could have consequences. For that matter, things were a lot different now. Just yesterday, when Mani strolled just a few metres into the market in the afternoon, he felt a strange tautness in the air in spite of the hustle. Things were the same...but the people, they appeared different. To start with, no one was smiling...gloom prevailed, and for some reason, people talked in whispers...huddled in groups. One got the feeling that something tasteless was brewing in the entire landscape. The flavor of the hill earth that had seeped into its globally renowned aromatic tea felt less delicious. Illegible pamphlets were stuck untidily on the fronts of shops and when Mani peered into one and read the slogan at the end of the page, it said, *"Maato ko balidaan ko lagi aaunuhos."*

'Ah...there! It IS about the soil.' Mani thought to himself. Mani brushed aside his observations thinking he was unnecessarily extending his state of mind on to the town, but his hunch said he wasn't really wrong, and it all probably led to a 'Laden la Road,' the second mention of which he had overheard in a conversation in the market. But where was Laden La Road? He suddenly became curious.

"Who is with her?" Asked Doctor Mazumdar, who came on

the fifth day. He was a pulmonologist who visited the hospital once a week.

The senior nurse pointed out to Mani and whispered something in his ear. "Hmm…" he replied.

An elderly man, probably in his 50s, he spoke softly in a heavy Bengali accent. "She is under observation. Treatment has started but we cannot say anything…maybe only after two days."

Mani failed to understand the 'anything' yet again, but straight away asked him the question Rubin Uncle had instructed him to ask. "Sir, can we please shift her to Kurseong Hospital? I come from Gayabari every day."

The Doctor retorted impatiently, for in the world of illness, innocence was suicide. "*Arre baba*… wait for two days. You can shift only if possible…if you need to at all." He probably felt offended that his grave statement that illustrated his status and authority as the only doctor, and therefore, almost God, had been trivialized by Mani.

Mani simply shook his head. The medical ifs and buts were beyond his comprehension, and the impending uncertainties were getting on his nerves. He thought of asking the senior nurse but did not want to be chided again, so walked out to sit under the tree. He wondered if he would return enlightened like the people who sat under trees, considering the time he spent here. To begin with, at least he could do with some medical knowledge so that the doctor and nurses would stop losing patience with him. He felt frustrated and lonely.

Just when he was about to sit down, he noticed a solitary nurse walking along the corridor at the corner of the building, her back towards him. He suddenly felt jolted, as if he knew that gait. The familiarity drew him in intensely and he had this illogical urge to run up to her and look at her face. He started following her and walking fast, pretending to have some urgent task at hand so that he could overtake her. He was simultaneously plotting in his mind as to how he would turn around or look back to see her face…or what excuse he would give if the whole thing turned out clumsy, and he was questioned. He had never done anything of this sort before and his heart was pounding with excitement. He did not even know why he was doing it at all. It was as if he was doing it involuntarily, a foreign energy was pushing him, and he had no control over his drive.

One, two, three…and there, he had crossed her. His heart skipped a beat in the thrill he felt. He bent his head down and walked on as fast as he could, and now the second feat would be to look back. How?

"Hey you…where do you think you're going?" A voice stopped him…in fact, paralysed him and he turned to stone. The voice was the same. He looked up dazed and saw a deserted corridor with shut doors and windows. He could see a staircase going up at the dead end. He was thinking hard what he would tell her but no excuses came to his avail. He turned around with only silence at his disposal and his breath stopped in his throat when he looked at her.

Yes…it was HER…Shahana, HIS Shahana.

Unaware of the gigantic waves of memories splashing in his mind and heart, she continued rebuking. "Don't you know it's the nurses' quarters? Who or what are you looking for? Are you new to this place?"

Tongue-tied, Mani remained speechless adding to her frustration. He stared at her, carried away to a lost land, wondering how time had washed away the radiance from her face. The same face that shone like the sun in his heart once looked freckled and worn out with faint lines now. He felt like holding her face in his hands and filling her in his embrace but in reality he did not even blink his eyes.

"Oh, sorry…I forgot," he said at last. Knowing how clumsy his excuse was, he suddenly became conscious about it, his height too, for Shahana was still taller (even though only because of the heels of her shoes). When he dreamt of meeting her sometimes, he had always imagined himself to be taller. He had felt protective about her that way. How disappointed he was with himself. He looked away wondering if she was able to recognize him but did not move from there. Such bombardment of thoughts in his head…who needed to know the Brownian motion in the books?

"Excuse me…Will you move now, sir?" She said in a sarcastic tone and he felt defeated and dismayed. She had not recognized him after all. But this moment, how would he let it go and what if he never saw her again? He had to tell her…but how? He stepped aside but stood there rubbing his hands. She was going…slipping away. He had to think hard, for a few steps more and she would climb up the stairs, never to be seen again. And what if she was not Shahana but a look-alike? He could not even be sure to ask for her by that name if she went away.

"Oh God…fast, fast, fast…do something please." He pleaded in his mind. He looked back once and found her staring at him peculiarly.

'Hope she does not think I'm a miscreant…I think she does… but what should I call her…Miss? Madam? Shahana *Didi*? No no… Oh heavens! Why is this so difficult?' He suddenly realized that he had never addressed her as any of these at the bungalow. He was finally settling down on an impersonal 'Madam' for the time being…at least till confirmation. Mani was shaken out of his thoughts when he heard her calling out.

"Hey you…come here…are you looking for someone?" She held the tip of her pen on her left cheek while she tightly held a file and a book with the other. Even as a million thoughts raced in Mani's head, he felt submerged in a pulpy feeling…how much he adored her. He'd never felt this way with any other human being…so surrendered. She probably grew suspicious of him and was playing detective. But was she Shahana?

"Speak the truth now or I'll report." Her tone said that she would not take any more nonsense. Mani's head echoed with the words 'fast fast fast…' but the more they echoed, the less he could think.

"C'mon…Tell me your name? I'll have to report it to the warden. And don't you go anywhere. In fact, come with me." She started walking back, probably to the Warden's office, and then like a boulder hitting its target it struck Mani. 'Name, his name…she'd know me if I…'

Without losing a second, Mani almost screamed. "Mani Raj Khaling. I am Mani Raj Khaling."

She stopped and stared at him like a lost deer. "What? Mani what…?" She murmured. "Mani…that small one?" She asked, her hand held till her chin to indicate 'small.'

Mani nodded his head and smiled, and he felt as if the irises of his eyes were swimming in water pools. She had not forgotten him after all. He felt his heart was throwing up through his eyes and unable to conceal it, he felt embarrassed. The remnants of childhood betrayal (as he had perceived it and would laugh at it sometimes) were still pricking Mani. It is strange how memories are embedded in our being, totally bereft of logic but so soaked in emotion. The body preserves it as the context and it surfaces no matter what.

Astonished and almost thrown off-balance, Shahana could hardly put things together. She held out her hand to hold his wrist and was almost shaking him as she asked. "But where did you go, dear? Why did you go?"

The next day Mani was ready by seven in the morning. Shiela Aunty was amazed by his energy and she wondered if the lad had slept at all. Norbu, who was accompanying Mani till Kurseong in the mornings, too commented on the spring in Mani's step…and thought it was about *Guru Aama's* recovery.

In fact, when Rubin Uncle asked him about *Guru Aama* last evening, Mani jestingly said mimicking the Doctor, "I asked them about shifting Uncle. That Bangali Doctor *buro* said "*Arre baba*…see two days if you have to shift at all." They will shift after two days of 'serious.' Why did they say that, Uncle?"

Rubin mumbled "Hmm…" his mind filled with doubts. *Guru Aama's* condition, Mani's ignorance…and the conundrum compounded by the moral responsibility he felt towards Mani. He thought, 'Should

I tell him? No no...why burden the poor child with worry, at least he's feeling positive. But then who will tell him the truth? No no...he's big enough, he should know the truth. What if something happens...what will the poor fellow do? *Chhya*...how can I even think like this? Oh God...this is so confusing. Hope she recovers soon.'

Mani, however, was restless. He couldn't wait to be under that tree, the tree of joy that was carrying the deep roots of his feelings for Shahana, someone who he had no name or address for, but the only person who felt like home. Would he feel the same way if he happened to meet his mother? His thoughts wandered far and he was astonished at his own musings.

Soon, afternoons with Shahana under the tree became the pivot of his life. She walked into his life like a messiah...as she had done years ago...a blessing from the Universe. *Guru Aama* came out unscathed from the 'serious' mode and Shahana took it upon her to see that she was shifted soon. Mani had blurted out every detail of his life, continuing it right from where he had left her, while she listened earnestly, marveling at how eventful his life was and how courageously he had survived it.

The only part he hadn't revealed was his dark story with KP as the antagonist and his psychosis surrounding it. He couldn't, even though his heart ached to, after she said, "You should not have gone away. How much *Kaki* cried...*Bada* refused to talk for days and *Dada*... poor thing. He went back to being the drunkard he was...as if he lost reason to live. I heard he's bedridden now..." Her thoughts trailed off.

'Ah...that monster. He's still alive? Why doesn't he die?' Mani thought to himself as he picked up a pebble and threw it at a mongrel passing by, as if to vent his anger. He hated the sympathy Shahana had for him. After all, Shahana was someone who had to be on his side...at least it was sealed that way in his perception. Ah! The illogical mind, it loves to tie, untie and create unnecessary knots, and then loses itself in the entanglement.

Shahana thought to herself and smiled. 'He hasn't changed a

bit…this little one. He's still so touchy about his surname.'

"Ok ok…Mani Raj Khaling!" Trying to ease the ambience, she imitated the way Mani had screamed out his name when he met her and she pinched Mani's cheeks as she laughed out loudly. Her laughter was still the same, looking up to the sky as the sun sparkled in her brown eyes. Mani stole such moments to keep them in his heart forever. Shahana rightly thought that Mani's life, as it had panned out so far, was about a search for identity or rather establishing his own…he detested a borrowed identity no matter how comfortable, and she never made him feel guilty about leaving Pradhan Niwas. She was unaware of the ugly triggers that had scarred his childhood and cemented his resolve to choose this path of endless escape.

After a long silence, Mani asked hesitatingly. "Can I meet *Kaki*?" He quickly followed it with "…but not if she still works at the bungalow. I'll never go there." Mani was assertive about it, and at the moment relieved that at least Shahana would understand his reasons behind his adamantine resolution.

Two days after Mani and Shahana recovered from the joy of their reunion, Mani asked Shahana what he was itching to ask. "Are you married?" For some reason he was crossing his fingers while waiting for her to answer.

She looked away into the distance and nodded unenthusiastically. Not knowing what to say…or ask…or what to derive from her response, Mani kept staring at her. She understood he had questions in his mind and said. "Yes…I got married to him, the same fellow… even before you had left. We eloped." And that explained her absence back in time. "But a year into the marriage I came to know he's a drug addict." She looked down, swallowing the shame on her husband's behalf that the latter never felt. Mani's heart was filled with sadness.

'The brute…he never deserved her. How I hate that scoundrel, the thief.' Mani raged within, feeling justified in calling him a thief, the one who stole Shahana from him.

"All he does is drink those cough syrups and remain stoned…

Codeine…" She used the medical term reminding Mani that she was a nurse. He, however, related to it through 'Corex.' He had heard in college how the longhaired weirdoes were actually overdosing on it, supposedly the latest fad to get high.

"One year after marriage, I took up this nursing course and have been here since then." She continued. "I haven't separated though… my in-laws live in Jorebungalow…I go there on my days off." She remained silent thereafter, her chin resting on her knees as she sat with her arms enclosing her legs. Mani could think of nothing to say, although instinctively he felt like wrapping her in his arms. He hated to see her sad and gloomy. She was his sunshine after all.

"I also had a miscarriage…" She whispered, her voice breaking and giving way to an unrestrained sobbing. Shahana knew that Mani was not someone who would understand her sorrow but she knew he was the only corner that she could weep in. She knew there was no one who would listen to her like Mani. He listened to her because he loved to…without the adult complexities like sympathy, judgment, analysis, or even stepping into her life in any way. Mani, moved immensely by her tears, hugged her tightly, slowly allowing the sobs to die down. These quiet minutes of unspoken affection would remain engraved as a forever moment in their souls as long as they lived. Words are indeed futile…all verbal promises are temporary and evidential in effect, subject to renewal and reassurance, but these wordless silent moments are the ones the human heart lives by. The knowingness in it is eternal, unquestionable.

CHAPTER 17

*G*uru Aama was to be discharged the next day, the 15th day since arrival.

"She is out of danger," the Doctor had said the day before, and Mani felt a sense of achievement for being able to decipher that. He responded with a gleeful smile. 'Dane-jaar…dane-jaar…' the doctor's words rang in his head and he would often imitate the Doctor to make Shahana laugh.

Guru Aama had not been introduced to Shahana, but she had noticed that a certain nurse was taking care that she was attended to properly.

"Won't you go to the temple Mani? You need to thank God after all…for putting your *Guru Aama* out of dane-jaar." Shahana asked Mani when they met under the tree in the afternoon. She enjoyed imitating the Doctor too. Dane-jaar, in fact, had become a laugh code between them. Mani remained silent for he hadn't made any transaction with God, at least not regarding *Guru Aama*. He suddenly felt slightly guilty too, like he did when Norbu told him about her illness. In fact, he had never been to a temple in his life, and didn't know you needed to thank God, for gratitude seemed such a human expectation; he doubted if the

Gods indulged in it at all or felt unacknowledged and small without it. After all, it was the human race that was born ungrateful. Didn't the Gods just go about doing what they had to? However, it would be nice to walk the lanes of the town with Shahana, reminiscing old times, so he asked, "Will you come with me? I don't know any temple."

"Ok then...let's go to Mahakal Dara tomorrow morning. Tomorrow's my off day. You can take your *Guru Aama* home after that." Mani thought she was unnecessarily stressing on 'your *Guru Aama*' and he wondered why. Was she kind of...jealous? He felt mirth within...any indication that Shahana considered him 'hers' or like in this case, disliked that he belonged elsewhere, made him dance inside.

"So you'll go away tomorrow, hmm?" She thought aloud with a tone of sadness. "...and I'll never see you again."

Mani felt happy and sad at the same time, happy because she was sad about him leaving, sad because she was sad. He had never understood his totally unstructured and misplaced feelings for her.

"No no...I'll come and see you...always," he replied instantly, emphasizing the 'always.'

Shahana looked at him quietly, finding his innocence so pure and honest. What did the boy understand of the trap of the 'always'? She thought to herself, 'The ambiguous 'always' that laces so many promises, ties down so many people in blind belief of eternity, only to reveal the ugly truth that forget forever, there aren't even tomorrows to fall back on....' Forever anyway is a relative concept...for after all, whose forever?

"You will not come to Gayabari to see me?" Mani asked hesitatingly, the tension slowly building in him too that he may not be able to see her again.

"To 'your *Guru Aama's*' house?" She asked jestingly, with raised eyebrows. "And what will you tell her...who am I?" She smiled mischievously as if she were playing a game with him.

Now this indeed was the most perplexing question. "Who was

Shahana to him?" There was no denotation such as 'my home, my world, want to be with you forever' in the dictionary of relationships. 'Ma'am? Ugh! No…moreover, calling her ma'am needed the mention of Pradhan Niwas…No, never…' Jumbled thoughts circled in his head.

Watching and understanding his confoundedness, Shahana came to his rescue. She came closer, ruffled his hair affectionately and said. "When you build your own home, get married and have a family, do come and take me there Mani. Will you? Promise?" She put out her hand and he covered it immediately, unable to speak because of the ball of tears rising in his throat that he was pushing down desperately.

"And where will I find you?" Mani asked earnestly after a period of silence.

"Jorebungalow…where else?" She said softly…the unhappiness and resignation blatant in her tone. "Also, Eden…or Sadar," she said right away, as if she was almost looking forward to him coming to see her. After all, where else had she found so much love and respect … and more than that a feeling that she was significant in someone's life, that she mattered and was important and wanted. Mani extended a whole-heartedness towards her that made him so endearing to her. He was like the protective brother she never had, the possessive lover she never had, the caring friend she never had…and probably also the adorable kid she never had…all wrapped in one. And yet, it felt so wrong to claim him as any of the above. Any claiming or naming felt like belittlement, such was the beauty of the nameless bond they had.

Mani took the first bus going to Darjeeling the next morning. He wanted to spend the entire morning with Shahana, at least now, even though he would have loved to spend every living moment with her. Now always equals forever in every teenager's emotionally unblemished mind, and Mani was no different. Rubin Uncle would be reaching the hospital in the afternoon and they would bring back *Guru Aama* together. She needed to be kept in isolation, but she did not need a hospital for that, the doctors and nurses realized after learning about her solitary life. Mani of course would have to play nurse and caretaker for a long time.

Shahana wore a blue sari the next day, the colour of the clear skies. She had left her hair untied, and they fell like a brown cascade. Mani felt a joy to see her old self. She looked like he always saw her in his dreams. Shahana walked him through quiet lanes to right where the bungalow stood.

"I thought you might have liked to see it once…and maybe meet Sushma *Kaki*." Shahana said, pretty sure that it would make Mani happy, it would help him overcome his past. But she was wrong this time for Mani suddenly started walking away.

"Wait…what happened?" she called out.

"I'm going back," he said curtly.

"But I thought you would want to meet *Kaki*…" she said a tad confused. "Ok, come back…we're not going here."

Mani returned but with a frown on his face that wouldn't go away. His face was red and he fidgeted with his hands, like he did every time he was in an unwanted situation or place.

"Ok…I'll just go in and get *Kaki* outside if she's there…will that be fine?" Shahana asked.

Mani just nodded for he wasn't sure if he wanted to meet *Kaki*… he simply wanted to flee…far and beyond.

Shahana went inside the gate, which was slightly open. Mani could see that the bungalow wore a shabby look as if it hadn't been painted ever since he'd left, and the open area was covered with tall, unruly grass. The place looked unkempt and neglected. Mani was sure Bansi was not around and wondered if he was still in town.

Shahana came out of the gate and said, "Let's go to Mahakal Dara now."

Mani did not ask about anyone but was curious to know why Shahana looked so grave suddenly, so he kept staring at her till she spoke up.

She looked at him and said, "It's in such a sad state…this

bungalow. There was only one servant who probably did everything. *Dada* is bedridden…I believe a paralytic attack last year. *Kaki* does not live here anymore. She went back to her *'kamaan'*…near Seeyok. I believe she refused to stay after you left. Samsher *Bada* is no more. The place has no life in it…it's dead."

Mani remained unmoved, unable to feel sympathy for KP but dug his face to the ground when he thought about *Bada* and *Kaki*. As much as he would have loved to meet them, he was somewhat relieved they were no longer a part of this bungalow, more so KP's life.

Both of them quietly walked through Mall Road and reached the upward slope leading to the temple. Shahana had just crossed the Windamere Hotel when four to five boys, aged 21-25 were running up the slope barefoot, brandishing naked khukris in one hand. They bore extremely fiery looks, as if in rage, and screamed "Jai Gorkha" in unison. Shahana almost lost her balance when they crossed her and Mani rushed to be by her side, covering her protectively.

Mani, startled, looked at Shahana and then at those boys. Shahana smiled and said, "Don't you know, stupid? It's a trend among the youth now…this oath. *'Maato ko lagi balidan'* they say. The other day, about 50 of them had gathered here to take an oath to fight for their *maato*…a huge crowd had gathered, it was the talk of the town."

Mani suddenly remembered the pamphlet he had peered into in the market, but of course could make nothing out of it then…or even now for that matter. He shook his head innocently.

Shahana laughed out loudly. "Which world do you live in, you dumb head? You don't deserve to be called a Gorkha. All young boys are ready to give up their lives for their *maato*…and look at you…as stupid as ever. Use your radio to listen to the bulletin also at times, my boy."

It struck Mani how naïve he really was and that Shahana had been noticing everything…taking note of all his little stories. She'd never stopped being his teacher.

"Where's Ladenla Road? That's where they have their meetings."

Mani blurted out just to appear informed, picking up bits from the conversation he had heard in Gurung Sir's house.

"No...it's not them, about the *maato*. This time it's different..." Shahana said.

They reached the temple entrance and kneeled down in front of the Shiva linga. Mani felt a calm come over him, especially when he watched Shahana pray with eyes closed. He kneeled down beside her and thought to himself. 'God...if I do have to be grateful...thank you for sending her back to me. Hope you won't take her away again. And yes...it's nice *Guru Aama* is well again.'

Mani realized talking to God was so easy...He never interrupted or judged you. But was He listening at all? Mani came out and looked up at the sky. The innumerable colourful flags fluttering high up in the breeze behind the temple filled his heart with immense joy, and he knew that the Gods did talk, but in a language beyond the limitation of words.

Both returned from the temple feeling blessed with love and experiencing peace and contentment in their hearts. How long they would sustain it would be a human feat...for restless humans cannot even carry peace for too long. Mental noise gradually converts it into an exclusively human phenomenon called 'boredom,' thus opening the door to let in chaos.

Shahana had arranged an ambulance for *Guru Aama* and Mani. Rubin Uncle also joined them, and as the ambulance left, Mani felt as if a piece of his heart was being torn away. Through his tears, all he could see was a blurred blue mass becoming smaller and smaller. He would have given up everything to stay back there...just so he could meet Shahana everyday, but he wouldn't even try because she wouldn't have approved of it and maybe would love him a little less if he did. She had set the standards of his life, she had taught him the value of the most invaluable asset one could have, and that was integrity. Losing it meant losing her forever...and having it meant having her forever, in presence and in absence. She was indeed his lodestar, his guiding light.

Looking after *Guru Aama* was a matter of his integrity now, she had made that clear before they left using the gratitude clause. Gratitude was not ever needed by the Gods, but it was essential that it resided in human hearts to make them more compassionate, more human.

CHAPTER 18

ani realized that if he had missed anything while he was away with Shahana, it was college. He was overjoyed to be back to classes, studies, his gang, and his routine circled around it all. The college crowd was all set to usher in the New Year, after which they would all be gone for a month and a half winter vacation.

The fog descended like a grey blanket across the valley and the winter chill was at its worst, with needle-like water droplets piercing one's skin.

Mani was fanning the charcoal *angeethi* outside to prevent the smoke from spreading inside… to prevent the house from being filled with smoke. He couldn't take chances with *Guru Aama*. Her asthma and wrath were competing these days, and it was all up to Mani to keep the house warm to subdue both. She seemed angry about everything… dissatisfied with everyone, especially Mani.

"I think it'll snow this time…don't you think so Mani?" It was Rubin Uncle.

Mani looked up, his stream of thoughts suddenly broken. "Maybe, Uncle…" he said indifferently.

"What happened? You don't look good," Rubin Uncle asked. "You hardly sing these days."

Mani simply shook his head. What could he say? It just didn't feel right these days. The feeling of having no place where he actually belonged to was digging a crater in his heart. As long as he was in college, there was some respite, but now he felt restless with the thought of having to stay put in the house during the vacation. Staying with *Guru Aama* had become extremely difficult these days. She wasn't her old self…the illness had made her a new person, a very unpleasant one. Previously, Mani used to find her indifference irritating…now her interference irked him. She behaved as if he had no right to exist by himself but his every breath was accountable to her. She never let him out of sight and screamed at his smallest mistake. And if that wasn't enough, at times she even burdened him with the mention of what would have happened if she had not taken him in. Mani felt suffocated all the time. But who could he share it with? He ought to be obligated to *Guru Aama* as per the world's standards of morality, even if she made breathing impossible for him. Even Shahana thought so….

"Oh!! I forgot to tell you. I was in town yesterday. I met the nurse who helped us and she was so glad to see me. She wanted to know how you and *Guru Aama* are doing."

Mani's face lit up with excitement. "And then….?"

"She gave me a phone number. She said it is the hospital's number but you could ask for her if you needed her help. Take it from me when you get time. Is she someone you know, Mani?" Rubin Uncle asked curiously, as if he had an inkling that there was more to Mani's life than the 'homeless child running away from an exploiting employer' story.

"No…no…not at all. I met her at the hospital. I don't know why she helped me." Mani said rather consciously.

"How's she?" Rubin Uncle asked, gesturing inside the house with his chin.

Mani smiled unenthusiastically and said. "Ok I suppose."

"She's become a dependent now." Rubin Uncle said thoughtfully. Then as if he understood Mani's state of mind, he said, "People become cranky you know…when they are not used to dependence. Sheila *tata* told me that she screams at you a lot these days. It's just her helplessness. Let the winter pass, she'll be better."

For some reason, Mani's eyes filled with tears. Thankfully, he could find escape in the charcoal smoke. Some people retained the kind heart they were born with. They did not have to labour to reinstall it after the vicissitudes of adulthood soiled it. Rubin Uncle was one such beautiful soul. The entire story of his life was about kindness. He was barely fifteen when his mother died. Sheila Aunty was his only sister but she was invalid, polio stricken. She needed a crutch to move around. She was thrown out of the house by his sisters-in-law, but Rubin Uncle did not leave her. He worked day and night, built this house and stayed with her. Sheila Aunty lamented it was time he got married and settled down, but Rubin Uncle remained quiet. Probably he feared history repeating itself and thought it was best to ensure such a situation never arose. He resolved not to marry.

Rubin Uncle probably understood *Guru Aama's* hara kiri and also Mani's predicament to bear the brunt of it. *Guru Aama's* insecurities were making her a person she never imagined she could become. Her attachment to Mani, her excessive dependence on him and the fear that he was actually not bound to stay with her, and hence, may leave her alone any time, had made her a suspecting, manipulative and annoying person. Such is the complexity of the human mind. When it finds love, it wants to hoard it, control it and bind it into a security contract, thereby snuffing the life out of it… for what is life without the freedom to be or let be? And then one wonders why love disappears even if the object of love remains, more often as an unyielding lifeless adjunct. It is certainly every human being's struggle to learn how to love rather than find someone to love.

"By the way, did you hear the latest?" Rubin Uncle said coming closer, extending the palms of his hands to feel the warmth of the fire.

"What?" Mani asked curiously.

"You know that Tamang boy…Lalit Tamang, the one who stays behind the school?"

Mani nodded knowingly and said, "Hmm…what about him?"

"I believe he has joined Ghising's youth wing…now he has managed some party portfolio and is out to expand his wing. 'Youth for Gorkhaland' he says… He is conducting meetings in his house and is convincing boys to join him. I thought he must have spoken to you… Anyway, be careful. They are a violent lot…and you can't afford to leave *Guru Aama* alone. Moreover, they are under surveillance and the 'Bengali' Police are already biased. They will be thrilled to beat up the lads if given a chance."

Mani nodded…but perplexed yet again, as to after all, what was all this that the world was suddenly talking about? He was still clueless. He needed to listen to bulletins as Shahana suggested. She was right.

"Mani…," it was *Guru Aama* from inside. "Does it take years to light a fire? And who are you yapping with…jabber as much as you like while I shiver inside. There is nothing you do properly these days…all you need is an excuse to stay away from the house."

Rubin Uncle and Mani looked at each other and smiled knowingly. Mani then hurried inside with the *angeethi.*

1:1:1986: The calendar changed. Mani had brought a new one from one of his Marwari friend's shop in Kurseong. A beautiful portrayal of Radha Krishna adorned it. He hung it on the wall opposite *Guru Aama's* bed so she could gaze at it the whole day, and hopefully feel at peace.

The New Year party was to happen at the college auditorium in the afternoon, as morning wasn't a time for parties, and night came in too soon during the winters. Mani was busy cooking up an excuse in his mind so that *Guru Aama* would release him. Just then, someone knocked. It was Rubin Uncle.

"Mani, Gurung Sir has asked you to go to college. Hurry up, he asked you to reach before two." Mani looked at him wide-eyed while Rubin Uncle looked composed as ever.

"Gurung Sir....? But why?" Mani was confused for college was closed today.

"Oh...you only told me the other day that he would be taking extra classes for the students appearing for higher secondary. Maybe he wants some help from you regarding that. How will I know anyway? Go and find out." Rubin Uncle then started speaking to *Guru Aama*. After some time he left, and Mani came out to see him off...in fact, as an excuse to clear his confusion.

"Uncle...," Mani looked at him questioningly.

"Dumb head...last evening you told Sheila about the party. She asked me to do this for you...she was sure *Guru Aama* wouldn't let you go anywhere." He laughed heartily like children do when they are successful in carrying out mischief.

Mani ran up to him and hugged him spontaneously. "Tell Sheila Aunty I'll get her grocery this weekend." He was thrilled to bits.

"Oh yes! Sure you can...now that you have to go to college every afternoon. You can't disobey Gurung Sir after all." Rubin Uncle winked at him and they both laughed heartily.

He rushed inside to finish all he had to for the day, so that he could be there for the party on time.

Mani met his Marwari classmate, Prakash Lakhotia, while walking up the college slope. Prakash was a tall and lanky guy and one would be more certain to find him at his stationery shop than in college. So Mani was pretty surprised to see him in college.

"*Arre yaar...kaisa?*" Mani called out to him, expressing surprise in his broken Hindi.

Prakash laughed and gestured 'it happens sometimes' with both his hands spread out. They laughed again. Prakash was not one of those guys one would seek for company, for he hardly had the time for it. But he was a quiet, soft-spoken guy with a clean heart and Mani was probably the only student he could claim to know in his class. No, they did not meet in college ever...but whenever Mani was in town, which he frequently was while buying things for almost half of Naya basti, he made it a point to wave out to Prakash or spend a few minutes with him if there were no customers around. In fact, Mani looked forward to meeting him because he reminded him of Kishan in some way. Prakash too had developed a fondness for Mani and it had slowly become a pact between the two...that Mani would share notes, etc. with Prakash and keep him informed of their progress with the syllabus. Mani had told him about this party last week.

The auditorium was already half occupied when they arrived. Girls were decked up daintily and the boys wore formals. Prakash and Mani were in their usual casuals but it hardly mattered to them. The place had been decorated with balloons and 'Happy New Year' banners. Far beyond, a girl was talking to a few boys and they were getting ready with the music and announcements. The girl put her hair behind her ears.

"Oh boy! That's Neetu...is she the Emcee for today? I'll go ask her." Mani thought to himself in excitement.

"Neetu," he called out as soon as he went closer to her. She was wearing a rose pink coloured bottleneck top with black trousers, and looked glamorous enough to give any female a complex, at least those present there. Mani skipped a beat when he saw her and he disapproved of his heart every time it behaved this way.

"Mani, you nut...I thought you wouldn't make it. I'm so glad you're here." Neetu replied. "So you'll sing for us today, right Mr. Kishore Kumar...," she trailed off in a teasing manner.

Mani blushed and joined them with the preparations. The party began with all hooting, whistling and shouting. Mani entertained the crowd with wonderful yodeling tracks and was cheered on with 'once more' a number of times. He hadn't been so gay in a long time, and the screaming and shouting cleared his chest in a way that all the heaviness he felt in the last few days had been released. The party was about to end, and all were invited to burn the dance floor. Boys and girls screamed out Happy New Year and Happy Holidays incessantly. Mani started looking out for his pals to wish them too.

Tearing through the crowd and din, Mani looked all over but Neetu and Norbu were not to be found. He found them at last in a dark corner of the auditorium…alone…distant from the crowd. They were sitting on a bench and Norbu's arm was around her. They were both looking into each other's eyes and smiling in a way every third person knew he had no place to be there. Mani stared at them from a distance, and felt queasy in his stomach. It was not that Norbu never wrapped his hands around Neetu…or even Mani for that matter, but in this moment, something didn't feel right. Mani felt as if they were no longer his friends, the same friends. He came back to where the crowd was and was pulled in it by Prakash. Mani danced along but something felt empty in him. He felt left out, lonely even in the thick of the crowd.

CHAPTER 19

Not much grew in Mani's vegetable garden in this cold weather. Mani did not want to go empty-handed to Gurung Sir's house, so he was in a fix. He finally settled on the few Chayote squashes, probably the last ones of this season, hanging from the creeper sprawling across the wooden fence of the backyard. Mani put a dozen of them in a cloth bag and kept it outside on the porch, so *Guru Aama* would not question it. He left the house at around quarter to two… like he would have to the entire vacation, or risk not being able to step out at all. That would be claustrophobic.

Mani walked up to the main road and sat on the parapet watching the vehicles zoom by. The weather was awfully windy so he pulled his yak wool cap lower to cover his ears. The chill felt like a spear running through his ears. He didn't want to disturb Gurung Sir so early in the afternoon. He could be resting…and he didn't feel like going to Norbu's anymore for reasons he couldn't exactly chalk out. He just didn't feel like he was his friend anymore. He missed Guard *Kaka* terribly and looked across at the desolate railway station. Guard *Kaka* had retired, and lived in the foothills now with his son's family. Mani realized Rubin Uncle had bailed him out for two to three hours every day from *Guru Aama's* clutches, but Mani didn't know where and how to use this freedom. And this abominable weather just added to the problem, for sitting outside was no pleasure at all.

Somehow, all he was brewing was resentment since last evening. 'Is this entire year going to be like this…full of resentment and doubt? Or is the malaise in the air?' Mani thought to himself.

Lost in his thought, Mani did not see a gang of boys approaching him.

"Yes bro…what are you up to these days? You've stopped coming to school?" Mani looked up. It was Lalit Tamang. A burly guy in his 20s, his face was full of pimples. Lalit was probably under the impression that he looked like Sanjay Dutt, the Bollywood actor. He imitated the latter's gait and had the same hairstyle, so he ended up looking like a rather funny version. He held a burning cigarette in his hand. Four others were accompanying him. He was flashing his best smile as if he had found his long lost brother.

Mani was taken by surprise. He had never spoken to him ever, and was even more surprised that he had been noticed in the school… Rubin Uncle was probably right the other day.

"No…not much. *Guru Aama* is very ill so… and they have also appointed an ad hoc so…." Mani, alert like a deer now, thought this excuse would make them take less interest in him.

"Oh! That's sad…don't worry bro…if you need any help, your brother's here." He had already picked up the mannerisms of a seasoned politician.

Mani simply nodded and smiled. He wanted to get out of there but the guys were all out for a fag, and they encircled him while they talked.

A short fellow said, "We have to do it *Dada*…it is just not fair, it never was! We are being treated as second-class citizens on our land, our *maato*. First it was the British…now the Bangalis." He was pointing to the earth as he spoke, enraged with resentment.

The word '*maato*' struck Mani. Yes…the malaise was very much in the air…the resentment was prevalent in the *maato*.

All the others nodded vociferously.

Another one added in a relatively composed manner. "Yes… they are running the show everywhere…ruling over us. See all the government offices…tea gardens…education departments, or even in business. All outsiders! And we, the ones who belong to this '*maato*'… we are the ones who end up as labourers, struggling to make ends meet." He smiled sarcastically, musing over the realization of injustice.

Mani was caught in the smoke and the conversation…for somehow, even though he was taking baby steps to understanding the depth of it, he was able to relate to the collective resentment in some way. It was about unfairness, probably the same way that life had treated him.

"We, the Gorkha Youth, will not take all this lying down any more *Dada*. We have to fight for our land, our rights." Another one pitched in with greater enthusiasm.

Lalit nodded all through and said at last. "The party is planning many *dharnas* and processions once this harsh phase of winter ends. Empty talk will not do, brothers. You have to take a vow to give up your lives if need be. Gorkha boys must come together as one, friends. Let's go to the party office now. We've got to get work done."

"Bro…come along. Coming?" It was meant for Mani.

Mani would obviously not disobey Rubin Uncle so he said. "I had come up to buy some medicines. Can't leave *Guru Aama* alone…"

"Ok…come when you have time." Lalit said. They all sauntered away.

An hour had passed and Mani had another in hand. He made up his mind to go to Gurung Sir's place.

"Ah! Mani…after a long time. How is your mother?" Gurung Sir was surprisingly forthcoming.

"She's better. *Dhanyawad* Sir." Mani joined his hands in gratitude and squirmed a little inside at the mention of 'mother.' 'Hard to accept…and harder to explain,' he thought to himself. He offered him the '*Iskus*' (Chayote Squash).

There was a prolonged silence thereafter, as Gurung Sir got absorbed in a book. Mani took a chair and sat down. He had no option but to spend his time there. At least it was warm inside.

After some time, Mani thought he should make conversation to make his sitting in Gurung Sir's house less awkward, so he said. "Sir, I met some boys on the road…they were talking about some *dharna*… processions. They said they will fight for their rights. What rights Sir?"

"Ha ha ha…," Gurung Sir laughed. "That Ghising chap…he's given them an occupation, our hot-headed youth."

Mani was baffled to see him laughing but relieved that he'd responded. "Who's Ghising Sir?"

"The GNLF party founder president. He vows this time it will be 'Gorkhaland' or nothing!" Mani would have to find out the expanded form of 'GNLF' for himself…his naivety could irk Gurung Sir.

Just to continue the conversation Mani asked, "This time…why this time Sir?"

"Oh! It's a long story that's why. People have been fighting for this land since almost a century, nothing new about it. India got its freedom but this part of the land remained in bondage…of the tea gardens. We could not build an image for ourselves beyond that of a tea garden labourer." He laughed sarcastically again.

Mani noticed that Gurung Sir was surprisingly talking in a quite uninhibited manner…as if he were eager to make that conversation.

"The Lepchas are the aboriginals of this land but they became the quiet spouse, and the migrants, the louder halves. You know when property disputes arise? Only after the spouses arrive, isn't it? The spouses, as always, are more vocal about rights, share, and what is rightly theirs…so is it here. After all, it is them who build homes and later divide them too." He laughed alone, for Mani could barely make sense of this rather strange analogy. Tangents and Gurung Sir, one could never keep them apart.

He continued talking, to Mani's relief, for the latter had run out of questions but still had to spend around half an hour here. Mani made sure he laughed along to appear actively involved in the conversation.

"1907…the 'Hills Men Association' was formed and a different administrative unit was demanded…but the efforts to raise voice probably got dissolved in India's Freedom Struggle. The voice did not stand out. In 1943, when the Bengal Famine was at its worst, Maila Baaje…Ratan Lal Brahmin did his best to see that goods were distributed fairly to all; that the hill people did not suffer. To bring this about, he ransacked godowns of hoarders, helped people establish numerous trade unions and workers unions with the help of the CPI. The CPI, in fact, had found the perfect platform to establish its ideology in the famine and the famished and therefore, lay the foundation of the communist identity in India through Bengal."

Mani marveled at Gurung Sir's knowledge. Awestruck, he was slowly being suctioned into a simmering mass movement. His interest was growing rapidly with every revelation by Gurung Sir and he stared wide-eyed at him while he listened intently. The realization was dawning on him that he too belonged here…very much here…to this earth, the 'maato' was his too and that his participation could make a difference. In fact, a feeling that he too had a moral duty as a Nepali, a Gorkha, was taking birth in him. And after all, the struggle was about a home…very much like his own. The tribulations of homelessness- who would know it better than him? A home was a vacant place in his heart that no other house could fill…neither the bungalow nor *Guru Aama's* house.

"But the boys…why were they angry with the Bangalis? They said they are like the British…ruling over us." Mani found himself asking spontaneously.

"Oh they must be for sure. All Ghising's language." He laughed again bringing his hand out and shaking it, as if to gesture dismissal. "He talks like that. 'Bangali' means Jyoti Basu…CPI(M). They are the enemies. And that too…currently. At one time, they were aides… brothers in arms." He laughed again. Mani had never seen him talking so freely. "In Ratan Lal's time, they accommodated his call for 'Gorkhasthan' in 1947. They, in fact, supported it. Maybe they liked the name better…Gorkhasthan…probably more upper- caste *bhadrolok*, more bangali.' he chuckled.

"But the worms crawled out when the States Reorganization Committee came into action in 1953. The census showed a distorted figure of only 19.96% Nepali-speaking people and that included only the Brahmins, Chettris and scheduled castes. The aboriginals, the tribals and the rest were conveniently sidelined. 'Divide and rule.' The CPI had learnt it well from the British. Of course, the façade did not last long. The show of support was washed away during the 1955 tea garden unions' unrest. The CPI slowly withdrew its hands. Probably, they could not find much purpose in fighting for people who somehow did not seem really important to them…either from a parochially driven empathetic point of view, or from the vote-bank point of view. That was the beginning of the discontent…rather, resentment against the 'Bangali.' What will today's poor Bangali officer do? He has labored, burnt the midnight oil to become one. It isn't his fault really that he serves a back-stabbing government."

Mani was confused where Gurung Sir belonged. Whose side was he on after all? He neither sounded disloyal nor offended.

"Sir, you like Bangalis?" Mani blurted out innocently.

Gurung Sir grinned. He had no answer to this, especially for a gullible mind like Mani's.

"Sir, you don't like Ghising?" Mani replaced his question.

"He's a fine man. Has labored his way to establish his one-point agenda…Gorkhaland. But our people? We need to become capable of ruling ourselves. Can the khukri-wielding youth alone give us a future? Already high on drugs and alcohol, if we push them into reckless killing and bloodshed, can we ensure peace for the next generation? Can we replace the Bangali Officer...Madhesiya Businessman... Marwari Tea Garden owner this way? Can we? We need to make some of us value the pen too. Our people are already restless, more disposed to physical activity. Will we not push them into labour again if we churn out a population with a herd mentality? We need to make them mentally evolved. We need thinkers and visionaries among us, more of our own to replace the outsiders we dislike. Disliking is not enough. We need to become. A true Gorkhali is about an unyielding, indefatigable, undying spirit...that of a fighter, a warrior...not about senseless violence because we have a weapon in our hands, for often, restraint is the biggest virtue of a warrior. Some of our leaders have interpreted it in an extremely shallow way...unfortunately too literally. "You are a Gorkha only if you agree to kill...else we'll brandish you as a traitor"...it has become this convenient these days, completely ignoring individual disposition. Youth needs purpose; the energy, the drive, it needs direction. A responsible leader needs to be careful about the integrity of purpose before risking lives and the future of an entire generation."

Although Mani hardly got his answer and the profoundness of the directionless information swam in his head, the line about '**valuing the pen**' made an immense impact on him. 'I'll study...I'll become an officer,' Mani resolved in his thoughts. It gave him a path, a goal for how to be, where to head.

Mani also realized to some extent that Gurung Sir was not about 'parties and groups'...likes and dislikes. He suddenly remembered the conversation of the gentlemen who had arranged the ambulance for Mani. Emotions ran high in the air these days and it was easy to chalk him out as a 'traitor' as per the louder version of what it meant to be a true Gorkhali...but Gurung Sir remained fearless and untouched in his solitude. A seer is always the Lion, walking majestically...without looking back ever to find the assurance of a herd. It was time to go now but Mani felt it had been worth coming here today. His respect for Gurung Sir increased many times over and he felt he was a changed person, suddenly a lot more grown-up in an hour.

"Can I come here to study in the afternoons Sir…in the vacation?" Mani asked hesitantly. Gurung Sir nodded as if it hardly made a difference to him.

Chapter 20

"Ah! There you are…," Gurung Sir said as soon as Mani arrived, as if he were eagerly waiting. "Will you go to the Library for me Mani? I need to return a few books and get a few."

"The Library remains open during the holidays?" Mani asked curiously. Gurung Sir nodded and handed him a list.

Mani gladly left for college. He hadn't been to town for many days and it felt like a fresh break. Mani went to the Library and did what he had to. The Librarian was an old man who insisted on speaking Nepali but betrayed its accent with excessive roundedness. In short, he had laced it with a Bengali accent. Mani loved talking to Mr. Ghosh only to hear him speak. He found it very endearing.

"What time do you come, Ghosh Sir?" Mani asked.

"What I will come…not one student comes. Nobody wants to read…all only fashion fashion fashion." Ghosh Babu always replied exponentially. He continued, "*Ei je*…all these fellows…long long hair like girls…all will fail. The exam is around the corner. You will see. In our time…O *baba*! How much we studied for Higher Secondary. West Bengal Higher Secondary means a 'biiiig' exam. All these girls…whole day haha heehee…what they will write? All will fail. Not one student comes. Then why I will come? You tell me…why?"

Mani smiled to himself at Ghosh Sir's lament.

Ghosh Babu took off again. "I have to come re *baba*…student or no student. It is my job…*chakri to*…in this spine chilling cold also I have to come. I come here after lunch…and go back after an hour. Some teachers come once in a while like you came with Gurung Babu's books. *Ei to*…that's it. Eight more months and I retire. They will know then. I have tended to these books like flowers in the garden. Books mean 'Vidya'…nowadays, who does all these? All these boys and girls…only English songs…dang dang dang…senseless noise. Hopeless! What do they know about '*vidya*?' This college will not find a Librarian like me, I can guarantee."

Ghosh Babu had served the Library for 30 years and had grown extremely attached to it. Moreover, he remained appalled and pained by the new generation's disinclination towards books, and endlessly complained about it to all and sundry.

"Yes, Sir…there is no one like you. But you are right. Books are '*vidya*.' I will come…read books. Will you guide me?" Mani said, enthused and freshly motivated since yesterday by Gurung Sir to 'value the pen' and now Ghosh Sir's '*vidya*.'

"*Arre* come *re baba*…the Library's yours." Ghosh Babu seemed delighted to find at least one interested student. He grinned from ear to ear.

When Mani reached the town, he felt like dropping by at Lakhotia's shop, and maybe if the latter was free, some hot piping *samosas* and tea in this cold weather would be fun. Lakhotia was alone in the shop and glad to see Mani.

"Hey, what a pleasant surprise…where to?"Lakhotia asked.

"Gurung Sir had sent me for his books. No customers today?" Mani asked in surprise.

"Vacation time...who needs books and stationery." Lakhotia replied laughing. "It's our chill time too...the rush will start next month when schools will reopen and new books arrive."

Mani bought *samosas* and tea from the nearby shop and both of them had a good time. Just then the phone rang. While Lakhotia attended it, a temptation started rising in Mani's heart. He thought of calling Shahana. She had sent her number but little did she know that Mani had no means to talk to her. But here was one opportunity. He hurriedly checked his wallet to see if he was carrying her number. He was.

He hesitantly asked Lakhotia, "Do you mind if I use the phone once?"

"Oh! Go ahead...my Dad's not around...he's gone for a pilgrimage." Lakhotia seemed to be enjoying his freedom and was only too glad to help Mani. After all, he was his only friend perhaps. "But who will you call?" He asked, knowing Mani did not have friends and relatives to call.

"The hospital actually....," Mani lied. "Just to ask when the doctor will come."

Lakhotia helped him dial the number and Mani waited with bated breath for someone to pick up the phone. A lady picked up the phone and he asked for 'Sister Shahana.' "Please tell her it's Mani Raj Khaling," he said.

After about five minutes of waiting, a voice answered. "Hello... Mani?"

Mani was thrilled to hear Shahana's voice. She seemed happy to hear from him too, but there was a suppressed sadness in her voice.

"Are you alright?" Mani asked after he had told her about Guru Aama's health, college, etc.

"Hmm...I don't go to Jorebungalow anymore." She said in a low tone. Mani could hear her sniffing at the other end. He felt helpless... totally at a loss of words.

'Telecommunication is a worthless discovery. It is just not suitable for those not easy with words. Is communication only limited to words? This black machine can make you feel incompetent and worthless in a minute.' Mani impatiently gritted his teeth as he fished for the right words in fear that she would keep the phone if he remained silent. 'Oh! The pressure of finding the right words!'

In a hurry Mani asked. "Why? You can't tell me?" Actually he wanted to say. 'Why? Did that ape do something nasty to you?' Ugh! How he hated him.

"He eloped again...another girl." She whispered, crying profusely. Mani hated to hear her cry...and that too, for that swine. He felt bile storming up his stomach with anger and disgust. All he wanted to do was bang the swine's head against some wall but he knew there was nothing he could do.

"Ok...I'll try and come next week." Mani said, in a way of assurance. He was still a teenager, not adept at dealing with an else's emotions with the sugar coating of words, and the telephone only made it worse. It made his incapacities seem as wide as a gorge. He vowed never to use it again in disgust.

"You never asked about the doctor?" Lakhotia asked...somewhat teasingly...as if he had guessed Mani was talking to a girl. "Doctor... huh! Where are you going next week, bro? Tell me...C'mon."

Mani smiled half-heartedly, for he was deeply saddened to hear of Shahana's life in such a mess. Not really in a mood to lie and then cover it up in a hundred ways, Mani said, "I'll tell you friend... someday...not today." Mani knew Lakhotia could be trusted with the story of his life so far, that he would not burden it with the weight of righteous opinions.

Mani took the bus home, his thoughts wet with Shahana's tears. If only he knew a way out to wipe them away forever...

The next week came in soon. Mani had spent hours thinking,

looking for an excuse to go to meet Shahana, for he could not go and come back in two hours. He needed a day for it.

Rubin Uncle and Sheila Aunty had become Mani's cushion… to fall back on for every problem that needed a solution. They had become the mediator between *Guru Aama* and Mani since their communication had grown cold and awkward. They were Mani's guides and counselors, in short, the warm corner when life felt too damp and awry. A cup of tea and a few jokes with Sheila Aunty by the fire rejuvenated Mani. And with Rubin Uncle around, Mani always felt looked after, cared for. It was Rubin Uncle again who showed him the way.

"You anyway have to take her for a check-up. Why don't you go and get an appointment done for next month? I'll come over and suggest in her presence…don't worry." 'Her' was always *Guru Aama* in their lingo. But this time he had a condition. "But only if you tell me who this lady is. You can't keep fooling us now…I know there is more to this story. What are you hiding from us and why? Hmm?"

Mani looked at the ground and nodded. How could he explain his entire life in a few words? And would they not judge him…in fact, start mistrusting him? In the first place, would they even believe him? If not, wouldn't they become more suspicious about him? He could lose their warmth and love. He didn't want to. How could he tell Rubin Uncle that? But yes! He was tired…tired of lying, hiding, and above all…still not belonging anywhere. In fact, he wanted to scream and say… 'Yes, I escaped…I ran away…but did I have a choice? Where was I wrong? I was wronged…I was not wrong.' But he couldn't… because he knew a homeless one is labeled pitiable…and is wrong if he dares to seek the sky. The burden of obligation is heavy; often, one who receives it also has to carry the sins of the one obligating. The Fox sold him but he was right. KP…was beyond right, even great! He was making him his heir. But why…and how? Who would know? *Guru Aama* would never be wrong, even if she stopped recognizing Mani beyond her own needs. It was Mani who would always be wrong if he did not stoop in obligation…here, there, everywhere. Did it matter to anyone…that he wanted to look up and breathe, not stoop?

Mani's eyes started brimming with tears and they ran down his cheeks…they were burning, as if emerging from a hot spring. He became conscious but couldn't contain them. They had crossed the threshold of their pain.

Rubin and Sheila were alarmed and watched him in silence. They hadn't seen Mani cry ever and were drowned in guilt. After some time, Mani collected himself and left. Rubin's curiosity only deepened for a human's spontaneous emotions express more truth than his words… always. Rubin knew the truth was deep…and painful.

Shahana smiled when Mani went to see her but her smile was dry, lifeless…only customary. It was too cold to sit outside under the tree…their tree, so Shahana suggested they go and sit in a small joint nearby where they sold pork momos. She told him in detail of how she had been cheated of her love, respect and money and Mani's stomach churned with hatred for that man. She looked pale and sick, hardly resembling the radiant Shahana he knew.

There was nothing Mani could do for her but the fact that he'd come all the way, even if only to listen to her, boosted her morale. She clasped his hands within hers and said, "You're such a sweetheart…to have come all the way only for me. Thanks Mani."

"What will you do now?" He asked her innocently.

"Live in peace…here in the hospital." She replied, trying to sound positive but in quiet resignation.

Mani said nothing, but while they walked up the slope to the hospital, he put his arm around her. All he wanted was for her to know that he would never leave her alone, and for that, he vowed in his heart.

On his way back home, he thought he saw the Fox's daughter walking down the main road. Of course, he couldn't be sure but his hunch said so. Grown-up and demure, she wore sindoor along the middle parting of her hair and a big bindi.

'Aah! So the Fox has got her married. I wonder if he hurried with it because of Kishan,' Mani thought to himself. He smiled to himself thinking how flashes of the life one thinks one has left behind keep coming back in subtle ways. The past does not allow one to disregard its reference totally. He hoped she was happy, the only human with a human heart in the Fox's house.

CHAPTER 21

The sun was shining for the first time after a long dark winter spell of about 50 days. People had put their bedding out to dry in the afternoon sun, and everything looked gay and spirited. The children were out playing and the women sat in groups laughing and enjoying fresh oranges sprinkled with salt and red chilli powder. Mani was out in his backyard garden…picking out the weeds and planting a few Chrysanthemums. He heard a familiar voice calling out to him. It was Norbu.

He looked different. His hair had grown till below his ears and he had allowed the few bristles he had for a beard to grow wild. It was as if he was trying too hard to put on a manly look. It disgusted Mani…actually, everything about him these days did…and Mani couldn't understand why. The fact that Mani just could not conceal his emotions angered him more. It showed in his screwed up expression, his distant body language and his conscious efforts to avoid Norbu and Neetu.

"Hey…what happened? You don't come over these days. It's been a long time. All fine?" Norbu asked in one go after he came closer and squatted down on one end of the garden.

"Hmm…all well." Mani answered in a disgruntled tone that said it was none of his business.

"You seem to be in an awful mood. She's fine?" Norbu asked pointing inside.

How could Mani say that now it was also about the outside… and exactly what it was, was still a question.

"Hmm…," he grunted again.

"Let's go up…hang out for some time." Norbu suggested, thinking Mani wasn't feeling to free to talk here. "College will be starting tomorrow…you'll be coming, I hope."

Mani left his work half done in the garden…he felt he would rather be done with Norbu first. He was feeling nauseous and asphyxiated in the latter's presence. He plotted in his mind to go up and then come back immediately, giving an excuse of some emergency. Moreover, walking would probably reduce the blatantly awkward silence between them. Previously, it was Norbu who spoke after intervals of Mani's monologues but today the silence between them was a shark's mouth…gaping to swallow and the teeth of bitterness glaring to strike.

Half way up the slope, Norbu asked again. "What happened 'som'…you're just not yourself." '*Som*', the most common word among youngsters, was rarely used by Norbu but today it had an intention… to reach out to Mani. Strangely, it sparked the fire of contempt instead of putting it out.

Mani suddenly said in a fit of temper. "Oh! Only me? And what about you? Are you yourself? Or Neetu?"

He turned to walk back home. For some reason, Norbu did not react and walked away slowly with his head down. Mani felt angry with himself about his outburst…and wondered what had come over him. Whether he was speculating a situation unnecessarily…whether he felt jealousy or betrayal, or everything blended into one, he knew nothing; but it confused and hurt him. He just did not feel like being with Norbu and Neetu anymore and he could not fake it. He felt a jab in his heart that college would never be the same. He somehow did not feel very enthusiastic about going to college. It would just be another lonely place on the planet for Mani…

While walking down in a huff, Mani met a gang of ruffians. They were fooling with each other and were cheering one of them, who was targeting a stray mongrel with a catapult. A sharp stone hit the dog and sent it into a loud crying frenzy as it jumped around in shooting pain. The crazier the dog went, the louder they laughed. Mani felt repulsed and his anger took a detour from Norbu.

"Hey you…scoundrels…you good for nothings! Don't you feel ashamed of yourself…hurting that helpless animal?" He screamed at them as he marched towards the dog in an attempt to protect it.

But they stopped him mid-way and stood up against him, trying to make him cower. "Oh! The goody-goody boy. Isn't he the same fellow *'som'*…the bootlicker? Gurung's bootlicker?" He was asking his gang. They replied with a laugh and hooting.

"Listen you," the roughest of them all grabbed Mani by his shoulders all of a sudden. "Just stop acting smart, you get it? This is my last warning…or six inches less, for both of you." He was wagging his finger below his chin to emphasize his threat. The others hooted and whistled again.

Mani shrugged himself free and the other boys pushed and poked him with their elbows as they walked past him. Mani felt good about himself, that he had fearlessly spoken up against those hooligans, but then came back home with a niggling worry. 'Why did they say BOTH of you?' He thought to himself. 'Was Gurung Sir being targeted? But why? And by whom?'

Evening was approaching already. He realized *Guru Aama* would be waiting for her tea…and he needed some himself desperately to clear his head. He was feeling somewhat dizzy because of the excess anger and doubt.

Feeling somewhat restless that evening, Mani thought of hopping over to Rubin Uncle's place to feel better. He needed to tell someone about what had happened today. There could be an impending danger in the hooligan's threat after all. Rubin Uncle was not at home and Sheila Aunty was sitting alone, staring at the wall deep in thought.

"What are you thinking about so hard, Aunty? Have you found your hero at last?" He teased her singing the number *'mere sapnon ki rani kab aayegi tu…chali aa, tuu chali* aa' in an exaggerated manner.

She laughed but not like always. Sheila Aunty was madly in love with Rajesh Khanna, the Bollywood star and the easiest way to make her happy was to bring him into the conversation somehow…but it wasn't working today.

"No Mani…why will he come to me. He is already amidst beautiful women swooning over him…." She went quiet after that.

"Rubin Uncle is not in yet?" Mani enquired.

"No…when does he come on time these days?" She said sarcastically. Mani had hit the nail on the head. Rubin Uncle was the pain point. "Does he even understand how worried I get? You know how it is these days…people carrying weapons, addicts and drunkards roaming in abandon. Don't you venture out alone after seven." She suddenly became cautious about Mani too.

Mani nodded. He had come here to relate today's incident but he changed his mind. Sheila Aunty was already paranoid, so he did not want to tense her more.

"It's not that I don't understand. He would come home on time… if he had married…," she was still talking about Rubin Uncle. With tears in her eyes, she continued, "He sacrificed everything for me, stupid fellow…but look at him, he's wandering all alone now. This house could have been so lively with the pitter-patter of children's feet…but he never listens to me. Who will marry him now? Who will give his or her daughter to an old man, tell me?"

Mani had nothing to say, but sat there to hear her out. In between, he was hit by a Eureka moment and he thought to himself. 'What if…? What? No no, she will not agree…she'll get angry with me.' His mind had wandered off to Shahana. The one thing he was sure about was that Rubin Uncle would never hurt her like that swine. She'd be happy and that was all that mattered.

There was no stopping Sheila Aunty. "Not all women are the same? Are they?" Mani shook his head vehemently with Shahana stuck in his mind. 'No no…she's not like *any* woman. She's an angel,' he thought.

"And what about me? An invalid, a liability forever…." Sheila Aunty choked and continued in a broken voice. "I can live in a corner anywhere, why does he have to give up everything for me? Oh God! Show some mercy…show me a way out. Drill some sense into the stubborn fellow. I don't want to die with this guilt in my heart of ruining his life."

Mani couldn't contain his idea and his excitement any longer and told her everything about Shahana except where he met her and what she meant to him. Maybe he would never find Sheila Aunty in such a vulnerable state of mind and he knew that for anything to happen, her approval would be the key. Sheila Aunty got equally excited and hopeful and the two of them hatched a new conspiracy. They plotted to bring Rubin and Shahana together. But how? Well! The logistics are always the bottleneck.

Just when they were giggling over their excitement, they heard a loud ruckus outside the main door. They looked at each other and Mani rushed outside. It was Rubin Uncle. Panting loudly and trying to get his breath together, he was sitting holding on to his left leg while blood was dripping from his chin.

Sheila Aunty had also come hopping fast on her crutches and she screamed on seeing Rubin Uncle like that.

"I knew something was wrong…I told you Mani." She was already wailing while Mani looked dazed, not knowing what to do.

"Shhh…shhh…tell this woman to keep quiet Mani. And hurry,

let me in fast. C'mon hurry! They're coming…fast…and don't you two speak a word right now." He was worked up and was panic stricken.

"Ahhh!! My leg…," He cried in pain. "Hurry child…lock the door and put out the lights…fast…quick."

"Who…who's coming?" Mani whispered as he helped Rubin Uncle lie down on his bed.

"Mani…go home…run. They'll be here any moment. Put off the lights and don't open the door. I'm warning you…Go."

Sheila Aunty was trembling in fear and sniffing away her tears at the same time.

"Go, you dope…don't ask questions right now. Do you want me killed?" Rubin Uncle said again on seeing Mani standing confused and unsure of what to do. Sheila Aunty hurriedly locked the house after he left and put off the lights. Mani ran inside his own house and did the same.

After about 10 minutes…he could hear footsteps, as if a troop was marching down. His heart started beating fast.

"What's that?" *Guru Aama* asked, sitting up in her bed alarmed.

Mani said nothing but was dead scared for he knew they were looking for Rubin Uncle. Then something came over him and on impulse, he put on the lights and opened the door.

There were around ten of them, some carrying khukris in their waist belt. He could hardly recognize them but he could spot one familiar face…of the guy who had threatened him in the morning. Their eyes met and the guy laughed out saying.

"Oh!! So you stay here goody-goody!"

Mani was frightened but he didn't show it. Sensing they were trying to identify a house, he gathered his guts and asked. "Who are you looking for?"

"Cowards like you, baby boy." The ruffian said again. "We want to pump some iron in the chicken-hearted. Like this." He was swinging an iron rod in his hand. "Want to come?"

Mani was perspiring but stood firm. He was determined to distract them from finding Rubin uncle's house…if that was what they were looking for.

The boy was getting fidgety and impatient…just then a firm voice stopped him from behind. A very familiar voice. It was Lalit. "Let him be. Stop it now. He's just a servant boy."

"Ok…Bye… savior of dogs." The boy was unstoppable, extracting fun out of every insult he could hurl at Mani. Another came running on the porch and scribbled 'YOUTH FOR GORKHALAND' on Mani's fence.

Mani waited till they were no more in sight and rushed to attend to Rubin Uncle. The latter was in excruciating pain. Probably he had fractured his leg…but there was nothing they could do at this hour. Moreover, the hooligans were hovering around looking for him. They had roughed him up because he'd refused to help them plant a bomb in the Intelligence Bureau Office in Kurseong. He was branded a traitor because he believed in humanity more. If you dared to disagree, you were ousted… and if possible, also taught a lesson. Dissension was not tolerated, however reasonable, by the one-agenda regime. In this strange world of dualities, so to say, one begets freedom at the cost of freedom.

Chapter 22

The night was a long one, and Mani spent it tossing between Rubin's cries of pain and Sheila's incessant crying bouts. They got ready to go to Kurseong Municipality Hospital as soon as daylight entered the windows of the house.

"Ah!! Look at this now…this lad here can't even wait for the sun to rise. He needs to escape this house so badly…this house that gives him shelter," *Guru Aama* said sarcastically. "Why care about me? I can make my tea…do everything…as if I needed anyone ever." She continued sulking, ignorant and insensitive to the fact that there could be a need greater than her own…Mani did not bother, for Rubin Uncle was a priority today.

As Mani was helping Rubin hop on one leg up the slope to the main road, he saw many people had collected below Gurung Sir's house and were talking in hushed tones.

"What happened out there, Uncle?" Mani asked Rubin.

"It must have been those hoodlums up to some mischief there too," Rubin tried guessing. "They were out to bring about senseless mayhem last night. Rowdies in the name of a cause…to justify pointless violence, that's what they are." Rubin Uncle was livid and the pain only worsened it.

Mani desperately wanted to find out what was up but he would have to wait…torn as he was between his two favorite people.

The left fibula showed a hairline fracture in Rubin's X-Ray report, and he needed a plaster to recover from it. The hospital was a deserted place today with hardly any employees or patients.

"What time are you leaving?" A ward attendant asked a nurse. "Hurry up…don't delay…everything will shut down in a while."

The nurse hurried up with her work anxiously as she said, "I know…day nurse didn't turn up, what can I do? He's the only patient today, I'll rush home then."

"But how did you manage to come so far today? They didn't stop you?" She asked Mani.

"An empty Sumo dropped us…I requested the driver." Mani said, half wondering what the fuss was about.

"I heard they've blocked all roads…and are beating up anyone daring to cross." She continued, edgy with all the news she had gathered.

Infected by the worried nurse, Mani looked at Rubin questioningly…Rubin usually had the answer to everything.

Rubin nodded and said, rather stoically. "They're protesting against police atrocities…some shooting happened near some tea garden I guess…."

Mani did not need to be educated about 'they' any more. The radio was always about the bulletin these days…and then there was a greater philosophy in Gurung Sir's talks…and a personal itch since last night after Rubin's attack episode. Mani had learnt enough to place his opinion about 'they.'

"Ah! So they think all this rioting will give us our freedom? How?

By telling us - join us, kill or die?" He reacted in rage.

The hospital ambulance passed through deserted streets with its siren continuously on, lest it be attacked if misunderstood for a regular vehicle. Rubin and Mani got off on the main road and it took almost an hour to walk down the slope. Mani would have to wait till tomorrow to visit Gurung Sir's house.

"Couldn't you tell me where you were going? Sheila told me what happened when she came today with food." *Guru Aama* was slightly mellow but not without expressing dissatisfaction with Mani. "Why will you? You're on your own these days…I'm nothing for you."

"The situation was such…it was urgent," Mani muttered. It irritated him, her inability to understand.

To avoid talking to her, Mani put on the radio. The bulletin followed.

In an interview with a local news publication agency, The GNLF supreme, Mr. Subhash Ghising reiterated a statement regarding the injustice meted out to the Nepali population by the Indian Government. He stressed the fact that "we have been trapped in this country" and that "India cannot decide the fate of all Gorkhas." He criticized the British for making Darjeeling a part of West Bengal. He also criticized the Indo-Nepal treaty of 1950 and demanded the abrogation of all such treaties. In an isolated incident, the house of a renowned professor of the region, Shri Jagat Bahadur Gurung, was pelted with stones…

Mani's ears stood up and he spontaneously got up to go.

"I'm going…," Mani informed *Guru Aama*.

"Of course…this basti won't run without you…everyone else's house needs you except mine," she retorted sarcastically. He felt disgusted…he felt like telling her that she wouldn't be talking like this if Gurung Sir would not have helped…but restrained himself. He did not want to get into a spiral of words from which there was no getting out. He left for Gurung Sir's house right away.

Gurung Sir appeared calm and composed even though he was hurt. A stone had hit him above his right eyebrow. Broken glass remained scattered all over the place, bamboo poles lay everywhere and the entire place was soiled with mud with conspicuous shoe prints on it.

"Ah! Mani…," Gurung Sir said as if he had been waiting for him since long. "The maid refused to work, you see…so this mayhem." He added as a matter of fact when he noticed Mani looking around in dismay.

Mani was surprised that he remained unaffected by what had happened…even the maid's refusal to work. But Mani could no longer retain his pent up anger.

"I know them Sir…those rowdies. I know who did all this. They think they have the license to do whatever they wish? They should be taught a lesson Sir." He continued relating all that had happened so far…their threats, Rubin…everything.

"Oh! Don't get so agitated Mani." Gurung Sir said. "This is how it happens. We are very small causalities in the larger scheme of the purpose. After all, not everyone is disposed to supporting a cause… joining movements, giving up lives, etc… There are different ways to stir the masses. The human race is unfortunately the most responsive to fear. Fear of loss. In spite of all awareness, humankind is always fearful of losing life, losing wealth and comfort, losing status in society, losing security in relationships. Humankind is the most selfish hoarder. When you want masses to respond to a cause, there are two ways to garner it. Either give humans a dream that is bigger than them, or create a psychosis around something that they fear to lose…so that they feel bound to support it. I am simply the scapegoat Mani…to put across the message that if you don't support, you'll meet a similar fate. Now who will not fear losing his life?"

Mani was amazed at how sorted Gurung Sir was in spite of the chaos. He got down to cleaning the mess. This was the least he could do for Sir.

"Don't worry too much Mani…some opportunists are surely on their way." He laughed. "They must be coming to sympathize with me. They will gladly clean the mess. After all, the scapegoat also needs to be shared in all fairness. If one has used me to send across a stern message to the people, the other will definitely wear the robe of righteousness and tell people how wrong the former is. The mass is after all, the only medium to the coveted throne and the chase is getting crazier by the day."

He paused for some time and then asked. "How are your studies going on Mani?"

It was the 30th day of Rubin's plaster. He was desperate to discard it as it had intensified his confinement, for he could not venture out of the house with the plaster on. Tired of limping around indoors, he had become rather grumpy. To add to it, Sheila Aunty had got a fine opportunity to stress how important it was for him to get married, and so nagged him day and night, and that made Rubin even more irritable.

"I don't care Mani…I'm going today," Rubin said, adamant on going to the hospital to get his plaster removed.

"But we need to confirm first if the doctor will be there," Mani replied, trying to persuade him to understand that it would not be safe to go. "Didn't you listen to the bulletin? A 72-hour bandh has been declared. You want to break your leg again?"

Rubin had lost all sense today. "You need not worry Mani, I'll go by myself. I can walk up the slope slowly. It's not so bad now…I'll find some transport on the main road."

Mani was at a loss for words as he hopelessly tried to convince Rubin not to go. Meanwhile, he strained himself to find a solution, for Sheila Aunty had already begun sobbing in helplessness.

"There…there…this is how he behaves with me these days. I told you Mani, didn't I? He thinks I'm his enemy…" There was no end to Sheila Aunty's emotionally weighted assumptions and melodrama.

"Fine…calm down Aunty, don't worry. I will go and find out first. We can go when we are sure the doctor will be there. Is that fine with you?" Mani replied to her, although he meant to speak to Rubin.

Mani rushed out before Rubin got a chance to stop him. He knew Rubin Uncle would never want to put him in danger, no matter what. Mani was walking up the slope but was clueless about his destination. He was absorbed in thought as to how Rubin Uncle would find relief. As he was about to reach the main road, he recalled a mention of a doctor neighbour Norbu talked about sometimes, a resident doctor in Tindharia hospital whose wife was having an affair with Norbu's brother…as per the town gossip. Mani remembered how disapprovingly Norbu talked about this lady, but very conveniently, never about his brother. Mani shook his head…wondering why no thought of Norbu traversed his mind without a taste of bitterness these days. But if it was for Rubin Uncle, Mani would have to swallow his distaste and ask Norbu about the doctor. After all, a 6-km distance to Tindharia seemed more logical than a 15-km distance to Kurseong in these troubled times. Moreover, the latter was one of the sub-divisional headquarters, hence more prone to an unpredictable situation cropping up any time. Mani hovered around in his thoughts but walked on straight towards Norbu's house.

Norbu's mother ran a tea and snacks shop, a pointless juncture in these 'passenger-less' days. His brother was hardly of help to his mother…or anyone for that matter, and was probably born to be a trouble-maker, or even better, a 'breaker,' of his own head first and families later, the doctor's to begin with. Mani's intolerance for the man had doubled with the cumulative effect of his repugnance for Norbu. He was yet to understand the reason but his gut secreted too much bile when he remembered the way Norbu and Neetu were behaving at the New-Year party. He refused to think about it, at least now…only that the closer he got to Norbu's place, the thoughts came crawling in with greater force.

'I better stay normal…don't get upset, don't get upset,' Mani was reminding himself to avoid any clash like last time. After all, he had no valid reason to behave rudely.

The shop was a deserted place with its shutters down, and the afternoon lull only worsened it. Only animals strolled outside these days. The human race had been bundled up and thrown indoors, so it seemed. A verandah circled Norbu's house and that of the other three shop-owners in that stretch, so each of them had a back-door entry to the house behind their respective shops. Mani had been there a number of times and had found it pretty interesting for some reason, the front and back doors and clandestine entries and exits.

The back door was also closed…so Mani knocked softly, still struggling with his hesitance. No one answered and he found it a bit strange for it wasn't latched from outside. He knocked again…but all he found was quiet all around. Well acquainted with the format of the house, Mani thought of peeping inside the room at the far end, Norbu's brother's room from the window opening into the verandah.

'Maybe they're sleeping…,' he thought to himself. 'After all, most homes these days are managing with only two meals, brunch and supper…and sleeping away the remaining hours.'

The curtain was slightly open and he had to narrow his eyes to look inside. He peeped through the white curtain and turned away, disgusted. On the bed lay a woman wearing a whitish flowing garment which had reached up her thighs…and on top of her lay a man with a naked torso…totally absorbed in the throes of passion.

'Ugh!! What a letch he is.' Mani thought in revulsion. 'And that woman…doesn't she have any shame left? No wonder they can't hear me knock…the desperados.'

It was not the first time Mani had witnessed something like this…the nooks of the college corridors, small roadside restaurants, and small hideouts in the woods, all were havens for passionate couples and more often lewd 'romeos' to get done with their raging thirst, but this was different…because he knew Norbu's brother and his lascivious ways. For a second, Mani got caught in doubt.

'What if she's not the doctor's wife? What if he is up to ruining an innocent girl's life?'

Mani's heart started racing as he thought of this possibility, almost concluding it to be true and his conscience started prodding him to save her. 'But…but how can I, it's not like he'll leave her…and what if she IS the doctor's wife…'

On an impulse, he peeped in again, although half of him was discouraging him to do such a voyeur thing. The man's hands were moving recklessly over the woman's breast as she put her leg around his. They were unstoppable but Mani still couldn't see her face. As if an obsession had come over him, he stood on his toes to get a better view and unintentionally hit the glass with one of his hands. The couple were alerted with the sound and got up instantly looking around. What Mani saw paralyzed him. They were no other than Norbu and Neetu.

Mani remained aghast and kept staring at them. His eyes met Norbu's and then Neetu's…they looked away consciously while he looked on…and left, not bothering to knock on that door, today or ever. Mani's palpitation was out of bounds and he just kept walking, completely forgetting why he had come at all in the first place. The insides of his being were feeling bitter and his eyes welled up for reasons he still could not chalk out. A drop even travelled down to his mouth and shocked him with the intensity of its saltiness. His hunch was not baseless after all. He felt Neetu had lied to him all along… she had never liked him. It disgusted him that she looked through the eyes of pity at him, as a product of his circumstances, and had never looked at him as an individual with dreams, desires and an identity of his own…like Norbu.

'Why did she have to act to like me at all? I never asked for it. Why did she lie…,' he thought, feeling betrayed. Neetu had made him feel small, very small…and Mani couldn't help hating her for it. He had felt sorry for her on so many occasions. He had felt as if he were wronging her by not reciprocating her feelings…and all for this lie?

'Moreover, Norbu…he never told me he had a thing for Neetu. We were best buddies… or so I thought.' Mani was filled with anger. He somehow felt both had not given him his due place but had showed some kind of haughtiness in pretending to be friends…in a way of sympathy for him. And sympathy he could not take for he refused to accept his circumstances as the signature of his identity. Whether his own perceptions and inner struggle had spilled over on the friendship, or whether Neetu's and Norbu's fatal attraction for each other had carelessly taken their friendship for granted…but this was it. The friendship, short-lived as it was, had turned sour. It had reached a point of no return.

Mani sat on the parapet opposite the railway station, his usual haunt, and brooded over what he had seen. He could not get over their intimate moves and retched every time it crossed his mind. It is with good reason that voyeurism is a vice. Human tendencies are such, that even though one may remain alarmingly indulgent regarding one's own lust, one cannot view another's without arousing judgment and detestation. It is inevitably ugly. So a little of lies, unintended or true…a little of losing that far-fetched dream about Neetu forever…a little of his disgusting circumstances and the final truth that the camaraderie was lost forever, made Mani's heart a wild, flooded river today, ready to ravage anything that came in its way.

After ruminating over the sickening incident for over an hour, Mani regained himself and realized Rubin Uncle would be waiting for him to be back with some information. He saw an empty Police Jeep coming and put out his hand out to ask for a lift. He made up his mind to go to Tindharia Hospital in person. He also had a good mind to tell the doctor about the latter's wife's infidelity in an unreasonably vengeful state of mind. He wanted to get even with Norbu in some way for his slyness. He convinced the Police driver with his story (he made *Guru Aama* fall sick again) and hopped on to the vehicle.

CHAPTER 23

Rubin was filled with guilt when Mani returned, sweaty and haggard. Mani had not found any doctor or vehicle. He had to walk all the way back. Rubin was unaware that Mani had had an abominably bad day and the 8-km walk was not the actual reason behind Mani's despondency, so he took it upon himself and was extremely sorry for having put Mani through so much trouble.

Moreover, Mani refused to go to college or talk to anyone even the next day, and it only worsened Rubin's guilt trip. Sheila Aunty called him over for lunch (she had cooked mutton) but it still didn't help. Mani was into an overthinking grind and was endlessly recycling what he had seen and hated at Norbu's. His emotions were swelling and waves of anger, revulsion, sadness and a feeling of abandonment lashed at him. It's a wonder humans never stop feeling, even if it means going through the same crests and troughs repeatedly. Interestingly, the pattern never changes, only triggers change, and yet we remain blind to it, unknowingly acting like a battery-driven toy that wobbles and dances to the mercy of an on/off button. Mani had brooded over Kishan…and now he was brooding over Norbu and Neetu. He hadn't learnt and couldn't change. No one does for no one belongs to anyone more than one belongs to oneself...even in the mould of any relationship, no matter how glorified. Friendships fade, homes break, love changes...all the time. Yet, we mark ourselves immune and continue to hurt, one another as well as ourselves. So absorbed was Mani in his own dejection that he was blind to the baseless misery he was causing Rubin. Mani finally came out of his hangover late in the afternoon and realized he had made Rubin unnecessarily miserable.

In a way to make up for it, he asked, "Shall we go to the hospital tomorrow...when the strike ends?"

Rubin, touched by his care replied enthusiastically. "Of course... of course dear...but I'll go by myself. You go to college. After all, 'she' hasn't kept you with her to roam around with me." Rubin chuckled trying to lighten the atmosphere with a *'Guru Aama'* joke.

"No. I'm coming and that's final." Mani said in an assertive tone, ignoring the second statement totally. Rubin and Sheila looked at each other in relief. They had got their Mani back.

Rubin got his plaster removed two days later at Kurseong Hospital after the bandh was declared over. He was advised to stay at home for another week to regain the flexibility of his limbs to a certain extent before he started going out. Rubin screwed up his face as he hated staying home but didn't have a choice.

"One more week of Sheila's lectures," he said in exasperation.

––––––––––

It was the 25th of May, 1986. Mani was dragging himself up the slope to college. It seemed the blood running in his veins had changed its texture. It was filled with so much energy and enthusiasm before the vacation started that he hated the idea of staying back home, even if he did not have classes. He had Neetu and Norbu then, and the camaraderie they shared made college feel like heaven, but now it appeared the blood had deteriorated into sludge...into a heavy and suffocating baggage of betrayal and misunderstanding. He hated coming face to face with them and he hated it more if he didn't see them around...because there was no guessing now what they were busy with. In anxiousness, the more he thought about it, the more he felt like pushing Neetu away and bashing up Norbu. He had no answers to why he felt this way but he couldn't help feeling this way. He hoped Lakhotia would come so that he would have some company. He realized that college was a sea of friends but you still felt lonely when you didn't have that small island to go back to, where your best ones could be found. Mani felt emptiness stab him like never before.

Lakhotia came for selective classes, precisely for the two morning classes coinciding with when students would be away in schools and the shop could do without him. Every breath and move of his was sanctioned by his father's stationery business. Lakhotia had come today.

"*Arre bhai*...nowadays all alone? What's up with those two? Something cooking?"Lakhotia winked and asked about Mani's friends, although in sheer innocence.

Mani felt his blood boil but he could be himself with Lakhotia so he hardly restrained his anger. "Oh yes! New lovebirds in town," he said sarcastically. He felt like puking out the bile he had collected for over a week now, but stopped. Although he was seething in anger, he did not want to malign Neetu's character.

"Heard he goes around with that weirdo these days...that addict guy in second year...haven't you seen? Some were saying he's into drugs, too. Last week, I was at the Library. He was there, smoking outside the Library and was given a good hearing by Mr. Ghosh. He was chased out by Ghosh Sir literally till the end of the corridor. I tell you, it was a sight with Mr. Ghosh screaming '*ekdom* outside...you go now...*ekdom* out...why you come here? You want to burn Library with cig-aa-rate? *Ekdom* out...' all along. You should have been there Mani, you'd have died laughing." Lakhotia related the incident about Norbu and laughed uncontrollably. Mani smiled along but if he was dying of anything, it was disgust. He was also aware of Norbu's new friendship...probably Norbu was trying to fit in too much, for the most conspicuous proof was his longish hair and goat beard these days. He evaded thoughts that Neetu would want him to do so...that she could be so shallow…was this how Norbu was casting a spell on her? He refused to think any further…

A strange phenomenon about thoughts is that they're amusingly very egocentric. If you try pushing them away, they regurgitate with greater stamina. You have to give them a selfish reason not to stay, you cannot tell them to simply go away. They don't like taking instructions. Thus, Mani had become a cud-chewing bovine these days, ruminating on the immediate past whenever he sat down, although not consciously.

On most days, Mani spent most of his time flitting between classes and the Library. Mr. Ghosh's face somehow brought more calm to Mani than any student's. Triggered by Norbu and Neetu, Mani was taking on a rather cynical view regarding shrilly girls and grubby guys hovering all over the place. He had begun thinking they had come to college only to have cheap fun. When has an else's cheer appealed to a melancholic human, after all? The easiest way out of this envy is to raise oneself to a pedestal of righteousness and Mani was no different today. He thought he had a greater purpose, a noble one, compared to the other frivolous ones around. This worked for his peace temporarily. As a result, he started taking his studies seriously.

The crowd coming to college had thinned down lately and classes were deserted most of the time. Instead, students were seen gathering outside the campus more often. A tall, fair guy with extremely sharp features by the name Dhruva Chhetri was often seen mobilizing students. He kept a moustache that differentiated him from the others, who had hardly any facial hair. Mani liked his ways and idolized him as a senior. He stood apart from the crowd, in the way he conducted himself, his courteous mannerisms, and above all, the substance and command his personality exuded without an iota of over-bearance. Mani was curious to hear him once when he saw him giving a speech in an empty classroom, but Mani never had had time. He was either running to class or back to *Guru Aama*. He did not have the time to indulge in any philosophy other than that defined by his life. Mani decided to return with Lakhotia today, as they had no classes. When they were walking out of the college premises, they noticed Dhruva Chhetri with a large assembly of students. Some pamphlets were being distributed and one had flown away to where Mani was. Mani picked it up quickly out of curiosity and read it. It read:

My dear Gorkha Brothers and Sisters,

We are the future of Gorkhaland. We have to fight for our motherland. We have long been cheated by the British and Communist regime of Bengal. We must come together to carry out the 11-point program chartered by our leader, Shri Subhash Ghising in his speech in Ghum. United in purpose, we must burn down the Article VII of the Indo-Nepal Treaty of 1950 and take back our destiny in our hands.

A meeting will be held at Kurseong College on the 1st of June, 1986. All students are requested to attend.

Jai Gorkha, Jai Gorkhaland

Dhruva Chhetri

President-Kurseong Subdivision,

GNSF

Yes, Mani had heard it. GNSF! It had been mentioned in the bulletin often. He looked sideways at the young leader again. He liked the promise in his eyes…it had truthfulness. Mani felt an admiration for the young man and secretly wished to be a part of GNSF, so that he could meet Dhruva and be like him. The sense of purpose that Mani saw in Dhruva was drawing him like a magnet. He too wanted to be a part of something great, greater than his life and its meaninglessness. 'Motherland.' That was the word that had hit a propitious note in Mani's head. It resonated with his internal struggle because he knew deep inside that only a motherland is home…anything else is merely shelter. Mani saw immense hope in the word, a worthy reason to live and die for, for there was certainly no life without it.

Mani walked away calculating how he would manage to attend the meeting on the 1st in his mind.

The town seemed unusually crowded today and the crowd did not seem to be the usual one, out for shopping on a pleasant summer day. He bid Lakhotia goodbye halfway and walked towards the bus stand. Trucks were lined up along the railway tracks and basti people were alighting from it. You could make out that they were not towners from their colourful attire and tightened skin, held together by sharp wrinkles, the kind that appear from working long hours out in the sun. Some of the older ladies wore nose rings in the septum of their noses. They were probably garden workers, Mani thought to himself.

Mani was looking out for a bus going to the plains but saw none. Hoping one would come along soon, he stood under the porch of a famous sweet shop by the roadside. It was a landmark for years and hence worked as a tacit bus stop for the town people. There was hardly any place to stand without inhaling body odour but Mani didn't have a choice. He looked around curiously, trying to understand the reason behind this assemblage but in vain. Far beyond, he noticed men in khaki gathering slowly and it gave him a sense of urgency…as if something was on the boil, ready to spill. The helmets were increasing, one by one, and a lady in a pink saree was trying to work her way through them…wait, the lady. Is she not Shahana? YES…Shahana… Mani lost all sense of the huge crowd and saw only Shahana, and without a second thought started pushing the crowd to cross the road and reach her.

'What is she doing here…in Kurseong?' Mani thought to himself in surprise.

The stubborn crowd hardly budged and Mani was flustered trying not to lose sight of Shahana…he'd be shattered if they missed each other and went their own ways. No…not with Shahana, he wouldn't allow it to happen that way. He would have to look for her fast. He had no sense of direction as he was being pushed and pulled with equal impetus and he clenched his teeth in frustration. He stood on his toes and looked around but couldn't spot the pink saree. Ugh!! No…his heart was already sinking. Just then, two more Landrovers came in, packed with young boys and girls. Far beyond, he could hear a faint siren…like that of an official vehicle approaching. Suddenly, the crowd in the cross-section screamed in unison "Jai Gorkha… Gorkhaland Zindabad." The crowd started running in that direction and Mani looked around helplessly for Shahana, allowing him to be ruthlessly pushed and elbowed by the frenzied crowd. Anti-Bengal slogans pitched higher by the minute and its echoes spiraled to the sky. Flashes of pink moved across in Mani's vision but he still did not find the one on which his eyes could rest. Amidst it all, it appeared as if a clash had broken out in the crowd far beyond and before he could comprehend what it was about, he heard a gunshot…and then another. The mob started running all over the place, and wailing and screaming women ran for shelter. The erratic crowd went haywire and no face was a recognizable one. Mani's heart was beating fast as he ran towards the road leading to Gayabari. He was torn between saving his own life and going back into the crowd to look for Shahana. He was weeping like a child in his confusion. Then something came over him and he started walking back…as fast as he could, against the crowd.

"Hey you…come back. Come back you fool…they'll shoot you, those demons. They'll kill you." A boy screamed at him but Mani remained deaf and walked on. As he was about to reach the sweet shop where he was standing first, he saw her…a frail and frightened Shahana, curled up in the corner of the shop. His joy knew no bounds and he cried louder…he ran up to her and without saying a word, grabbed her hand and started running towards home. She was shivering and in a state of shock. Both ducked in reflex as they heard gunshots one after another in the distance. Mani was weeping profusely as he ran holding her hand, and silent tears started streaming down her cheeks while she stared at him in disbelief all along. They must have run continuously for about 2 km till the crowd almost thinned down to a handful of people. Tired and thirsty, both had run out of breath and tears. There was a small cottage on the roadside and Mani requested the owner to let them rest for a while. The owners, a middle-aged couple, eagerly took them in. News of the shootout had travelled and they were worried as their son had not returned home from work. They were hopeful they would get some news.

"I don't think he'll be able to return, Uncle." Mani said as he gathered his breath. "They must have blocked the roads by now…we escaped somehow."

The man nodded his head in resignation as he offered water to them.

Mani and Shahana had not spoken a word to each other as yet. Shahana was still in a daze and not stable enough to speak. After resting for about 10 minutes in silence, Mani asked Shahana, "Shall we go?"

"Where…go where Mani?" She asked softly. He noticed she had developed dark circles and looked as if she had been ill.

"Leave that to me today," Mani said…although he was also not sure what he would do. He knew he could not take her to *Guru Aama's*. She would bluntly refuse and probably shower insults too. He wished his relationship with Norbu had not gone sour…at least he would have a solution for today.

Changing the topic, Mani said. "Maybe we'll find a vehicle in Mahanadi. We may have to walk for a few kilometers. Can you walk?" Shahana nodded for both knew that they didn't have a choice today.

They walked on slowly through deserted streets. Mani gradually eased her out of her shock with his warm conversation. He carried her handbag and took her hand when she felt she couldn't walk more. She smiled back at him lovingly. Mani, meanwhile, had made up his mind to request Sheila Aunty to keep Shahana. He was apprehensive that Rubin would ask too many questions and dig into his past...but he had no choice. He was simultaneously knitting a story in his head... in case it was required. Then he brushed everything aside...deciding he would speak the truth, at least about how they happened to meet today. He could obviously not have left her alone in that situation after she had helped him so much, during *Guru Aama's* sickness. He hoped it would be sufficient...this explanation. He planned not to act so familiar with Shahana in their presence...so that they would not smell a rat.

As they walked, Mani asked, "Why were you in Kurseong today? Why on earth 'today' of all days?" He touched his forehead with his hand exasperatedly.

"I had an off today. One of the sisters who had brought me up at the orphanage is very ill. She stays in St. Helen's. I had come to see her today. I was returning when all that happened," she explained.

"You didn't think of meeting me even once?" Mani sulked.

Shahana laughed. "But where could I meet you Mani? I wasn't even sure you'd come to college. You never called after that day. I had given you my number." It was her turn to sulk.

Mani felt relieved that she was returning to normal. They joked and giggled and the strife they had just been through was slowly taking its burden off their palpitating chests.

"You know something Mani," Shahana said with sudden excitement. "Guess who had come to meet me? You won't believe... Sushma *Kaki* had come," she screamed. "I told her about you. Oh boy! She was so happy. She's desperate to meet you. She has asked me to take you along to meet her some day at her place. I was just hoping you'd call me some day so that I could tell you this."

She became slightly somber again said. "I believe *dada's* lawyer has made a will at his behest. Sushma *Kaki* will be coming again on the 20th of next month. She wants me to be there too, as a witness."

Mani hated to hear anything about Pradhan Niwas but he was happy he could meet Sushma *Kaki*. They started planning right away when they would go to meet her.

"In October…," Shahana said.

"No no…not this year," Mani interjected.

"Who knows whether I'll be alive or dead next year?" Shahana said.

Mani, angered by her statement, looked at her accusingly and refused to take it as a joke. "I'll go only after my higher secondary exams next year," he said softly.

"Ok ok, Maniraj Khaling…as you say." Shahana always referred to him with this name when he became angry.

They both laughed.

They had walked almost 7 km and evening was approaching. Mani noticed a van parked by a dried-up waterfall. The driver had probably got down to relieve himself. They stood by it for some time. A man emerged from the nearby bushes in a while. They had guessed right.

Mani almost pounced on him and animatedly related what they had been through. He started requesting the driver with folded hands to drop them at Gayabari after he learnt that he would be going up to Tindharia.

Shahana was so tired that she could hardly hold herself together. As soon as they sat inside the van, Shahana dozed off, unknowingly placing her head on Mani's shoulder. Mani smiled, for in spite of her age and travails, she had a child-like innocence that was very endearing. Mani looked at the fading clouds in the summer sky as dusk covered them and wondered what would be of her…would he be able to keep his promise to her? The uncertainty of life had knocked hard on him today in the midst of the furious crowd. He had felt life slipping away like sand for the first time…his as well as Shahana's.

Chapter 24

Mani consciously walked a few steps ahead of Shahana as soon as they walked into Naya Basti. The skies had darkened and the entire basti seemed still. These were not times when people ventured out after seven, and the blazing news of the ruthless shootout had passed a shock wave through everyone today. Mani, however, was relieved to see the deserted lane. He walked up to his house and asked Shahana to sit on the steps of the porch while he stealthily knocked on Rubin's door.

"Oh my God!! How worried I was my boy," Rubin exclaimed. The radio was on. "This bloody foot of mine…I was desperate to go searching for you but…"

"Thanks to the grace of God, you're back. Sit sit…I'll make some tea," Sheila limped to the kitchen.

"No…first listen…," Mani stopped her. He related everything bit by bit. "It was horrible…people tearing off each others' clothes, running over each other to save their own lives. I was running away too when I saw her…the 'SISTER *didi*', terrified and feeling lost in the crowd. It was impossible for her to cross the chaos to go in the opposite direction…and she had no place to go this side. So I brought her here…but *Guru Aama*…" Mani looked down at the floor praying Rubin would understand.

"Where's she?" Rubin asked. Mani pointed outside.

"Oh…I see…bring her in, don't worry," Sheila Aunty suddenly said excitedly, a tad unusual for the situation they were in.

Rubin looked at her, rather surprised.

She justified it by saying, "In humanity *bhai*…shouldn't we reach out to people in distress? What if it were me in her place? Bring her in Mani, I understand. She can stay with us." She was limping hurriedly towards the door. Mani and Sheila exchanged looks…the kind that said 'Good Lord! Look at Destiny.' It was as if their conspiracy had been blessed with an Amen. Mani just hoped Sheila would not blurt out some rubbish in her excitement. Mani made a stop signal with his hand at her…as if to say he would go get Shahana but it actually meant to tell her to hold her excitement.

Rubin remained stunned…a mere witness to all that was happening. Before he could put the pieces together and express his informed approval or disapproval post analysis as per his habit, Sheila had let in Shahana.

Shahana, meanwhile, had been sitting awkwardly on *Guru Aama's* porch. *Guru Aama* had sensed Mani had arrived and was at her wrathful best, screaming from inside.

"Come, come…I'm waiting for you with a *Khada*. I regret the day I took you in, an irresponsible vagabond that you have turned out to be… Here I am, paying your fees so that you study but you have no shame, roaming day and night on the streets as and when you wish to. You think I've kept you to cook for you and serve food?" *Guru Aama* was livid.

Shahana's eyes became wet when she thought of Sushma *Kaki's* Mani…he was the apple of her eyes… Her wandering thoughts were broken by Mani. He came close to her hurriedly and whispered hastily in her ears. "We don't know each other, hope you understand why? I know you only as 'Sister *didi*.' Ok?" He said the latter statement rather shyly.

He took her to Sheila Aunty'shouse and said aloud at the door to alert everyone, "Come inside, 'Sister *didi.*'

Shahana entered Rubin's house as per the will of God. A harrowing day came to an end at last…end or perhaps, a new beginning if God smiled upon them.

The next morning came in with joyous newness. It felt extremely exciting to have Shahana living next door. It felt like a dream. Mani's heart ached to jump over to Rubin's house but he had his limitations. *Guru Aama* had become uncontrollable last night and Mani had put on the radio hoping she would find her answers in the bulletin. She was quiet after that, although she didn't ask Mani a single question, not even out of curiosity. She could never put herself in another's shoes anyway. It was a glaring disability and Mani knew it well.

After finishing his washing and cooking, Mani slipped out quietly. Rubin's door was half open and he entered without knocking. Rubin was reading a book and sipping on tea while female voices could be heard in the kitchen. Mani apparently did not show any interest to peep inside although he was dying to ask Shahana if she had been comfortable last night. Instead, he walked up to Rubin and sat opposite him on a cane stool.

"Any idea if vehicles are plying, Uncle?" Mani asked.

"No…there's a curfew in town." Rubin looked worried. He continued talking. "Your Sister-*didi* wanted to leave early in the morning but we got news of the curfew just then from the milkman."

"Curfew? What's that?" Mani asked curiously.

"You can't go out to town. All shut down." Rubin simplified it. "It's a government order."

"Which government's…if we refuse to be a part of Bengal?" Rubin was stunned by Mani's question for it was interestingly very pertinent. Rubin stared at Mani in disbelief and then looked away. Some answers, you needed to wait for…

Just then, Sheila came limping in, Shahana standing timidly behind her in her awkwardness. Shahana was wearing Sheila's clothes, which were slightly oversized for her. Shahana and Mani exchanged a smile. Sheila Aunty's excitement, however, knew no bounds and she babbled continuously. She was all praise for Shahana and with intention.

"You know Mani, *bahini* is so sweet. She did the entire cooking in the morning. I tell you, I have not had such delicious potato curry ever. You must taste it." She beamed with joy. She was desperate for her words to have some effect on Rubin or at least draw a hopeful reaction from him but he sat unmoved like a boulder. She did not stop trying though and continued.

"See Rubin, *bahini* has made a home-made ointment for you. She says it will help strengthen your bones." Sheila Aunty was holding a bowl with an oily concoction in her hand. "Come. Let me put it for you." She started stretching out Rubin's leg even before he could voice his consent. He simply looked exasperatedly at Mani for he was unable to express any irritation at Sheila in front of Shahana.

"Is this how you do it, *bahini*?" Sheila asked Shahana.

The soft soul Shahana, and a conscientious nurse, had no inkling what she was getting into. She offered to apply it unknowing of the conspiracies of the earth and heavens combined.

"Not that way, *didi*. Let me show you how." Shahana took the ointment from Sheila's hands and rubbed it on Rubin's leg in a circular motion like a professional. Rubin wriggled in awkwardness and Sheila giggled. Sheila was rejoicing inside and smiled at Mani with a gleam in her eyes.

Mani quietly slid away, smiling to himself thinking if that moment could be arrested for the four of them. He was holding too many secrets in his heart and all for the sake of love, but it was weighing down on him. He could not tell anyone who he was and what Shahana was to him…he could not tell Rubin or Shahana that he had conspired about them with Sheila Aunty…and he could not tell Sheila Aunty that he was actually saving Shahana through this conspiracy. If they knew, he would become a culprit in each one's eyes…if they didn't, there was a glimmer of hope that they would all be saved. So would he have to walk away from them eventually to save them? He realized that even though he occupied a throne in each one's heart, he didn't belong to their home and never could. He felt a hollow crater in his heart and wondered where his home was…that yellow cottage with chrysanthemums, a Tibetian terrier and his mother in the red knitted blouse…

The next day they received news that the curfew had been replaced by 'Dhara 144' (Section 144 of the Indian Penal Code).

Mani was to drop Shahana at Kurseong Bus Stop and leave only after she got a vehicle for Darjeeling. This was Rubin's instruction and Mani smiled to himself thinking there could be people more worried for Shahana than him. Only the Gods knew how he had gone back into the crowd, ready to take bullets on his chest to find Shahana… because he had promised himself that he'd never leave her alone. Even Shahana was unaware of what Mani had put himself through only for what he carried for her in his heart. None of them, including Mani, knew that if the heavens operate through serendipity, it has a greater significance in the hearts and minds it is placed in through the incidences and coincidences of life. There is profound redemption in it, beyond the limits of human logic and comprehension.

Mani nodded obediently, feeling secure in the sense of responsibility Rubin was extending towards Shahana. Even if the basis was simply humanitarian, it held hope. Mani looked at Sheila and she stood smiling in deep contentment as if her life's purpose had been attained. Yesterday's excitement was replaced with a peaceful silence.

After Shahana thanked them for being so hospitable and caring, all of them exchanged goodbyes. Sheila refused to leave Shahana's hands and repeatedly said, "Come again *bahini*…come and meet me.

This is your home too, don't forget that."

Shahana nodded in affirmation, overwhelmed by Sheila's affection. While walking up the slope, Mani looked back once. He expected Sheila to be there but instead saw Rubin standing, looking at them walk away. 'What…is he waiting for Shahana to look back and wave?' Mani thought to himself and smiled. Spontaneously, Mani dropped his wallet only to distract Shahana so that she'd look back. She did. Mani bent down to pick his wallet and peeped through his own legs. He saw Rubin waving out to Shahana. He smiled looking at the bright summer sky and his heart leapt up like the pair of eagles soaring across, gliding on their magnificent wings.

Mani and Shahana finally left for Kurseong in a bus, which was almost empty. They went and sat in the second last seat. The bus was going to Darjeeling so Shahana did not have to worry.

"Why so empty *Daju*?" Mani asked the bus conductor. He was wondering if Shahana would be all alone in it after he would get down in Kurseong.

"Which tourist will come now, *Bhai*? Thousands of them are already stranded in Darjeeling because of the curfew. Things are pathetic right now. We're not the daily up and down carriers on this route…we've been sent to bring the tourists back to the plains." The conductor explained.

Shahana took out some money from her purse and gave it to the conductor, "Tickets. One for Kurseong, one for Darjeeling."

The conductor was busy crushing tobacco in his palm with his thumb. He laughed to himself and said, "Not needed sister. Don't you see, this is government duty bus? Keep it, keep it. We'll drop you wherever you want to. That '*dada*' in the first seat…he is also going to Darjeeling…on government duty."

"Madam is also a nurse…going for government duty." Mani suddenly pitched in, emphasizing 'duty.' Why he had to say this, no one knew. Probably, he felt it was his duty to ensure her safety and the conductor looked like he had a preference and reverence for the word 'duty' so he used it as a connect.

Shahana found it somewhat funny, rather witty of Mani, and smiled at him. She pulled his ears affectionately. She then covered his hands with hers and said, "Thank you Mani…I don't know whether I would have survived that day if I hadn't met you. I think you are God's most valuable gift to me. She came closer and kissed him softly on his cheek." Mani felt his eyes going hazy and looked away to the other side consciously. He had never imagined that she would also feel what he had felt about her his entire life, that SHE was God's most valuable gift to HIM. His hand was still in Shahana's and he made no effort to release it till they reached Kurseong.

As they were approaching the town, he said very hesitantly. "Can I come also? I'll return by the same bus…Promise." He said it fast as he was afraid Shahana would scold him.

"Are you mad?" He was right. Shahana would not allow. "You know how uncertain these times are? Just get going to college and your studies. Enough of all this now…I'm not a kid, I'll manage. Trying to act very big, huh."

"Ok ok…I'm going." Mani had to surrender but with a heavy heart. "But how will I know if you reached safely?"

"I have your Rubin Uncle's office number. He gave it to me to keep in touch with you. I will let him know when he joins office. Satisfied now?" Shahana tried her best to pacify Mani's concern.

A jubilant "Oh!" escaped Mani's mouth for reasons other than Shahana's understanding. Mani got down from the bus and as it started moving away, he cupped his mouth and called out to Shahana sitting by the window. "Please don't forget to call 'MY' Rubin Uncle, dear 'Sister-*didi*'." He smiled at her in a teasing manner.

She smiled back shyly and showed him her fist. They waved out to each other then. Mani stood there watching the bus fade away and then walked up to college.

Chapter 25

Five lives were lost in the police firing, and life had become grim after that, somewhat like the dark monsoon clouds taking over the skies with an impending gloom. Faces looked glum and it seemed as if everyone was experiencing the dull ache that creeps up after the initial searing pain of a bruise. The pain was that of being cheated on, of lives having been taken for granted. The innocence of the unsuspecting hill people gathered to protest non-violently had been quelled by a sly move by the police, and the wave of resentment refused to die down thereafter. College corridors these days were filled with conversations about the current firing, and all in hushed tones.

Gurung Sir had many times explained the communist ideology in class and it had seemed to Mani that there was no ideology as noble. Marx was almost a God in his eyes for being able to propound such a humanitarian theory. Confusion, however, started, as the ideology started trickling down to a list of names one after the other…Leninism, Stalinism, an even more concocted Marxist-Leninism, Chinese Maoism, the recent Euro communism trying to eradicate excess Soviet influence…and closer home 'Bengalism.' By the end of the list, Marx appeared unrealistic in the ideology and the nobility of it had turned sour in Mani's mouth, especially after this incident.

Gurung Sir had conjectured, "It is not only with communism but with any ideology…regimes fuel it as a promise to propagate it and then cleverly localize it in a manner laced with their convenience. After all, ideologies don't run governments, individuals do, and not outside the limitations of human nature. Look at our own…we'll go around in tatters, khadi, crumpled cotton…scorn silk, satin and all luxuries to uphold fairness, equality of wealth and talk about breaking down divides drawn by it but will never look into the intellectual arrogance we rightfully carry. We feel justified in the haughtiness derived from our conditioning that we are born with greater minds and all others are smaller minds, hence smaller beings. When there is no equality at the root of your thought, it is but obvious that it will extend to your attitude…how can we think about bringing about equality and fairness in something as superficial as wealth then? Wealth is anyway secondary in the larger scheme of psychology."

A mum class had listened to his lecture and no one had the courage to question his 'we.' Thoughts swirled in Mani's head. 'We… meaning? Is he a communist? No, no…how can he be? He's not Bengali….' It was another matter that Gurung Sir never believed in favouritism of any sort…he never resorted to blatant communalism even when it was running rampant like a fever in the hills now. This had irked many and he was branded a traitor and thrown stones at. He remained sadly misconstrued, inside and outside his homeland… inside because he believed in being human first, Gorkhali second… outside because he was counted as Gorkhali first, human second. The soft humanitarian was suffering the perils of intellectualism. He was a vivid picture of it.

After class, Lakhotia had given an atrociously oversimplified interpretation of Gurung Sir's lecture. "Yaar, he can't be communist… he's unable to select his community. He will have to live in Siliguri, the no-man's land. Poor thing." Mani disapproved with a frown while Lakhotia laughed without a care. "*Madhesiyas*, my father and Gurung Sir, all will go down." Lakhotia added wittily pointing to the plains visible from the class window. Mani knew that Lakhotia was blabbering just for the sake of it and his words didn't contain any malice, but ironically, humor was sometimes dark.

Over a week had passed since the firing incident. Mani was in the Library, writing assignments. Suddenly, he heard a commotion outside. His heart started racing again…muffled voices could be heard from outside the Library. Mani tried ignoring it but couldn't after he heard Mr. Ghosh's shrill cry, "*O re baba!*" Mani ran outside and saw Norbu holding Ghosh Sir's collar. He had that 'addict' guy and another filthy-looking guy for company. Mani's blood boiled at Norbu's audacity and without a second thought he ran and pulled off Norbu's hands from Ghosh Sir's collar and stood in front of Ghosh Sir to protect him.

"How dare you? Have you lost your mind?" Mani screamed at Norbu.

"Move away you scum…bloody servant boy! Do you think you'll become a hero…trying to save this Bangali?" It was the other guy threatening Mani and Mani realized he was the same guy, belonging to Lalit's gang. Ghosh Sir stood astonished and shaken, for never had he been treated so disrespectfully in his entire career.

Mani looked at Norbu with piercing eyes, unable to digest the ugly change that had come over the latter. The addict guy meanwhile came forward and slapped Mani without uttering a word of caution. A crowd had gathered and all remained stunned by their brazenness. Probably the news of the scuffle had spread, for just then, Dhruva came and took control of the situation. He took those hooligans and asked a few others to attend to Ghosh Sir and Mani.

Ghosh Sir was so shocked he could not speak. He remained quiet even in the Principal's office later. Dhruva spoke in favour of Mani, and Norbu and the addict guy were suspended from College. The third guy was not a student and had been sent off with a warning. This incident left a very bad taste in Mani's mind. He wondered how many youngsters really understood what it meant to not have a homeland…

if they used it to justify and masquerade personal biases. He wondered if all felt the depth of the real battle. He felt sad that exhibiting biased and violent behaviour had become the barometer of support for a noble cause. He felt depressed as to how the parameters of right and wrong had changed. Else, why would Lalit appear to be more popular than Dhruva? Why would Ghosh Sir think of stop coming to College? Why would Lakhotia's father think of winding up his business here? And why would Norbu walk around like a monarch and Mani have to avoid the accusing gaze of hundreds around him?

Mani volunteered to help operate the Library till a new Librarian was appointed. Ghosh Sir opted for voluntary retirement and left the town without meeting any one. Although things didn't transpire too pleasantly and Ghosh Sir left a gaping absence in the Library, Mani found his haven in the Library through this voluntary service. The books became his closest companions and he did not miss not having a friend in college any more. And the fact that he was entitled to come here even on weekends made it even better…he did not have to think of endless excuses to slip out of the house to find relief from *Guru Aama's* bickering.

It was 7th August. Mani was sitting in the library as usual. He was reminiscing a day from a year ago. It was Neetu's birthday. Neetu was wearing a white and red dress and she looked like a princess. He recalled how he had sung a song for her in the deer park and the fun they had had…he suddenly missed all that intensely and wished he could wish Neetu today. Just a year had changed the dynamics of every atom of their existence, but the hurt remained stagnant. Memories always came back to sting and sway. Mani sighed hopelessly, for things could never go back to being what they were…. In fact, they had only worsened with the latent enmity between Norbu and him that was no longer limited to the confines of their soured friendship. Lost in his thoughts, he didn't notice a girl had come to issue a book.

"Hello! Excuse me," she was thumping her hand on the table, rather irritated. "Where are you lost? Tired of this job already?"

"Uhh….no no," Mani said apologetically. She was a senior in second year and had come to return a book. She was staring at Mani while he went about searching the catalogue box.

"Aren't you that singer guy…Neetu's friend?" She asked.

Mani looked up surprised. 'So Neetu talks about me…,' he thought to himself. He nodded his head. She smiled in response.

"I'm her cousin. I'm sure you know about her then…almost half the town knows," she assumed.

Curious as ever, Mani blurted out, "No…what? I mean what happened?"

"Don't you know?" she said, surprised. "Neetu's in a horrible state after she returned from Kalimpong last week…she's very ill. She's in the hospital."

Mani was shocked. "Oh!" This was all he could utter.

Mani sat down in his chair and wondered what to do. His conscience was prodding him to live up to his friendship, to go and meet Neetu… but the part of him that had felt cheated struggled against it. Everyone in the hills had been shaken up by the callous killings and mayhem that had happened in the shootout over a week ago in Kalimpong. Those who stayed miles away also shuddered as they visualized the heart-wrenching stories of the strangulation of innocence and manipulated bloodbath that had made the rounds. A shiver ran down Mani's spine at the thought of Neetu being caught in it. He had known how life appeared so elusive, like a fleeting image on screen, when he was caught in the firing in Kurseong. He trembled to think that a rocketing bullet could have hit Neetu…and she'd be gone forever. Just one hit and it would hardly make sense, thereafter, who she cheated and who she exalted. The story could be abruptly cut short there, and that was just how meaningless it was. In a flash of a second Mani realized that it was his regret that mattered ultimately… if he were to die, he wouldn't like to die with the regret that he chose to turn away when his heart told him that Neetu needed a friend. He'd love himself a little less if he turned away. He decided to go and meet her in spite of his displeasure.

It wasn't too tough to find Neetu. The entire hospital staff knew 'the girl who had dodged death.' The aftermath of the ruthless Kalimpong firing by the CRPF on the peaceful protestors was such that people lost total faith in being true. Every individual was showing a wound of the stab, the sly stab on one's back, and hence more hurtful. It was the 27th of July, innocent people had gathered to abolish a piece of paper that had marred their destiny for years, which had made their existence on their very own land a tennis ball in the hands of two neighboring nations enjoying the game in the name of a treaty. This day, people had come to speak for themselves and not against any nation, but their voices were quelled and how! Faces were expressionless but tears of blood trickled down insidiously in each heart…this time, even in those hearts, which had remained unmoved so far. Like Mani, people had pulled out the grief of subjective injuries and poured it into an objective one. The sorrow was one, deep and vast. A newspaper rightly construed that 'a Jallianwala Bagh had happened.'

Neetu opened her eyes after half an hour of Mani's waiting. She was being injected with tranquilizers to contain her anxiety attacks that she was suffering due to trauma and shock.

"She's not saying anything…just screaming and shouting for help when she's agitated," her mother informed Mani, her tears knowing no end. "She has also fractured her arm and hurt her head."

Mani nodded. He felt as if he had lost his speech too. There was really nothing to say but only to feel, and his blood boiled at the unfairness of life and the helplessness of the situation. Neetu stared at him for a long time but said nothing. He tried to smile at her but his smile didn't spread out enough. It couldn't. He came back feeling heavy and stared long at the mist rising from the valleys as he rode back to his basti on the State Transport bus.

Mani felt like visiting Neetu again the next day so he bought some ginger cookies for her from the bakery in the market. She loved them and gorged on them when they used to be together earlier. Mani realized that his anger did not want to stay inside him when he saw Neetu frail and helpless. Her mother was sitting beside her on the hospital bed. Although Neetu was awake, she was lying pale and inert under the effect of the sedative.

"Oh! Good, you came…," Neetu's mother smiled lovingly as she saw Mani. "She's being discharged. She asked about you last night… that's the first time she spoke normally in the last ten days."

Mani smiled at Neetu but she looked away, as if in pain. Mani felt guilty. Did she not want to see him? Was he causing her more sadness by coming to meet her? He wished he knew. He stood there for five minutes and then kept the ginger cookies at the bedside table. He turned to go, when he heard Neetu speak softly.

"Will you come home, Mani?" She asked imploringly. Mani's heart softened and he nodded right away.

Not knowing what to say, Mani simply smiled and said, "Get well soon."

A renewed friendship thus took off in the context of Neetu's recuperation. Mani usually packed up early by an hour, so that he could drop in to Neetu's, and Neetu spent all her waking hours in anticipation of this one hour. She hardly spoke the first few days he dropped by but asked him to visit her again, unfailingly in the same imploring manner when he got up to leave. Neetu's mother insisted too, and Mani felt obligated to visit, for probably she could see the positive impact it had on her daughter. Mani had unknowingly become the harbinger of hope for both mother and daughter that Neetu would go back to being the same radiant bubbly youngster she once was with his support.

"Why didn't you come, Mani?" Neetu's mother asked once when Mani did not drop by for two days. "She was extremely restless. We had to give her extra doses." She informed miserably.

Mani felt guilty and responsible. Unaware, he was getting sucked into the greatest trap of human attachment, that he was needed and hence, indispensable. It was for life to decide whether this feeling would imprison him or bail him out, but he took it upon himself to be more committed to Neetu's recovery for the time being. Just a month ago, he hated her…and now he was almost adopting her. There is nothing as unpredictable as life and nothing more unreliable than feelings, and yet, humans believe in them more than anything else. Mani believed with all his heart that Neetu needed him.

A month went by. The day Neetu spoke first, she sobbed uncontrollably. Mani sat beside her in silence. Probably, that was what she needed to recover, a patient calm listening. She related the horrific series of events one by one and howled as she described the one image that had clogged her mind forever…that of a headless torso of a uniformed man with blood oozing out, running towards her… She hugged Mani and cried her heart out till her tired mind and weary eyes surrendered to sleep. Something moved inside Mani's heart that day. He started feeling that Neetu was a part of him, an extension without which he felt incomplete. Meeting her, talking to her, and knowing how she was keeping became his emotional compulsion, a part of his sense of well-being.

Neetu recovered slowly over the next two months, and Mani gradually started driving her towards her studies as their higher secondary exams were approaching. He took books for her and shared his assignments with her. She was slowly regaining her previous self, but there was still a moat between their hearts, especially Mani's heart, and the crocodile in it was Norbu. It disallowed Mani from crossing the moat.

Neetu probably sensed it and knew Mani would never bring it up in any conversation so out of the blue, she said one day, "I know you're angry with me…"

Mani knew where the conversation was directed but chose to act ignorant and asked, "No. I have no reason to."

Neetu looked down quietly for some time and then said, "Norbu…Norbu and I…"

Mani did not like thinking about that day. It made him feel sick.

His feelings were showing in the changing colour of his face, even though he chose to remain quiet.

"I thought he loved me Mani. When you were away during *Guru Aama's* time, we became close. I believed him when he said he loved me...," she sounded repentant. Mani was caught in intense rancor but was suppressing it with all his might because he was afraid any reaction would affect Neetu. After all, she was still recovering.

"Slowly I realized he was not the Norbu we - you and I - knew. He started spending time with that other guy, that second year addict guy. He got swayed perhaps... He used me...I started feeling so. We fought last month and I don't want to meet him ever." She spoke as if she owed this explanation to Mani.

Mani, however, could no longer conceal his resentment and with the hurt burning in his eyes, he said. "But did you also not love him, Neetu? You chose HIM after all. He couldn't have used you if you didn't choose him."

Neetu was on the verge of crying. She was sniffing, trying to push back her tears. She could not defend herself as she knew where she had wronged Mani. She knew how much she liked him but did not believe in him enough to wait for him. Her haste and excitement of romance had got the better of her. She knew Mani's worth now, but could not ask for it to be hers. She realized bitterly that she was no longer worthy of it.

Mani was conscious about her state of mind, however, and decided to end the conversation by not participating in it any more. He was careful of not hurting her though, so he said, "I'll come tomorrow, I have some work right now. Please finish reading those assignments I gave you. We'll discuss tomorrow."

Neetu said nothing.

CHAPTER 26

Monsoons were over and the bright festive season was on its way. But this year the ambience still seemed damp. After all, when were festivals about the weather? Of course, the weather sometimes marked it in time and added fervor at other times, but festivals are senseless without human cheer. This is how 'Tika' was approaching this year, senselessly. After losing so many loved ones senselessly to a purposeless Quixotic firing, few had the heart to celebrate. It was more a less a chore to be completed in most households. This year, Mani was not even interested in the dusting and cleaning. Fortunately, *Guru Aama* had started going to school again and Mani realized it made her less intrusive, and therefore, made life easier for him.

The first day *Guru Aama* returned from school, she simply collapsed on the bed and went off to sleep without a word or dinner. Mani was worried to death thinking she had fallen ill again like last year, and spent the entire night hovering around her like a bee. Tired of waiting for her to confirm her well-being, he had fallen asleep at her bedside by dawn and was woken early in the morning up by a shrill "Mani, you lazy bum...is this the way you sleep?" Mani was more than relieved to see her all ready for school even though she was in a horrendous temper to find Mani sleeping without a care, and the chores left unattended. She had walked up the slope screaming at Mani and the entire neighborhood woke up to her sorry opinion of 'the useless lad Mani.'

Later, Rubin Uncle joked, "I think we should send Sheila off to work also, what say Mani? It is important everyone is tired by the end of the day…there'll be more peace around, don't you think so?" He laughed wickedly while Sheila Aunty sulked and threw a plastic tea strainer at him. Mani laughed along too, enjoying the camaraderie of the siblings and the aromatic tea and breakfast Sheila Aunty pampered him with to get him off his stupor.

Rubin Uncle took some leisure time getting ready for work. He looked at himself consciously in the mirror and Sheila Aunty winked at Mani.

Teasingly, she thought aloud, "People take so long at the mirror these days…what for? Wonder what's up? Mani, do you know anything?"

Mani went red in the face and shook his head in haste. Guilty of being an accomplice, he was terrified Rubin would easily uncover his conspiracy. He bit his lip. He knew Rubin was a habitual prober. At times he wondered why Rubin worked at the Electricity department… he was so much better at being a detective. Mani, nevertheless, looked up to Rubin Uncle and dreaded his disapproval.

Sheila meanwhile was enjoying Rubin's discomfort. She continued with a chuckle, "This change is quite recent you know… since the time we had a pretty guest in this house." She then took a long breath and said, "I was hoping this Tika will be different this year…there'll be a new addition to the family but let's see what God has in store for us. Only God can help, people will spend their entire life staring at the mirror and doing nothing I suppose." Mani fiddled with his food trying to not look anywhere, for he was worried his eyes would meet Rubin's and the latter would know his part in Sheila's rhapsody.

"There there…enough of your day dreaming Sheila…," Rubin said in irritation. "Oh! That reminds me. Mani, I received a call from your Nurse *didi* last week…"

Sheila laughed and interjected excitedly, "See Mani, did I not tell you? See for yourself. Did I take anyone's name? But he is reminded of 'someone' out of nowhere. Now you know who that 'someone' in that mirror is?"

Mani knew he had no business to be in the conversation but was being used as a medium to communicate, so he sat quietly in spite of his restlessness. Moreover, his ears were alert now… curious to know what Shahana had to tell.

Rubin ignored Sheila consciously and turned to Mani. "You need to go and meet her one of these days… she said it was very important."

Mani nodded, although he was craving to ask if she was fine. He swallowed his concern and began scheming in his mind as to when he would go…

"I have work in town tomorrow. If you want, you can come along." Rubin said casually as he walked out of the door.

Sheila jumped in again, "YES Mani…say yes, you dope…you have to go…" Mani knew what she was plotting and felt awkward.

Rubin looked at them skeptically and smiled to himself. They were probably walking through different paths to the same place. Whether Shahana was a destination or simply a milestone for Rubin, only Shahana could tell. Rubin, however, had made up his mind about her.

The next day Rubin and Mani were ready to take the 8AM bus. Rubin wore a crisp new burgundy shirt and stone-washed jeans and looked dapper. Mani smiled brightly on seeing him and Rubin returned an equally bright one. They walked up the slope, Rubin's arm around Mani's small shoulders, making a happy picture of sincere affection.

"Some special occasion?" Mani asked, tugging at Rubin's shirt. Mani had a wicked smile on.

"Yes Mani…very special," Rubin said shyly. After a pause, he continued in a hesitant but serious tone, "I want to ask your Nurse *didi's* hand in marriage. Will she agree?"

Mani felt as if every pore in his body was dilating with joy. He felt ecstatic…as if someone was showering flowers on him. He couldn't believe his silent prayers would be answered this way. However, the tingling feeling came to a halt when he tried finding an answer to Rubin's question. Would Shahana really agree? He was trying to play angel for her without her knowledge but what if she did not agree? This uncertainty made its significance felt for the first time…and also the realization that one can inspire but cannot conspire for hearts to unite. It had to be left to destiny.

Mani said nothing for a long time, although Rubin kept looking at him questioningly. After they had travelled almost halfway, Mani simply said, "I can try convincing her…I'll try if you're sure of yourself."

Rubin smiled and nodded his head. Mani meanwhile wondered if Rubin knew about her past…and whether he'd change his mind later if he didn't approve of it. What felt dreamily possible an hour ago was ridden with ifs and buts now….

The bus meandered through turns and twists till it reached Ghum. Mani always got lost in his thoughts in this stretch from Ghum to Darjeeling. The view of the entire town resting under the shimmering Kanchendzonga range…it never failed to enchant him. The more he gazed at it, the more mysterious and mesmerizing he found it. Today, under the clear blue skies the entire landscape appeared like a piece of art, like the face of a regal woman wearing a crown, the green slopes at the outskirts of the dense town flowing down like her beautiful tresses. The dense town looked like the myriad emotions her face expressed, the dreams that she saw and the philosophies that her fascinating mind held, to find the depth and root of which, one had to delve deeper into her bewitching world. However, as he entered the congested road leading to the town, the image vanished and he could sense being caught in the turmoil of emotions behind the beautiful face. He was closer to the truth perhaps, and the visage in his imagination was probably an enticing mirror, reflecting the angst of the people living behind it...

This was a stretch that invariably made Mani reminisce about his life, and he ruminated upon the bends he had crossed and the events that had thrown him over on this stretch time and again. Today, as he was approaching the town yet again, the new question that popped up in his introspection was that where was he headed to, after all? Where would he halt? Did he know where he was going? He hazily thought about the day when fire consumed his world and gutted his life. Barely ten or eleven years old, he knew nothing beyond his existence as Maniraj Khaling, son of a simple man named Giriraj Khaling. He remembered his father going to work to some post office nearby. Mani's world was a fairytale between the warmth of his yellow cottage and the school he went to a kilometer away. The stretch in between was a dreamy road with a small wood with pine trees on one side, and a daisy-filled slope on the other side. Mani and his friends loved playing 'chor-police' in these woods. He was busy playing that ill-fated day too while the flames were slowly eroding away every layer of his existence. A heavy smoke crossing the woods had disrupted their game... and Mani never imagined that he would trace them to his house. Confused and terrified by the gigantic flames, he remembered how he hid in a jeep that was parked on the road below his house. Huddled and trembling with fright in a corner of the back of the jeep, he remembered watching the chaotic flames soar and his countable neighbours cry in helplessness...he recalled the jeep slowly starting off, unknowingly carrying him away to another world. Consumed by his thoughts and the intensity of pain in his memories, Mani choked as he almost felt the smoke in his eyes. A deep longing slashed his heart...he felt like leaving everything behind and going back to those woods. Soureni...Yes! That was the name of his little world, which he preferred to forget, and so never mentioned it to anyone, not even Shahana. The name drilled a dry hollow well in his heart because it was of no meaning now. Soureni was simply a barren mass of debris. He no longer had a home to go back to.

"What happened?" Rubin asked, alarmed to see Mani's eyes filled with tears. Mani became conscious and immediately jumped backed to his present. He smiled and said, "Dust probably...," the overused adult cliché for hiding tears. Mani realized that instead of diminishing, the sting of his memories was adversely becoming more severe as he was moving away from them in time. He probably no longer had the insurance of childhood with him. He could not allow distractions to dismiss his pain now as his awareness grew day by day. Although faces were fading, the cries of pain of his dear ones were growing louder now...as much as the understanding of the immensity of his loss...and the gnawing desire to go back and reconstruct his world, his home that was not only rightfully but also soulfully his.

"Aren't you too silent today?" Rubin broke Mani's stream of thoughts. "Tired? Didn't you sleep last night? Come now...we've got to get down. What 'important' work could Shahana have with YOU by the way?" Even though indirectly, Rubin was at it now, digging his hunches that would inevitably lead to Mani's grave, i.e., Pradhan Niwas.

"I don't know...," Mani said, somewhat worried if it would be a can of worms but he was too exhausted of hiding the truth and revealing lies, so he just lay back and decided to wait.

As they were climbing up the slope leading to Eden Hospital, Mani asked Rubin, "Does she know about you...I mean that you'll be coming with me to meet her?" He was curious if there was any context to Rubin's decision.

"No...not exactly. Just that I told her over telephone the other day that I'd come and meet her if I came to town..." Rubin said, carefully placing his words. He did not want Mani to doubt his intentions.

Mani still could not fathom the depth of their acquaintance and wondered how Shahana would react. Anyway Rubin would have to take a chance...

It was around 11a.m. Mani knew Shahana would be on her morning rounds, so he thought of looking for her by checking the wards rather than asking for her at the Nurses' common room. He liked surprising her to see that happy smile on her face. So Mani asked Rubin to wait outside and went off to look for her. He found her in a ward upstairs, attending to an old patient and waited for her to finish her work. As soon as she turned to go to the next patient, he purposely coughed in her ears.

She turned around instantly and exclaimed, "Oh my God! Mani!" She laughed joyfully. "What a surprise! Why didn't you let me know you were coming? I'd have taken the day off." She said, already flustered as to how she'd take out time with Mani.

"Don't worry, we won't take much time," Mani said.

"We?" She asked.

Mani teasingly said, "Yes yes…someone is quite eager to meet 'MY sister-*didi*'…she seems to have applied some magic ointment on his legs." Mani laughed heartily while Shahana blushed and pulled Mani's ears.

"Ok, wait for a few minutes under 'the tree'…I'll come and meet you there." Shahana said.

Mani nodded and turned to go. Then suddenly turned around and blurted out, "What was it that you had to tell me?"

Shahana guessed his apprehension and said, "Don't worry, I'll take care…. Ok, you wait outside. I'm coming, we'll go down together."

She explained a few things to the nurse accompanying her and came out.

"Hadn't I told you about the will? I'm talking about the bungalow…," Shahana wasted no time. She was boiling inside with things to tell Mani. "Sushma *Kaki* had come to visit me and took me to the bungalow. We both signed the will as witnesses. *Dada* is totally bed-ridden…these days Sushma *Kaki* visits once a week to see to the house and *Dada's* needs. She said she vowed never to come back… but she feels indebted to the bungalow and now that he's lying on his death bed…." Abruptly changing the topic and with excitement soaring, Shahana said, "Do you know something Mani? The will is in your name…can you imagine, you're filthy rich now. Sushma *Kaki* convinced *Dada's* lawyer that you are the legitimate inheritor as *Dada* had adopted you. She was adamant you inherit it after knowing that you're alive and very much around. You just need to sign it and the lawyer will hand it over to you in our presence. Can you imagine? You're the owner of Pradhan Niwas."

Mani cut short her excitement with a curt: "I don't need it…I'm not going there." His entire being experienced a bitterness that was beyond comprehension. He did not want anything from that bungalow to even touch him…he was so allergic to it. And this property? His soul could not accept it. Every cell in his body was rejecting it and he actually felt an urge to vomit. The news felt like venom moving through his capillaries and he struggled to repel it, eject it. It was not the property he would inherit…but the name, and he would never be able to free himself of the shackles of the darkness that the name carried. He wanted to break free from it.

"What happened Mani?" Shahana asked after noticing his face change colour. The excess rage inside pumped so much blood to his face that it made it appear almost purplish.

"How is the man still alive?" Mani asked, unable to conceal his acute detestation.

"Hmm…maybe a few months more. That's what the doctors said…hence this will…," Shahana appeared confused. She knew Mani hated the idea of going back…but she also knew this inheritance could change his life. She could not understand his fuss, which she considered somewhat childish now. She thought it was time he'd realize that he didn't have anyone after all…and that this inheritance would change his destiny, if he wanted…. Shahana wanted to play angel for Mani here. 'The gift of the Magi' with a twist was being enacted here in pure innocence.

They were walking towards Rubin now, each lost in their individual web of thoughts.

"Please don't tell him…Rubin Uncle…anything," Mani said.

"Hmm," Shahana said.

Rubin and Shahana greeted each other on meeting. Rubin appeared slightly conscious, probably because he had come with an agenda.

After some time, Rubin asked, "What happened? Why did you want to meet Mani? Something important?"

"Uhh…yes, somewhat…," Shahana replied. "There is a vacancy here in the hospital. I'm asking him to apply…but he doesn't seem very eager. He says he wants to complete his graduation first."

Shahana and Mani exchanged a knowing glance.

"Oh…ok. I think he's right. He's a bright boy after all." Rubin said, smiling at Mani.

Mani sensed Rubin was getting fidgety and so butted in. "I need to go to the stationery store. *Guru Aama* has asked me to buy a few things for the school. I'll come back in an hour…is it ok, Rubin Uncle?"

"Fine…go, run." Rubin Uncle said. "We'll leave by the 2 o'clock bus so be back by then." Rubin intended to tell Mani not to come back before two. After all, this period in time was a crucial turning point in his life. He could not miss this opportunity.

Mani was eager to go, too. He needed some solitude to neutralize the turbulence inside him. He was unable to process the negative emotions that overpowered him at the mention of the bungalow in any capacity. He could not help feeling it and hated his inability to conceal them. He hated himself when he was not his best self with Shahana because he knew how pure her intentions were. What he could not logically express were the repugnant vibes that he was soaked in at the thought of KP…and his intense repulsion of any thread that associated him with KP. He had seen the latter's darkness, had been terrified by it but still had no access to any understanding of his intention behind it even now. It had seemed extremely reprehensible and criminal, yet he could not explain it to anyone because no explanation seemed acceptable in terms of the limited worldly outlining of criminal behavior. After all, how can one derive evidence from a child's feeling…even if it holds the purest truth?

Mani walked away, nonchalant to the hustle of the town. The noise in his head was so heavy and unmanageable that he could hardly lift it to look around. He thought of drinking tea to feel better, and for some reason thought of going to the sweet shop Kishan worked for. He was not fearful of looking into old faces any longer, for his frequent visits to the town made him realize that people moved around carrying their own islands in their minds, and he did not live in any, not even in the Fox's island. Even in the Fox's island of thoughts, he was like a broken bottle thrown away in the corner for the seawaters to carry away, a mere object long forgotten after use. If there was any threat of the past, it was KP…but he was immobile. This anonymity, however, suited Mani. He found comfort in it.

He sat in one corner of the shop and called out to a boy attending the customers. "One tea and two *singharas,*" Mani said.

The owner looked the same except for a few white strands above his ears. He was oblivious to the fact that Mani could be someone he had known once and was busy exchanging change and taking orders.

"Kishan," the owner suddenly called out.

Mani's ears stood up when he heard that name and he strained his neck to see Kishan. He was contemplating if he would speak to him…when a little boy came running up to the counter.

"Yes *Kaka,*" the boy said. Mani smiled to himself. He was watching a replay of his life in many ways. He ruffled the boy's head when he walked past him in affection because he could see a shadow of himself in the eight-year old.

Mani felt a lot better after drinking the tea and walked over to the counter to pay. Beside him, an elderly lady was fiddling with her purse. She had probably come to buy sweets. Mani waited for her to finish paying.

"I've no change…why don't you believe me. You earn so much, still you harass me for change every time I come," she said, talking in a familiar manner like a regular customer does.

"Search *Didi*, search," the shop owner replied jestingly.

Mani did not need a second to know the voice, the built…she was Sushma *Kaki* and his impulse told him to just go and hug her but his feet remained arrested with shock. She bent down to pick a heavy bag with groceries and left the shop. Mani hurriedly paid and ran after her, walking behind her closely. He could not make up his mind about how he'd stop her…or tell her who he was for obviously she wouldn't recognize him…so he went and caught her heavy bag that she was struggling to carry.

"What on earth are you doing?" she almost screamed, terribly startled.

"I just mean to help you," Mani said. "I noticed it's a bit too heavy for you so…."

"Oh…you're such a good boy…where do we find such lads these days…." She laughed, feeling a bit awkward and affectionately said, "Thank you so much, child."

"Where will you go, *Kaki*?" Mani asked, just to make conversation.

"Pradhan Niwas…that old bungalow, you must be knowing… Who doesn't? It's a landmark." She said.

"Yes…I do," Mani said.

"Do you stay that side, too?" *Kaki* asked. "Oh…it never struck me to ask you. You must be having work, child. I wouldn't like to trouble you…I'll manage, don't you worry." She came forward to take the bag.

"Don't worry *Kaki*," Mani said, reassuring her. He realized she was still the same *Kaki*, affectionate, sensitive and committed. His heart was aching to tell her who he was but he could not find the right words. He was sincerely hoping she would guess…but how? He was no longer the small child she knew.

"The knees…they betray you…too bad." *Kaki* was trying to make some conversation going. "There was a time when it barely took me half an hour to get to the bungalow. Now it takes me a good one hour. Where do you stay, child?"

Mani could no longer bear with the small talk. They were about to take the road that went uphill towards the bungalow and he had no intention of going there.

So without mincing words, he said, "I'm Mani, *Kaki*…your Mani."

She stopped, and shocked as she was, she stood staring at him. Feeling awkward, his face turned red and he looked down waiting for her to say something.

"Mani…my child…my *nanu?*" She asked softly, her eyes brimming with tears.

Mani nodded, trying to push back his own.

"My *nanu*…my child…," *Kaki* cupped her trembling hand around his cheek. "How I've hated myself all these years *nanu*…I could not forgive myself…I couldn't keep you…" *Kaki's* tears were flowing down her cheeks uninhibited. "Why did you have to go away, my child? Why…?"

Mani came forward and hugged her close to his heart with one hand without saying a word. Realizing they were in the middle of the road, they composed themselves and walked on.

There was a deep silence for some time.

"Shahana told me about you…I'm so grateful to God you're alive." *Kaki* said after some time. She just could not have enough of Mani and looked at him lovingly every two minutes.

"How did *Bada* die? Was he ill?" Mani asked, carefully choosing not to talk about KP or the bungalow.

"It was his time to go…there was nothing to live for, that's what he told me a month before he expired. The bungalow is a house of ghosts and demons, that's what he said." She paused and then said, "He said he had found hope in you but…." Changing the topic, she asked, "Did Shahana tell you about the will?"

"Yes…," Mani said reluctantly. "I don't want it, *Kaki*. I ran away to be away from that bungalow forever…I don't want it to hang around my neck like a noose."

"The bungalow is deserted…except for a ticking clock that may stop functioning any time," she said, implying KP. "You can secure your future dear. After all, you did not choose to come here asking for it. It fell in your lap." *Kaki* tried to instill sense in Mani. It was insane to reject a fortune like this.

There are riches, and then there is richness of life. What exactly makes one wealthy? Man has forever struggled juggling between seeking riches and richness of life in the illusion that the former begets the latter. But Mani had known how to live beyond this trap. He had spent his small life in acute scarcity, but it had not hurt him so much to eat a meal only once…what had hurt him more was when the value of his existence was equated to a meager meal…by the Fox, the bungalow, or *Guru Aama*. Circumstances and intensities may have been different but the trade was the same. Take a meal, live and hand me your life. Mani realized he was standing alone in this battle because it was his soul that was seeking freedom. He knew how pure and noble *Kaki's* and Shahana's intentions were…they were fighting to give him a secure future they thought he deserved but he was dismaying them with his adamant rejection…and without a viable reason that he could frame in words.

As they were about to reach the bungalow, Mani asked out of the blue, "What happened to *his* family, *Kaki*…before me?" This was a question that had always been the biggest question in his head but he had never had the courage to ask it, when he was staying at the bungalow. It didn't matter much but he thought he had the right to know…and probably *Kaki* agreed on this.

Kaki became pensive. She sat down on the parapet on the

roadside sandwiched between two shops and spoke slowly and softly, "Hmm…I guess you ought to know. After all, you're the sole inheritor of the clan. She was beautiful…Brinda, his wife. Young and vivacious, I remember her running around little Mohit, fussing over him all the time. He was a prankster, too…the precious one," She laughed. "It used to be so lively, the bungalow." She looked far away, not at any object in particular but as if caught in a different span of time, she said solemnly, "It was the month of March…It was Mohit's ninth birthday. They celebrated it so joyfully…but a day later, something happened. The child fell ill. For some reason, Brinda fought with *him*. She was so violent, she almost stabbed *him* with a knife. She was never the same after that. She became psychotic, always protecting Mohit…sometimes talking to him even when he was off to school. We were all worried. It seemed as if she was losing her mind. The child too fell ill often. On his tenth birthday, they said they were going for a vacation. We were all very happy for them, hoping things would go back to normal again. But a week later, *he* returned alone. *He* said they drowned in a river and *he* drowned himself in alcohol thereafter."

Mani heard her patiently but felt restless within. He eerily recalled his birthday celebration at the bungalow and the night that followed. He had fallen ill too out of fear…but the monster? Did *he* have more to the story? *He* probably did something beastly…and to *his* own son? Did he really want a son…or someone like his son? *Kaki's* narration didn't convince Mani. He was rather convinced that *he* WAS a devil after all…it was not mere projection. What he was told today disquieted him from the inside even more. He was almost convinced that there was more to this story but he could not explain it to *Kaki*… or anyone.

"The bodies were never recovered. I remember Samsher *Bada* having an altercation over it with the police but everyone was helpless." *Kaki* said gravely.

Mani stood quietly, chewing on his own thoughts. His resolve to reject this inheritance grew only stronger after all that he'd heard.

"I'll go now *Kaki*. I've got to meet Shahana," Mani said.

"Won't you come to the bungalow? I'll make you some tea," *Kaki* tried persuading Mani affectionately. "It's yours after all...."

"NEVER! I left it to go away, never to come back," Mani replied firmly.

"Oh Mani...my child," *Kaki* said in dismay. "Give up your anger...now it's only you."

Mani walked up and kept the grocery bag a meter away from the gate. He then came back to where *Kaki* was sitting and bowed to take her blessings. *Kaki* blessed him and kissed him on his forehead. "I'll always have a place to come back to if you come back, my child," she said, her voice breaking.

Mani knew he did not have the answers today so he held her close to his heart once more and walked away.

Rubin was waiting alone. Shahana had gone inside as she was on duty.

"You took pretty long?" Rubin asked.

"I was giving you time," Mani said wittily.

Rubin smiled but not very heartily.

"What happened?" Mani asked. "It went well I hope... Did she get angry?" He was worried how Shahana must have reacted.

"Not really... I didn't ask her or tell her anything as such. I just asked her where she belonged to...and things like that, you know casual questions." Rubin said, appearing somewhat dismayed. "She said she's married..." And that, according to Rubin, probably seemed the end of hope and the reason behind his sadness.

"Did she?" Mani tried to look surprised but he felt anger at her illogical commitment towards that wretch who had conveniently abandoned her. "I'll just meet her and come before we go...just five minutes and I'll be back." Mani ran off to ask for her in the Nurses' common room.

She was sitting there and came outside on seeing Mani. Mani was feeling somewhat irritated…he usually did when Shahana showed her loyalty to that wretch. He could not generate tolerance for that man ever. He'd felt irritated when he was a child…he felt irritated even now, at the threshold of manhood. It was still too early to understand that as much as we calculate the modalities of life and try moulding it with our best interests, it is but just another perception we have of things at the end of the day. In reality, we are always driven by mathematics of the universe. Otherwise, why would Mani want to reject what was a 'windfall' in worldly view…and why would Shahana remain blind to love carving a way into her life?

"I'm going…just wanted to tell you that I met Sushma *Kaki* today." Mani told her in detail how they met but not what he had been told. Mani wanted to convince her about Rubin Uncle but did not know how. His intentions were obvious, and he knew Shahana knew about Rubin's interest in her even though she was trying to act ignorant. So like he did every time, he shot off straight away with a slight tone of impatience.

"You know what…I haven't known a better man than Rubin Uncle so far. And just like you don't understand why I cannot accept the bungalow as my inheritance, I also cannot understand why you need to remain so loyal to that husband of yours who is actually not even yours…"

Mani knew that was a rude but he walked away…he had said what he had to.

He heard her call out his name from behind but he didn't turn around. He just waved his hand. Rubin and Mani took the 2 o'clock bus back home, not exchanging a word with each other, each replaying their own conversations in solitude.

CHAPTER 27

Exams were approaching, and Mani spent most of his time with his books. Once in a while, he went over to Sheila Aunty but he hated to see a dispirited Rubin, as if he had compromised with the lonely life he had. The spark of hope ignited by Shahana had dimmed. Sheila Aunty kept asking what happened that day but Mani had no answer. Every time she asked, he had the same reply. "I don't know. I wasn't around…had left them alone deliberately to talk."

"He didn't say a word to me…he won't," Sheila Aunty lamented. "He'll just sit alone staring at the wall…I just hate to see him like that."

When a week was left for the exams, Mani's nervousness heightened. It was important for him to do well. Just last month, based on Gurung Sir's recommendation and Mani's sincere voluntary service, the principal had promised him that if he passed the exam with a first division, he would create an *ad hoc* post for him as 'Assistant Librarian' and pay him a monthly stipend of Rs. 1500/month. Mani had been overjoyed and was aching to share this news with someone. He had told Rubin Uncle and the latter had responded with a warm smile and a hug, but Mani was so excited, he wanted someone to jump and celebrate with him. After all, it was his first job…his first as a literate.

He wanted to tell *Guru Aama* too…adding that she would no longer have to pay the fees for his studies, but something chained him. He postponed telling her. He missed the old times' Norbu and he knew Lakhotia wouldn't have time… He zeroed in on Neetu…although he wasn't really sure if it mattered to her…or if she'd be able to understand his joy and share it with him…

Neetu's face perked up on seeing Mani. It was a cold February day, and she had wrapped herself in a shawl and was sitting by the fire in the kitchen.

"How did you forget your way home today? The Library must be shedding tears, I'm sure?" She asked. Mani knew she was being sarcastic. After all, he was coming to visit her after almost a month.

"Oh really?" Mani said laughing. "I was letting you sit by the fire and become fat. See how your cheeks are going to fall off now." He teased Neetu.

She ran after him with a wooden ladle and both laughed heartily.

"Come, have some hot *thukpa*, Mani." Neetu's mother laid out the bowls for Neetu and Mani. She was fond of Mani, and even more so because she knew he cared for her daughter.

Mani had brought some pastries for Neetu.

"What's this for?" She asked. "Some occasion…your birthday? But you said you don't remember?" She was confused. In their first phase of friendship when they were trying to get to know about each other, birthdays made for an important conversation. They had laughed when Mani had said with a straight face, "My birthday falls on the 366th day of every year."

"For you, stupid. Does it always have to be an occasion?" Mani said.

Neetu picked one up, gobbled up one half and thrust the other half in Mani's mouth. She then laughed, pointing at his cream-soiled nose. Neetu's mother smiled contentedly.

Later when they were by themselves discussing their studies,

Mani told Neetu about his job. Neetu squealed with excitement and hugged him spontaneously, her cheeks brushing against his ear. Mani had not expected anything like this and blushed in surprise, joy and embarrassment combined.

"Oh my God! I'm so happy for you Mani," Neetu screamed.

Mani was overwhelmed with emotion. Life is lonely without selfless friends by your side…Mani had missed it so much after Kishan, Bansi and Norbu, but he felt fulfilled today. Neetu's happiness for him made up for it…and perhaps was far more sincere than Norbu's or Kishan's….

"Now you don't have to depend on that foul-mouthed *Guru Aama* of yours, isn't it?" Neetu continued in her excitement.

"Hmm…," Mani said smiling. "She's good Neetu…just bad-tempered… In spite of everything, I owe my education to her."

"Yes, that you do…," Neetu said. "But it's good if you don't need to depend, I meant that actually."

"Of course," Mani said agreeing with her.

Neetu knew the circumstances in which Mani had ended up with *Guru Aama*. She had seen closely how devotedly he managed her life but had felt pity for Mani often, when she saw him tolerate *Guru Aama*'s insensitiveness and wrath with such patience. Neetu knew in her heart that Mani was a caged bird in *Guru Aama's* house and this would at least allow him to flap his wings. It was a precursor to his freedom.

Neetu stared at Mani, as if in awe, with such a pure smile that it made him conscious.

"Working man, huh!" She teased him. "Will you always work at the college Mani? Like…forever?" She asked him. "Is this what you thought of doing always?"

"No…I didn't really know this was coming. I never thought what I'd do…I just thought I'd study. But Gurung Sir says we should aim to become big officers, join the administration. Only then can we influence policies pertaining to the welfare of our people. I think he's right."

Neetu listened interestedly, noting his every word.

"I don't know if I'm dreaming too big…but I want to join the administrative services." Mani said hesitantly. He was scared people would make fun of him if they heard him say this. 'Servant boy,' this was his second name and he knew how hard it stung…

"No Mani…all of us have the right to dream." Neetu placed her hand on top of his. "And you will definitely make it. See how far you've come. You have it in you." She was sincere in her encouragement. Mani felt a gush of energy in his resolve. He saw such hope in his dreams, he felt as if he was flying. This was the first time he was sharing his thoughts, his dreams with someone and it felt liberating. In his subconscious mind, he always had Neetu with him when he dreamt about his future, but he wasn't aware in what capacity she would always be by his side. He thought it was a given…she would be there when he would finish studying…join the administrative services…build his home…she'd just be there. From the very beginning he was aware of the fact that he was not looking out for a hook-up with Neetu…or with any girl for that matter. This was in no way an agenda in his dreams. Moreover, he had become cynical about the boy and girl thing after Norbu. In fact, he perceived it as a hindrance. Moreover, which girl would feel happy going around with a 'servant boy'? He was also, in fact, aware of the ways of the world, too. But this was different and yet unknown…it was like a latent truth that could not be analyzed within the boundaries of liking and disliking that their juvenile minds had yet to learn, and therefore buried in the sands of time, waiting for the right moment to reveal itself.

Chemistry alone may unite bodies but not necessarily hearts. Sometimes, it is that one chord of genuine feeling that someone other than you is joyous in your joys, and sad in your sadness, that sings a tune of love. It is wonderful to find a human shrine on this earth where one can open one's heart without the fear of judgment, and Mani and Neetu had set off discovering it in each other. It was strange, as both had been interested in each other but both had drifted away along the way. But now that the interest factor had been struck off from their minds, connecting was easier. Not having to be with each other in a certain way, to be able to be themselves without inhibitions, allowed a free and unrestricted flow of communication between them. It allowed them to be their true selves with each other. They were coming closer to each other, far more than they ever were, without any premeditation. Sharing every bit of their lives, their confusions, their feelings about everyone and everything, and their half-baked philosophies, slowly became a habit with both, without which they felt incomplete.

Mani helped out at *Guru Aama's* school after his exams if he returned from the Library early. One such afternoon, he was sitting in a corner of the staff-room reading the newspaper. He turned the pages every day as the results could be announced anytime.

Mani read the headlines:

"It is a Grey Spring this year: Tourism Industry suffers a huge setback."

"Ghising warns center; Says total poll boycott during March 23 elections greatest political victory for Gorkhas."

"Subhash Ghising has become irrelevant to the agitation, claims DIG Handa."

Mani chuckled and thought to himself, 'this man seems to have gone bonkers...talking rubbish. How could Ghising become irrelevant? The one man, the God on whom lakhs of Gorkhas had pinned their hopes to regain their motherland from the clutches of Bengal...irrelevant? Impossible! Ridiculous! This Handa is not even a Bengali...God knows what's hurting him so much? Why doesn't he just go back to where he belongs?' Mani thought in disdain. He was yet to know that one's sense of duty, one's commitment was the spine of one's integrity. There was no running away from it. One would know if one was DIG Handa.

Mani was living in interesting times though. Somewhat misdirected, the battle at this point of time seemed to be drawn out between the Gorkhas and the deployed forces, rather, between Ghising vs DIG Handa. DIG Handa was rising like a colossus against the GNLF radicals (as he called them) and had almost taken a personal vow to wipe them out, especially after he almost lost his life in an attack last December. A bullet tore through his shoulder, barely missing his lungs, and made him stay under medical supervision for almost a month, but he came back with an even stronger resolve. It almost became his personal mission. So adamant and forceful was he, and so unpopular, that these days, every poster bearing the slogan 'We want Gorkhaland' was paired with another slogan: 'Go back Handa.' The 'Militant' or 'Extremist theory' was, in fact, put forward by him...although he remained confused about whether the Militants on the Indo-Nepal border were a wing of the GNLF or against them, so it was sometimes even more confusing as to who was fighting whom. However, post some major attacks on the major officials and administrative properties in the recent past, the administration had been strengthened with an 'Anti-terrorist Act' to curb insurgency and militancy. This violent approach was supposedly the new strategy of the GNLF, as hypothesized by Handa, and so offended were the center and the state with this change of strategy that they secretly came together and planned to give up on the consideration of Gorkhaland altogether. This Act, however, had a local meaning. An entirely new concept of 'Raids' was the trending conversations among the commoners this year.

Although Mani lived in an almost immune part of this agitated world, he had heard from friends in college how the forces had just barged into houses, picked up youth and put them behind bars, branding them as terrorists. Mani had also heard that Dhruva had developed his own intelligence cell that worked on finding out about prospective raids and the probable areas they would be conducted in, so that the targets could be intimated beforehand. Mani wondered if it could happen in Naya Basti too...he shuddered at the thought of being put behind bars with the likes of Norbu and Lalit.

Mani finally came across a small snippet of news at the corner of the local daily that said-

"WBCHSE Class XII results to be declared in the first week of June."

He did not need to read the newspaper any more.

A week passed by in acute impatience. Mani was in the Library, dusting and settling books. Very soon it would be decided if this dutiful dusting would be held in parallel with Handa's 'curbing insurgency,' calling upon his integrity. Very soon it would be decided if he were capable of becoming Ghosh Sir's successor.

Lakhotia came running and panting with excitement. "Hey you…come fast *yaar*, results have been declared. Let's go and see the notice board. I'm shivering; I'll pee any moment. There are rumors that only 50% students have passed…Jai Shri Krishna, save me…save me…. I saw good luck, a basket filled with coal while coming. Hope it works God. Uff! So much tension. Jai Shri Krishna." Lakhotia seemed to be talking in delirium.

Mani's heart started palpitating too, although he tried his best to remain calm. "Don't worry…there's nothing that can be done now so what's the point. We'll see what happens…" Mani was actually doing some self-talk. He was confident he'd do well but these rumours and in these times…it made one doubt one's performance. Last year's results had not been good too…and victimization of hill students by the board had been the most convincing conclusion, so the threat and uncertainty was looming at large.

The notice board was thronged with students. Many girls were bawling in corners whereas most of the guys were going around with long faces…including Norbu. Norbu's and Mani's eyes met once but Norbu quickly turned away. The list had a P/F with a division (I/II) against the exam roll numbers. Mani looked through an entire list and then another. His heart beat faster with every 'F' he crossed. He finally found his number on the third list.

JUNE 7, 1987: Mani had passed his higher secondary exams with a First Division.

Neetu and Lakhotia had thankfully passed too, although with a second division. In fact, Mani was the only student from the Arts Section to get a first division. Mani became conscious and hurried away to the vacant Library. He went to a secluded corner and let the rivers of joy flow silently. His dedication had paid off. He had won over life. This time, HE had defeated fate.

Mani stayed back in the library till the college was deserted. He then got up to go late in the afternoon. He had three people to thank, and in that order- God, *Guru Aama* and Gurung Sir. He had Rs. 300/- with him that he had collected over a period of time. He had to divide it among the three of them to buy gifts as a token of gratitude. He was unable to decide on a decent gift for all three so he finally reasoned.

God would be happy simply with the purity of intent in his heart…it was all He asked for. He was THE giver, what could one give him?

Gurung Sir was not a 'things' person anyway. It would be meaningless to him…anything bought with money. He would be happiest with Mani's promise and sincerity to study further, achieve greater academic success…just that.

Guru Aama…what would make her happy? Mani remained confused. Of course…completing the chores, etc. but that had no connection to the results. When Mani had passed his matriculation exams, she had just responded with a 'hmmm'…as if she meant 'that's what you're supposed to do anyway.' Mani racked his brain but could not think of anything that would make her exceptionally happy. So he finally decided to use the money for her. He set out for the market to buy a saree for her. At least, the reaction would be different in some way this time…hopefully.

CHAPTER 28

Mani was returning from his first day of class. 1st year BA with a major in Political Science: Mani felt pride in it. His education meant a blessing to him. Neetu had opted for Geography as her major subject, so they would be in different classes most of the time this year onwards. There were barely ten students in his class and Mani missed the classroom ruckus and commotion of his higher secondary days. He looked around for Lakhotia in all the classrooms but did not find him. He wondered what subject Lakhotia had taken up. Not finding him anywhere, Mani decided to meet him on his way back home. After all, he was the only guy he could categorize as a friend…even if stationery hardly gave him time to nurture friendships.

Lakhotia's shop was closed. Mani found it rather strange, especially now when the new session was in full swing and students flocked to stationery shops. He knew Lakhotia's house was on the first floor of his shop so he climbed up the dark wooden staircase leading to it after another hardware shop in the row. There were a number of leather sandals and slippers in front of a door so he assumed that was the entrance. The door was open and the house seemed full. An old man wearing a dhoti and red vermilion on his forehead was sitting on a chair. Some others, all dressed simply, were sitting on a durrie spread out on the floor. They were all speaking in a language Mani was used to listening to, in the vicinity when he worked at the Fox's coal godown…the sound of it was familiar, although he could not catch the words or their meaning. The only word that rang a bell was 'koni' meaning 'not'.

A person saw Mani standing at the door and made a 'what' gesture by raising his brows.

"Prakash? Is this his house?" Mani asked shyly.

The man nodded and asked him to come in. He assumed Mani had come with a purpose like all of them.

Prakash, or Lakhotia as Mani called him, was sitting on a divan kept in the innermost corner of the room. His head was tonsured and he looked frail and down. He shifted in his place on seeing Mani and gestured at him to sit beside him. He said nothing and sat with his head bent down. Sensing the grim environment, Mani asked him nothing.

The men spoke to each other, some softly…some angrily…but Mani could understand nothing as much as he strained his ears and mind to do so. In between, some female voices interjected from the other room. One voice sniffed constantly, giving out a cry in pain, calling out to God once in a while. After about 20 minutes, Mani started getting restless. Mani held Lakhotia's forearm softly as if to assure he was with him in his sorrow, and left the house. There was no guessing. Someone had died…but who and how? Mani did not know much about Lakhotia's family. As he got down from the stairs, the intensity of the light on the road almost shocked Mani. He walked slowly, not knowing exactly where to go. He wanted to know what had happened but there was no one he could ask. Then it struck him- the hardware shop. He went to the shop. He called the helper (a hill boy in his teens) aside and asked him.

"What happened?" Mani pointed to Lakhotia's shop.

"Six inches of the owner gone, what else?" The boy said casually.

"What?" Mani exclaimed. "But why?" His heart was beating terribly.

"I believe some two weeks back, he closed the shop late…at around ten. The place was totally deserted as it was raining heavily. A number of rowdies came and asked him for money for some party fund. He asked them for proof and then got into a squabble with them. The beggar who usually sleeps on the porch of the garment shop on the opposite side was watching it all and told us the next morning. I believe the fight escalated and in a fit of rage, one of the guys took out a khukri and slashed his neck. He cried out but the hooligans fled. His son came running down and fainted in shock to see so much blood oozing out. By the time people gathered and rushed him to the hospital, his pulse was silent."

Mani was filled with sorrow…he knew how painful it was to lose your dearest people. His eyes brimmed with tears. He felt a surge of anger, almost sure that those heartless rowdies were Lalit's boys… or maybe drug addicts like Norbu. His heart went out to Lakhotia.

The boy then came closer and whispered in Mani's ears. "Don't you dare tell this to anyone, understand? The police are investigating but everyone is mum. The beggar was the only witness but he has fled, no one knows where. No one is saying a word against those rowdies. Everyone is scared it could be their turn next."

"Hmm." Mani nodded and walked on. His heart felt tired today because of the times he was living in…no human could trust the intent of the other. There was no unanimity in the perspective of right of wrong any more. It depended on the faction you belonged to, the fearful one or the fearless one. The latter also justified murder. It was conveniently given the name of war. When was war fair or democratic? People were living in fear, they feared fighting for what was right, they feared fighting against what was wrong. Suddenly, your surnames decided your loyalties, friendships and your beliefs. Beneath the blind veil of parochialism, humanity no longer existed.

Lakhotia had lost his dad, and Mani lost Lakhotia forever. This incident sketched an unfathomable distance between them. Lakhotia left Kurseong forever, the place his grandfather had chosen to establish a business in. He later heard they went back to Rajasthan, their native land. Mani wandered if Lakhotia was still studying or had left studying, as he had to shoulder all the responsibilities. He wondered if they would ever meet again. Mani wondered, 'Would he not miss the green slopes he pranced about on throughout his childhood? Would he not miss the mist that danced around him as he grew up? Would he ever be able to identify with the desert sands as home? What was home after all? After what had happened, would he hate the place like Mani hated Pradhan Niwas?' Mani searched for the deeper meaning of home through himself, through Lakhotia and through the hearts of the people who were ready to give up their lives and kill others, fighting for their homeland. In this struggle of the masses, the lateral damage was not counted, in fact, it was not even acknowledged. There were many who lost their loved ones, which therefore diminished all meaning of home, no matter where. There were many who felt uprooted from the place they called home, not because they could trace their origin to it but simply because their heart resided here.

Mani missed Lakhotia deeply. There was something incredibly forthright about him. He was miles away from diplomacy, sometimes even to the point of embarrassment. Lakhotia's simplicity, lack of any pretense in his personality and the fact that he did not have even a pinch of superficiality in him was what Mani had found endearing. Mani thought about him often. Till he was around in town, Mani felt he had a place to go to, but now he felt an emptiness walking around town. In fact, he avoided taking that road where his shop was. This incident and Lakhotia's leaving had made Mani philosophical.

Mani was helping Sheila out with making momos one evening. He was sipping tea while making the dumplings and chatting with Sheila Aunty. He asked her, "Is this the case with life always Aunty? Do we have to lose every person we find?" He was contemplating on his own friendships in retrospect.

Sheila Aunty was taken aback by the depth of his thoughts and realized what he was saying was so true. "Yes dear," she said, agreeing. "Life has a funny way of walking you through relationships. Usually, either you lose yourself in finding them or you find yourself in losing them."

Mani appeared confused. He could not make head or tail of her statement. Even she was surprised by her own unusual observation and laughed aloud.

"Oh my my, Mani! What's wrong with you? Cheer up, c'mon. Isn't Rubin enough that now you too?" She bit her tongue as she realized Rubin was listening to their conversation. "You'll make sages out of us if you talk like this. Why don't you sing a song instead?"

"Naya naya sajaun hai sansara,

(Let's build a new world)

Sukha dukha bataun hai mile-ra,

(Let's share our joys and sorrows)

Ghaam ko pahilo kiran,

(The first ray of the sun)

Chhunchha gara gara,

(Touches every corner)

Afnai dara-kada, aafnai dara-kada..."

(Of our own hilltops and bends, our own hilltops and bends)

Sheila started humming the new hit song asking Mani to join her with her hand.

"You know, Mani, the whole world has seen this movie except me. But I have a brother who's good for nothing. Can't he take me to Darjeeling just once to watch it? He always has this excuse that the situation is not right outside." She sulked. Then she limped up to where Rubin was sitting and said, "Ummm...that reminds me. I saw a sealed letter on the table *Bhai*...a big envelope. Who sent it?"

"It's from Darjeeling," Rubin said uninterestedly.

"A letter has come from 'Darjeeling' but he won't tell me about it. Fine…don't. I'm no one of yours, why should you," she complained. She had already decided that it was from Shahana. "It could be for me also, you never know…it was so sweet of Shahana *bahini* to send that beautiful stole for me last time, I need to reply to say thank you."

"Oh come on… It is not for me…or you," Rubin said, irritated at the mention of Shahana.

"Then?" Mani and Sheila asked unanimously with wide eyes.

"It's for Mani," he said.

"Mani?" This time it was only Sheila Aunty.

Mani's curiosity knew no end. 'A letter for me?' He thought to himself.

"It's probably some document…some form for Mani maybe," Rubin said, linking it to college admissions. "She sent it by post…and had called me to tell me to deliver it to Mani."

"Oh…ok," Mani said, lunging to take that letter.

Mani kept it aside to read it later and got back to making the dumplings. To take his mind off the letter, he kept bringing up some topic or the other to chat. Sheila had gone inside the kitchen to see to the steaming of the momos. Rubin was fixing an old clock.

"Uncle, do you people never go to Mirik side for work?" Mani asked. His mind had wandered off to his yellow cottage again. Mirik was a scenic spot with a beautiful lake, a small but significant town near Soureni. He knew Rubin worked in the rural electrification department and hence kept going to far-off villages and bastis for work.

"Of course we do…or have to," Rubin said. "It comes within this subdivision too. But who wants to go that side these days. The border area is so risky…bombs and explosives blow up any time. Don't you know, it's Handa's favorite spot!" Rubin laughed as he said this. "Handa has become obsessed with that part of the world. All his militancy hideouts are behind those valleys near Manebhanjan on the Nepal side," Rubin added.

Mani nodded knowingly. The area, in fact, was not only incredibly picturesque but also very fascinating. Spread out into cascading hillocks with a carpet of tea plantations on one side and enormous valleys on the other, the landscape was divided by a road, which functioned as the borderline for India and Nepal at many stretches. Funnily, a whole hamlet was named 'Simana' meaning border, but it had no border for people from both countries. They lived like twins, with individual identities but inseparable in essence.

"I'll be going next month…to a place called Soureni, very close to Mirik. I wonder if you know…Have you been to Mirik? Want to come along? If you come, I might take Sheila too…you people can go for boating on the Mirik lake while I finish my work." Rubin innocently laid out an entire plan, unaware of the earth shaking below Mani's feet at the mention of Soureni. "Give it a thought. If you want to come, I'll speak to *Guru Aama*. Sheila will also stop eating my head…she needs a break." Rubin continued thoughtfully. Thankfully, Sheila was busy in the kitchen or else she would have brought the roof down with her excitement.

"Hmmm," Mani said softly, feeling both sad and happy at the mention of his small town. Half of him wanted to go, to see those lakes and valleys once more, and the other half wanted to run away from it, as it reminded him of that day when his world came crashing down.

Changing the topic right away, Mani asked, "What else did Sister-*Di* say?"

It was Rubin's turn to become gloomy and silent, and utter a monosyllable, "Nothing."

Mani realized it had been months since he had spoken to Shahana, not even after his results. He was eager to know if Rubin had told her over the phone but he had no courage to ask him anything about her after the monosyllable. He was angry with her the last time he'd met her because of her unreasonable devotion for that worthless man she was married to, but Mani couldn't stay angry with her for long. He missed her and was hoping he'd meet her soon. She'd be so happy for him…his results, the part-time job, he had so much to tell her. 'She was so thoughtful to send the form,' he thought to himself, itching to open the envelope. He finished making the last batch of momos and hurriedly cleared up the place. He needed to slip away quickly to read what was inside.

Mani went and sat on the porch of *Guru Aama's* house and opened the envelope.

DRAFT WILL

I, Khagendra Pradhan, son of Shri Dhirendra Pradhan, aged 54 years, resident of Pradhan Niwas, Dr. S.M. Das Road, Darjeeling, do hereby revoke all my former Wills, Codicils and Testamentary dispositions made by me. I declare this to be my last Will and Testament.

I maintain good health, and possess a sound mind. This Will is made by me of my own independent decision and free volition. Have not been influenced, cajoled or coerced in any manner whatsoever.

I hereby appoint my Lawyer, Mr. Uday Yolmo, as the sole Executor of this WILL.

The name of my adopted son is Maniraj Pradhan, I own following immovable and movable assets.

1. One bungalow, Pradhan Niwas on Dr. S.M. Das Road, Darjeeling.

2. One office and godown on Hill Cart Road, Darjeeling.

3. One ancestral property in Mungpoo.

4. Ancestral land in Mungpoo.

5. Farm land in Lebong

6. Jewellery, ornaments, cash, National Saving Certificate, cash with certain banks.

All the assets owned by me are self-acquired properties. No one else has any right, title, interest, claim or demand whatsoever on these assets or properties. I have full right, absolute power and complete authority on these assets, or in any other property which may be substituted in their place or places which may be Acquired or received by me hereafter.

I hereby give, devise and bequeath all my properties, whether movable or immovable, whatsoever and wheresoever to my adopted son, Maniraj Pradhan, absolutely forever.

IN WITNESS WHEREOF I have hereunto set my hands on this _____ day of _____, 20__ at _______________.

TESTATRIX

SIGNED by the above named Testatrix as his last WILL and Testament in our presence, who appear to have perfectly understood & approved the contents in the presence of both of us presents, at the same time who in his presence and in the presence of each other have hereunto subscribed our names as Witnesses.

WITNESSES:

1. Smt. Sushma Rani Thapa

2. Smt. Shahana Josephine Subba

Another note lay beneath the document...in Shahana's handwriting that read:

"Please come soon, he does not have time. Let me know when you come (through Rubin Daju) so that Sushma Kaki can be informed too. We all need to be present to sign the document.

How were your results? What are you studying now?"

Mani's hands were trembling. Things were happening beyond his control. He had run away so far from everything…yet it had him in his clutches, this document. Who can deny the ordainment of this universe? There is a math to it…a calculation of intents, motives, desires, and actions that probably lead to redemption, somewhere through the intertwined paths of the many lives it touches. Mani hurriedly put the document back in the envelope. He was perspiring. His legs were shaking and he felt restless and nervous. What would he do now? He did not understand much of the will except that he was trapped…he could not deny the existence of Maniraj Pradhan and he could not give up the existence of Maniraj Khaling.

Mani went inside and hid under his quilt to sleep, but couldn't… the bloodshot eyes pierced through him like bullets from all over. At times, he felt it so intensely that he sat up, perspiring and breathing heavily with fear. He was the same Mani today…the 13-year-old Mani who saw shadows on the wall, the horror-stricken desolate boy. That bungalow reeked of alcohol and the darkness mixed in it- the desperation of *his* wife, the mysterious illness of *his* child, their sudden disappearance, Mani's unknown fear…and the deep suspense of his impure intentions looming all over the place. How could Mani ever own that dungeon…that hell? How could Mani call it his own…the ghosts of *his* fears lived in those very walls. He hated it…hated it with every inch of his being…and would not take it ever, not for his sake… not for Mohit Pradhan's sake. Mani knew in his heart that he was never a father but only a monster in disguise who had disowned one son and owned another, only to fulfill *his* beastly desires.

Mani, attacked by sleeplessness, was desperately waiting for the morning. After *Guru Aama* left for school, Mani sat down to plan to get away from this whole trap. He would have to confide in someone… he needed guidance. But who could he turn to? Confiding also meant opening his life up to someone…and that would be tough. No, he could not risk telling Rubin anything…Shahana was already a delicate thread between them. Gurung Sir…Mani could never muster up enough guts to talk about his personal life at length. *Guru Aama* was anyway a dead end with understanding. Shahana or Sushma Kaki would have it no other way. They were blinded by their goodwill for Mani. For them this was an opportunity to secure a future for Mani. At the end of the day, he was tired and drowsy with overthinking. Before supper in the late evening, he usually lit an incense stick in the small temple he had made on a rack in the corner of the house. Sheila had coaxed him into making it. As he closed his eyes to pray, a name played like a tune in his vision…*Uday Yolmo*. Yes, Uday Yolmo, the lawyer mentioned in the will. Here was the awakening moment. But who was he? Mani decided to take the 8 a.m. bus to Darjeeling the coming Saturday to meet him secretly. Maybe he'd know a way out?

Uday Yolmo happened to be one of the best lawyers in town. Mani was guided to his office located behind the swampy vegetable market. After having to wait for some time, Mani was led to the lawyer's cabin by the latter's receptionist. He introduced himself as Maniraj.

"Come in, I was looking forward to meeting you," Uday stood up to greet Mani and even hugged him. "KP was a close friend," he said to explain his behavior to a perplexed Mani.

Mani had no intentions of rekindling relationships here…in fact, he had come to abolish one for once and all. So he took out the will, kept it on Uday's desk and said in one breath.

"I am Maniraj Khaling, son of Giriraj Khaling. The rightful owner is Mohit Pradhan…who is no more. I have no interest in becoming Maniraj Pradhan."

Uday was taken aback. This was definitely not what he was expecting.

Their meeting lasted an hour and the world remained oblivious to what transpired within the confines of the cabin, but thereafter, Mani walked out in freedom, as if the shackles of destiny no longer weighed him down.

CHAPTER 29

Apiece of paper, nevertheless, did not change the way Mani lived his life. It was a sunny Sunday morning. Winter was approaching and *Guru Aama* insisted that the bedding be put outside to sun-dry. Mani, however, was fishing for excuses, because today he had to help Shahana shift. He had to leave for Kurseong to receive her. She had been transferred as a senior nurse to Kurseong Hospital. Rubin was sitting in his cottage, patiently waiting for Mani to join him. Rubin's excitement was palpable even under his calm demeanor.

"Library, library… All the time, library this, library that. I'm sick of your excuses," *Guru Aama* was out of her mind. "Why don't you put up a tent there and spare me? A lazy bumpkin you are… Don't you try my patience anymore. Just because you're earning a little doesn't mean you can do as you wish. You're living in my house and you better do as I say." She was on a screaming spree today.

Rubin was losing his patience. He had to reach Kurseong and *Guru Aama*'s senseless screaming was getting on his nerves.

"Enough *Guru Aama*," he pitched in. "He's not what you're making him out to be, we see him toiling day and night. Think what you'd do without him. Can't you allow him some peace?"

"Oh! Yes, yes, why not?" She continued sarcastically. "It's you people who have made him think like this…all your doing, brainwashing him against me. I feed him but he spends the entire day at your place…not for nothing!" She shifted to picking on Rubin and Sheila now.

Rubin was losing his cool. He was shocked that she did not think twice about lashing out at someone who had gone all out to help her when she had no one by her side. Sheila made it a point to share everything she cooked with her…no neighbor was as considerate. He could not believe one could be so ungrateful and rude. And then this false accusation…It was becoming an ugly spat today.

"Do you even know who he is? You think he's your slave?" Rubin blurted out in a fit of anger.

Mani ran to him and held his hand, shaking his head vigorously so that Rubin would say nothing more.

Guru Aama was unstoppable. "Some prince? Really? I don't care who he is. If he's someone so great, why does he have to stay in my house? He can go where he likes…as if I need him. Go, get lost… whoever you are."

Rubin was red in the face. Mani had hardly seen him so angry. Mani took him inside the house. Sheila looked offended too by *Guru Aama's* words but was quiet in a bid to pacify Rubin.

"She's like that…you people know it. Why bother? Please don't bother." Mani was feeling guilty, as he was the bone of contention. Rubin had spoken in his support. Moreover, he knew *Guru Aama*…she had a foul mouth and insecurity had made her worse, as she tried her best to cover it up with arrogance. Mani could see beneath the brittle shield of her temper.

"How can you take it Mani…and for what?" Rubin said in frustration. "Do you really need to stay with her? Why don't you just leave her and go to the bungalow. You can also stay with Shahana now if you like."

Mani smiled. "Yes, I need to stay with her no matter how she treats me, Uncle. If she wouldn't have brought me home that day, I could have ended up like a dog on the street. Today I'm going to college only because of her. I can never forget that…I shouldn't. And please don't ever tell her about me. It will make everything awkward. I want to finish my graduation. I'll have to leave after that anyway once I get a job. Besides, I have got used to living with her, why make it such an issue? And the bungalow, or what you were referring to… none of it is mine, it never was. It belongs to Mohit Pradhan. Please don't mention it again. I request you." Mani folded his hands.

"And Sister-*Di?* How long will you take to get her here? Then we can all stay together…I think that would be great fun. Don't you think so, Sheila Aunty?" Mani teased Rubin with a chuckle, trying to change the mood of the day.

Rubin nodded and smiled. His fondness for Mani grew even stronger when he realized how much integrity and humility the latter had. He was truly a gem…as his name suggested. Mani and Rubin no longer had to pretend not knowing. Shahana had untied the knots between them in a way that they valued each other even more. They had to proceed so that Shahana could be received on time, but Mani said he'd join them after finishing his chores at home.

Rubin had arranged for a small flat near the hospital for Shahana. Shahana seemed happy and excited about her stay there, and Rubin overjoyed, although restrained in expression. His destination seemed to be slowly walking towards him and he was swelling with hope. Mani was the happiest of them all and most transparent about it too. Now he could meet Shahana more often…and also keep his promise of caring for her. He only hoped she would throw that wretch out of her life and allow Rubin to walk into it.

The days were getting extremely cold. The college was a totally abandoned place as the winter break was on, so Mani went to the Library every alternate day these days. He was at home today, cooking soup and reading a book. *Guru Aama* and Mani had a new family member since a month ago and it had already made the winter less harsh. It was nothing less than *Guru Aama's* lifeline. The colour television, a small red portable box, was the most attractive thing in the house now. It was placed on a table in the middle of the room, as is a deity in a temple, visible from all sides. Children from all over the basti crowded inside *Guru Aama's* small house on Sundays to watch the phenomenon of the decade-'The Ramayana.' Mani enjoyed the liveliness it created since it came, and above all, *Guru Aama's* change of focus. Now all she thought of was ogling at the box and Mani's 'laziness' did not bother her much.

It was late evening, and *Guru Aama* was watching a show for farmers. Mani had cozied up in his bed with his book. Suddenly, there was a knock at the door. Mani was surprised. No one usually ventured out after six these days.

'Who could it be? Must be one those kids, already addicted to the TV,' Mani thought to himself in disgust. There were some ardent 'viewers' in the neighborhood who swarmed in as soon as they guessed the TV was on.

He unlatched the door to find Shahana standing there. She looked worried. Mani was shocked to see her at his doorstep but did not know how to react in *Guru Aama's* presence.

"Come in please," Mani said shyly.

"What happened?" He whispered in her ear.

She looked at him expressionlessly and proceeded to speak to *Guru Aama*. Mani was even more perplexed.

"*Namaste, Guru Aama,*" Shahana greeted the former with folded hands.

"Hmm," *Guru Aama* responded with a nod.

"I'm that nurse you met at the Eden Hospital," Shahana said, introducing herself. "Actually, I'm Mani's cousin...you might have guessed. I happened to meet Mani at the hospital by chance." After a pause, she continued, "He had run away when he was small… and fortunately landed at your place. I am so thankful to God you found him and gave him shelter." Mani had no idea why Shahana was blabbering all this rubbish.

Guru Aama listened, although as stoically as ever…as if it never mattered to her.

Shahana continued. "We had lost hope that he'd ever be found… but I met him at the hospital by God's grace. He made me promise that I don't mention it at home because he did not want to leave you alone. He said you needed him as you were ill. I kept my promise but I had to come today, I did not have a choice. Actually, Mani's father expired… and Mani is the only son… He needs to come with me for the rituals. Please can you allow me to take him for 15 days?"

Mani was totally in shock. Shahana had come with a plan but he could not exactly figure out what. Where was she planning to take him for 15 days? What was happening?

"Hmm…,"*Guru Aama* said, half believingly. "Where is he from? What did his father do? What about his mother?" *Guru Aama's* curiosity was increasing. Her grip on Mani's life seemed to be loosening and she realized that it was Mani who stayed back for her…and it wasn't her who was 'keeping' him, as she'd comfortably thought. Her illusions seemed to be disintegrating.

"His father worked on and off as a labourer in the Cinchona plantations in Mungpoo. Mani does not have a mother. She died when he was small. She was my Aunt, my mother's sister. He has an elder sister who is married now. Mani's father was a hopeless alcoholic. He used to beat Mani all the time. That's why Mani ran away I think…"

Mani felt he'd faint now. Another story was being imposed on his life and he didn't know why. He was already tired of so many identities he was carrying, and now this one? But it was Shahana who was making this up…he had to trust her. She would never do it on a whim. She probably had some very serious reason to do it.

There was a silent pause in the room. After about five minutes

Guru Aama said, "Mani, make tea for your sister…and pack your bags."

Permission granted. The lines of worry on Shahana's face vanished slowly.

They left the house after a while. As soon as they were out in the chill, Mani asked, "Why all this? What happened? Where are we going?"

Shahana said, "*He's* no more. *He* died in the afternoon. Uday asked me to get you as soon as possible for the rites. I knew you'd not know what to do so I came. Your Rubin Uncle asked me to make up this story. We'll stay at my place tonight and leave early morning. You'll have to stay at the bungalow till the rituals are over. Sushma *Kaki* has already reached so you need not worry." Shahana was talking faster than usual. Probably, it was the urgency of the situation. After some thought she said, "I thought you'd guess…by the description of your fictional father. Anyway, let's hurry."

Mani took some time to digest it all. It was happening all too soon. Mani saw Rubin standing a few yards away at the forked junction and understood that Shahana had not come alone in this pitch dark and unsafe times to get him. He felt relieved about it. The hospital ambulance was waiting for them on the main road. Rubin returned after seeing them off.

"You'll come to town, Uncle?" Mani asked Rubin innocently before they separated. He wanted Rubin to be with him.

"Tomorrow," Rubin said, patting his back.

Chapter 30

The 15 days were a totally spaced-out experience for Mani. He was actually internalizing the meaning of death. The lifeless body that lay before him, the stillness of it, evoked a strange vacuum inside him. So many times he used to think in wrath, 'why doesn't *he die*?' But today, Mani felt no anger…instead, hollowness laced with regret. 'If it all came to this…why did he do what he did?' Mani thought in regret. 'What a worthless life it was, what a waste…so many years of mindless living, if only he would have known the value of *his* time. Now it's all over…' Mani realized how fleeting life actually was in retrospect to KP's lifeless body in front of him.

Rubin came in the morning and assisted Uday in getting things ready for the cremation. A crowd was slowly gathering at the gates of the bungalow as news of KP's demise spread across the town. After all, KP's end also signified the end of a lineage. He was taking away with him a legacy that would be written down in the history of the hill town. Mani was no more perturbed by all this though. A serene calm had descended over him after he had given back Mohit what was rightfully his, and had taken off the burden of being 'Mani Pradhan' forever. Even the bungalow no longer disturbed him…the ghosts that were following him no longer lived there, in body or in spirit.

Mani performed the last rites for KP. Uday and his assistants rallied around him, looking into every detail of all that had to be done. Rubin pitched in as and when he got the time, during the next two weeks. Sushma *Kaki* managed the house, and with all the noise around, the bungalow looked as if it had come alive again. Mani had to live an ascetic life for ten days post the last rites, but whenever he found some free time during the day, he cleaned the garden and the wild growth all around.

"There you are again. Can't you sit in peace indoors? I'll get it done, *baba*...why do you have to toil in the freezing cold outside?" Sushma *Kaki* fussed over him like in the old days and Mani smiled at her lovingly.

"All for you, *Kaki*. You're old now, how will you keep the bungalow?" Mani was implying that she stay back there. He, in fact, *wanted* her to stay back. He knew her children did not really care and that she was more at home staying at the bungalow. She had spent her entire life there after all.

Mani even went to 'the prohibited' part of the bungalow, KP's room upstairs. He walked in and looked around. It was of course, like any other room in the bungalow. For some reason, he opened all the curtains, and even the windows, allowing the cold mist to wash away all essence of darkness that may have been left behind within the walls of the room. In a week's time, the bungalow looked neat and livable again.

In the meantime, many well-wishers of the Pradhan family paid a visit to the bungalow to pay their last respects to KP. On the ninth day, a dozen people gathered at the bungalow claiming to be KP's relatives.

"Come in," Sushma *Kaki* had said half-heartedly. "Where were you all when he was ill? He spent his last days orphaned...and now that he's gone, everyone is his kin." She was her sarcastic best, careful not to allow anyone in Mani's vicinity. She was worried they would try influencing the good-soul Mani in their favour. She knew they were here with an ulterior motive.

The next three days passed by in a whiz as there were rituals to be performed from morning to evening. A huge feast was organized on the thirteenth day, and everyone associated with the family in any way attended it. Uday ensured all the poor people who came did not go back hungry. Mani looked at him in admiration and wondered if KP really deserved a friend like him.

The rituals ended and the bungalow was still again with only Sushma *Kaki*, the attendant and Mani inhabiting it. Mani was to return in the afternoon and Sushma *Kaki* was already tearful.

"As if there aren't colleges here…,"she sulked. "Students from far and wide come to study here but he has to return to that small town to study. Go. Let this place become a jungle again."

Mani smiled. He had no words to explain his situation, and telling her that he did not belong here was useless. Nothing would convince her, not even the papers.

Uday came to meet Mani in the afternoon.

"So, what have you thought, Mani?" He asked.

"About?" Mani asked in reply.

"About the bungalow, the property…all that he has left behind. What else?" Uday said.

Mani remained flabbergasted. "Was he still not free?" he thought.

Uday understood the boy's dilemma and spoke to him very gently. "Listen Mani, I understood what you told me…every word of it. I understand your dilemma. I even respect you for your decision… that is why I suggested the making of this Trust and you the Trustee, not the inheritor. But please understand that you are still bound by duty, and ever will be. Even I am bound by duty, till you grow up and are able to manage it on your own."

Mani looked perplexed. Uday read his expression and came closer to him.

"Ok…you did it all for Mohit, didn't you?" He continued affectionately. "You felt he had been wronged…and that you would not let KP erase his identity. Is this not what you told me? But what's the point if you behave in the same manner? KP never valued what he had, not even Mohit, I guess… But you know it all. You should make it right for Mohit's sake…for your sake. Else, there's no difference between you and KP."

Uday was not an accomplished lawyer for nothing. He was attacking where it hurt Mani the most. He knew how to make stubborn minds come around in the gentlest of ways. He continued, "If you want Mohit Pradhan's name to live on, you will have to work on this Trust. It's senseless without a future and it is your responsibility now. Of course, I'm there with you all through but you are the actual Trustee of this Trust. Do you understand how big the responsibility is? And you have chosen it so you should not run away from it. You are, after all, a smart, intelligent boy. This Trust could not have found a more sincere person to helm it." Uday placed his words in such a way that Mani would do it for the sake of his own integrity. He knew it was his weakness, and that he would always choose it over everything else, even his freedom. He would not have come to meet Uday on his own otherwise.

Uday was using the right words to convince Mani. He knew how pliable his mind was at this stage of his life. A desperate search for establishing one's identity is the foremost struggle at this stage, and Uday knew it well. He was also aware what a large legacy KP had left behind and the potential it had if invested in properly. Uday was conscious that in spite of all sentiments that had led to this decision, Mani had the first right to it and he needed to shape Mani to give the Trust a direction, a vision. Uday also understood Mani's potential. Few boys had the sense of values that Mani had at his age. Uday had noticed how responsible and sincere Mani was in the last few days. The only hitch was his stubborn hatred for KP and all that was KP's. Uday had to change Mani's outlook somehow, to make him believe that the responsibility was solely his, and he was successful to a certain degree. It was dawning on Mani that this bungalow and all that the Pradhans owned was not his…but his responsibility. He felt a sense of deep brotherhood towards Mohit, whom he had neither seen nor met, especially in solidarity of the way they had been wronged, and he felt a strong conviction in Uday's words. This would actually be a victory over KP's wrongdoing - Mohit's victory as well as his own. He was slowly being suctioned into this belief.

"What do I have to do?" Mani asked Uday innocently.

Uday was elated. "Oh, nothing as such dear…you finish your graduation first. I'll take care of everything till then. But you need to look after the bungalow, keep coming here once in a while. If you want, you can stay here too…forever." Uday wanted to make it all look very casual so that Mani would not feel overwhelmed all at once.

"Can Sushma *Kaki* stay here?" Mani asked hesitatingly.

"You want her to? Of course she can, if you are willing. In fact, keep the attendant, too. He'll come handy later on." Uday said. "It is good. She will take good care of the place." Uday said to encourage Mani's involvement.

Mani felt overjoyed. The bungalow was a warm place to come to as long as Sushma *Kaki* was there.

Uday gave Mani a warm hug before he left. "Come soon, my boy. And don't forget to meet me whenever you are around. I'll let Shahana know if something urgent comes up."

Before Mani left, he bowed to take Sushma *Kaki's* blessings with folded hands. He read the uncertainty on her face and said, "Don't you think of leaving this place even for a second, got it? Who do you think will look after it in my absence? I have to come here every month now. Uday Sir will see to the expenses. And don't let that attendant go. He'll stay here with you. I'll have the black lentils when I come next. You'll cook it for me, won't you *Kaki*?"

Kaki's eyes were brimming with tears, and, unable to speak, she held Mani's face in her hands affectionately. Her Mani had given her a permanent home at last.

CHAPTER 31

Mani missed the last bus going to the plains. He fortunately found a jeep going up to Kurseong and hopped onto it. He decided to stay over at Shahana's if he did not get a vehicle to go further. At least he would not miss college tomorrow. He could go back to the basti in the evening.

Mani could feel the chill in his ears even through his woolen cap. It felt somewhat light and strange, his tonsured head. He looked at himself in the side-view mirror and thought he looked older by ten years. He also felt years older now…he had so much to do all of a sudden and he wondered what he'd do…and how he'd do it. Heavy with thoughts, Mani was on the verge of dozing off. From a distance, he could hear a hundred voices scream in unison, the volume gradually increasing. 'Jai Gorkha, Jai Gorkha' echoed in the air. He got up, startled, thinking it was a dream, but he could see it right before his eyes…innumerable flames approaching him with one collective voice. A huge procession was coming up around the bend with inflamed torches. It looked intimidating in the dark as one could only see the light and sound approaching, getting bigger as it got closer. The few vehicles plying had parked aside to let the procession pass. The rhythm of the slogans moved the insides of Mani, and he began palpitating. Mani wondered who the faces in the dark were, what made them believe in what they were doing…what made them become one voice of solidarity resonating in the skies? Solidarity is quite a shallow phenomenon. It is not found in happiness; human nature is such that people usually like being happy in comparison-relatively, rather than completely in themselves. People usually truly unite only when there is a sense of deep inadequacy in each heart, reaching out to one another for support to fill it. People are not wired to fight another's battle. Even in a collective, each is fighting his or her own inadequacies, trying to complete his or her own life. Mani was beginning to learn this, although not consciously. Circumstances were totally different for him today, only because KP was a wrong man… and had wronged his own son as well as Mani, hence the solidarity. But would things be the same if KP had been a good father…to his son as well as to Mani? Would it even be the same if Mohit were alive but unable to accept Mani as a legitimate shareholder? Maybe not… maybe one would not have met a glorified version of Mani then, but an ordinary boy chasing his greed. It was only because Mani was also fighting his own sense of incompleteness, a hollow inadequacy that was fuelling him to find his voice in that inflamed cry for freedom. At present, he had a number of homes; he did not need to think about where he'd go tomorrow. He knew *Guru Aama* was terrified of him leaving her alone under the veil of her abhorrent behavior…he knew the entire bungalow and much more, everything was dependent on him for its deliverance…but his heart, his heart was still craving for that one home, his yellow cottage that the fire took away from him forever. Nothing else, no riches, qualified as, or made up for a home for him…and it was this inadequacy that was driving him to do what he was doing, no matter what the situation was. He stood by the procession, screaming 'Jai Gorkha' with all the air in his lungs…it was a vent for all the suppressed tears his heart was filled with - a deep longing to be home, his home.

People got into their vehicles again. The driver of the jeep said, "Come on, hurry or you'll be left to scream alone here…got to reach as soon as possible, never know what may happen."

Mani got in and asked, "What may happen? Why *Daju?*"

"Oh, don't you know? The old man has a new plan now… indefinite strike from tomorrow. Do or die for Gorkhaland." The driver said, focusing on driving to get out of the town as soon as possible.

"Oh, really?" Mani looked surprised. He had been in another world the last few days, hardly listening to the radio or reading newspapers as he usually did in the Library. He was worried now. He had already stayed away from the Library and college…and now an indefinite strike meant staying locked up in the basti…would he even reach there?

"People are already suffering, no income since the last two years…barely surviving on two meals. What is left to fight for? The old man is almost permanently living in Delhi now…what does he know about survival here?" The driver was openly cynical, probably because he knew Mani was the only passenger.

Mani could see what he was saying…he could see it all around, but he knew that no sensible person openly said what the driver was saying. It could be a breach of trust…a betrayal of sorts, and he could lose his head if he voiced his opinion is the wrong place. Everyone was to believe in the greater vision of the movement…and were set out to believe so in the beginning, without knowing that it would test their will to survive…it would get tiring and formidable. Thousands in their innocence had believed that voicing a few slogans for some days would beget them their land…in the beginning, it sounded exciting too. But almost four harrowing years had passed with barely any accomplishment…instead, with the loss of dear ones, burning down and shattering of homes, no income, and even starvation of many inconspicuous stomachs in the nooks of the Himalayas. Very few were prepared to face what they were facing…passions failed to be roused now…the agitation was losing its vigour in the face of hunger.

Mani stayed back at Shahana's that night and left for the basti at dawn, in a van carrying milk cans.

So began a new regimen with the strike. Bored of having nothing to do, Mani spent his days at Gurung Sir's house where he studied and made almost sugarless black tea (as milk was scarcely available and Sir refused any such favour to be provided with from any faction) for the 'opportunists' who never stopped pouring in. Mani got to listen to conversations that shaped his cerebrum to a finesse no formal education could. They made him think and ponder. Sometimes a desire with a sincere intention is answered in strange ways. Mani always had a tremendous inclination and zeal to learn, to know. He was drawn like a magnet to the world of books and what they held. And here was destiny that had unusually placed him in a place where he could soak it all up like a sponge. It was up to him, to do that bit, to realize that it was an opportunity. He had access to an erudite teacher, a philosopher par excellence, the best books, and the quietude to absorb everything he could access.

Mani spent the nights at *Guru Aama's*, and the mornings and evenings were spent finishing chores so that he could save the day to be at Gurung Sir's place. A major part of his work at home meant thinking of a new recipe involving the Chayote squash…for that was the only vegetable available these days. No part of the plant remained unused, so sometimes it was the squash, sometimes the roots, and sometimes the soft stems and tendrils, each cooked in different ways. Sheila Aunty helped Mani with the recipes, for all *Guru Aama* did was complain about how awful the food was these days. Sometimes some small seller from some basti would come with a different produce like radishes and carrots, and it would be swept away in no time. It was all about luck if you got to buy some, and a celebration later, for the meal would include a new ingredient. What joy! Someone basking in abundance would never know this joy.

While families struggled with depleting ration and the mounting stress as to how long this situation would extend, the movement was at its peak as far as protests were concerned. Violence erupted in pockets and the subdivision headquarters were being covered by patrolling CRPF battalions that had been deployed to curb insurgency. Gradually, a normal sight to behold was that of a burning basti. As dusk approached, one could see flames rising from a yonder hill. A dull pain emerged in the insides of the heart as the ravenous fire spread across the green hills, but all one could do was look away in regret and go back to the squashes. Life was becoming a strange mix of chaos and stillness. It appeared as if nothing was moving, not even the breeze between the leaves of trees. But suddenly something pulsating happened...like the spreading of news that a head separated from the torso had been left for display in the town's marketplace, or all of a sudden in the stillness of the night, one could hear slogans of –'*Bangal hamro chiyan ho* (Bengal is our graveyard)'- and then witness a procession passing by with burning torches and hearts. A purely engaging phenomenon was the 'raid.' The anti-terrorist act had equipped the police and CRPF to catch hold of suspect youth and trouble-makers in anticipation of violence, so out of the blue, one would witness a grand chase where youngsters ran all over the place to find hideouts and shelter and the booted men would soon follow, pushing their way around and knocking on all doors with their rifles to check for hiding subjects.

In one such instance, Mani stood trembling for two whole hours while Lalit kept hiding under *Guru Aama's* bed. The rifled men did knock on the door ruthlessly, but *Guru Aama* saved the day...she coincidentally got into a choking fit and Mani was so flustered bringing her water and stroking her back, the entire attention was misdirected. The soldier poked the wooden partition walls, dropped a few utensils but thankfully left the bed alone.

Observing how whimsical everything was these days, Gurung Sir opined, "How convenient it is to have your way around terrorism. Who knew it would turn out to be an ugly militant war… a violent power struggle between two power centers. It is people who are ultimately suffering. It has never worked this way. The moment power starts concentrating in one person or party, democracy suffers. Can there be freedom without democracy?" He was saddened by the violent direction the agitation had taken and the hostile approach of the government. "There is no governance…only suppression, and sadly, at both ends."

The strike was finally called off after 40 long days. People breathed again…this time asking for normalcy more than anything else. Mani rushed to town to see Shahana, go to college and buy groceries, in that order.

"I've never been so busy," Shahana said. "So many patients with injuries these days, so many emergency cases. Didn't suffer for supplies though; that's the advantage of working at the hospital." She added, to rest Mani's worry that she had been starving. "It must have been really tough for you people, isn't it? See how worn out and thin you look."

"Oh yes, the wonders of the squash…that's what we've been eating for over a month. I'm dying to sink my teeth into meat. I've almost forgotten the taste of it." Mani exaggerated and Shahana laughed.

"Ok…I'll cook some for you tomorrow if available in the market. Get going to college now, I have to go the electricity office too." Shahana said.

"Oh! So that is why I'm being shooed away…electricity office, huh," Mani teased her. He thought Rubin had called her over.

"Will you shut up," she said with a slight blush on her face. "I have to straighten out some long-pending hospital bills…"

"Hmmm…40 days…a long time if you miss someone too much…" Mani replied in a long-drawn tone to tease her. Shahana threw a comb at him, saying, "Will you get lost?"

Mani laughed and fled, saying, "Ok, I'm going…I'm going…."

A normal day became the biggest luxury in the days to come…a day when one could buy and eat what one wanted to, a day when no one had to hide in fear of being caught or killed, either by the police or the rogues, a day when no houses were burning on a yonder hill and a day you could choose peace above everything else. The violent unrest was finding less support with every passing day, although no one was explicitly vocal about it. The agitation was retracting very slowly and subtly. Even the honchos were realizing that the fiery speeches were no longer igniting a suitable response…they could not use the people for a cause without feeding them. In retrospect, an agitation was launched dismissing Maslow's hierarchy of needs. A sense of identity and esteem is at level 4. One cannot fight for it by compromising the first three levels. Food is a foundational hierarchy…a basic need, not a choice.

CHAPTER 32

If collateral damage of the agitation was to be accounted for, the ones to bear the most glaring loss, even though remaining largely unacknowledged by the society, were the students. A generation's education had been put at stake, a secure future compromised for thousands. The loss of lives was numbered, valuation of damaged property established by the press, but no one mentioned the loss of education. It was not blatant but many children would perhaps carry the burden of this struggle for the longest time. Mani, Neetu and many others like them were living witnesses. They had had no classes for months, had no inkling of what they were studying and why, and had no idea if they would be able to appear for their university exams coming up soon. Students were lucky if they reached school or college, they were lucky if teachers showed up, they were lucky if they had a supply of books and stationery, and were the luckiest if they could appear for their exams without a hitch.

Classes were always uncertain but these days the Library started filling up as students relied on themselves for their education. One could even see Dhruva digging books rather than mobilizing students. He had missed his exams the last two years...the first year he had been busy boycotting the University exams, and the second year, he was caught in an ambush. Probably this year, his personal loss was staring hard at him.

Neetu came to the Library too but not exactly to study. She preferred sitting opposite Mani and watching him engrossed in his work or books. Many times, Mani grew conscious of her stare and even chided her for not studying seriously, but she just smiled breezily.

"You don't even sing these days…it's been such a long time. You've become such a bore." She said one day. "Can't we go someplace…and spend time singing, just hanging out?"

"Oh yes! And the University will sing a lullaby for me and put me to sleep forever," Mani retorted to evade her. He was aware Neetu was eager to rekindle old times, but he could never tell her that it hurt him the most. It reminded him of what a fool he was. That they were drawn to each other was a fact but Mani concealed it better. Neetu was dismayed often for he never reciprocated her rather undisguised feelings, but still carried hope that he would come back to her some day.

"Oh…just say you don't want to. As if I don't know," Neetu said, losing her calm slightly. "Always running away from the truth… Why did you come back at all? Why did you help me when you hate being with me so much? To show me how noble you are, right?"

Mani had not imagined his evasion would trigger such a reaction. He looked up from his work, shocked to see Neetu on the verge of tears. She walked off in a huff. Mani ran after her, not really knowing what to say.

"Neetu…wait…" he called out.

"Don't you dare come anywhere around me. I've had enough of your greatness." Neetu was blabbering endlessly. "You can keep your favours to yourself."

Mani was still confused about what irritated Neetu, but one thing was for sure. He did not feel at peace. He knew his intentions were not as were being interpreted by her, but he also did not know what his deepest intentions were. He thought reaching out to her when she was ill had been about forgiveness, but it was long over. Being with her or having her in his life was a habit now…and he was scared of losing her again, although he never confronted the feeling for a reason. He had comfortably thought she would always be around now. But her getting upset and going away made him feel empty and disturbed. Neetu, on the other hand, only saw the surface of Mani's behavior…and interpreted his evasion as dispassion. She was tired of carrying guilt and she thought Mani made her feel worse with his endless favours. They were weighed down in truth by their own web of misjudgments and inhibitions, and therefore, were unable to give each other a chance.

———————

This time, the University exams rolled by relatively peacefully. Neetu and Mani exchanged glances when they saw each other but Neetu was too uptight and Mani too hesitant to talk. It was Mani's last paper. He left the exam hall and stretched out in the open corridor. He felt free at last and just loitered in the corridor. After some time, he noticed Neetu walk out of one of the doors, too. He wanted to call out to her on impulse, but was hesitant, thinking maybe it would upset her. He, however, started following her. As they reached the college slope, it started raining heavily. Neetu took out an umbrella. Mani was still walking behind her in the dilemma whether he should talk to her or not. But the more he dwelled on it, the more desperate he grew to talk to her. He walked faster and simply ducked in to get under her umbrella.

"YOU?? How dare you?" Neetu said in a fit of temper.

"I'm not carrying an umbrella," Mani said timidly.

"Then go get drenched… Go die. I couldn't be bothered," Neetu argued.

Mani firmly caught hold of her hand around the handle, which she was trying to pull away from him.

"Will you stop trying now?" He said calmly. "Ok, where are we going?" He said in a jovial tone.

"Oh...so doing me another favour just because I said it the other day, right? You'll never get it." She was still unable to get over her anger. "You think I'm this desperate woman and you this GREEEAAAAT man out to do some charity, right?"

Mani put his arm around her and whispered in her ears in a naughty tone. "No...this time you're doing the charity...Do me a favour please, I'm the desperate man." Mani laughed out loudly. Neetu could not help laughing along and she punched him and pinched him saying, "How I hate you...you mean thing. Making fun of me all the time..."

They spent the afternoon together; arguing, getting drenched in the lonely woods and cuddling over hot tea and snacks in the nearby stalls. Mani sang songs in her ear in between, sometimes laced with his feelings and sometimes to tease her. There was definitely a thread between them that could not be broken. They were meant to be together, in love or in war.

August was around the bend and Mani was enjoying a few casual days lazing around at the basti before his classes resumed in a week. He was contemplating slipping away secretly to Soureni for a day, to find out if the debris of his childhood could still be found... maybe he needed to go one last time for closure. His thoughts were filled with remorse. He had seen everything up in flames and knew nothing remained. 'Even the ashes must have been swept away by almost a decade of rains,' he thought to himself.

Just then, Rubin came back from work and said, "What are you guys up to today? I'm sure some mischief...both of you had ample time today." He was in a happy mood and was fooling around with Sheila and Mani.

"It seems you had a good day today," Sheila said, implying Shahana. "Tell us...if there's something you want us to know."

"You people really have nothing to do." Rubin laughed at Sheila's adamant resolve to get him married. "Did you listen to the news Mani?" He suddenly changed the topic.

"No…why?" Mani asked apprehensively.

"I believe it's over." Rubin said. "Talks to call off the agitation are going on. The old man has settled for a Council."

"Really?" Mani said. "After all this mayhem…"

"Hmmm," Rubin agreed. "It isn't unanimous though. Some in the party are not agreeing…however, people are tired now and there is so much pressure from the government to bring back peace to the hills."

"My department has also finally resumed work," he continued. "I'll be going to Soureni and Mirik next week. You people want to come along?"

"First let's ask Sister-*Di* to take leave that day," Mani said slyly.

"You two are impossible," Rubin shook his head and smiled.

"As if you don't want her to come…huh," Sheila added. "So when are we going exactly? Mani will convince *bahini* and we'll all have a nice picnic by the lake. Agreed…everyone?" She was looking at Rubin for his affirmation.

Mani jumped at the idea, in fact more in amazement as to how his thoughts had travelled to Rubin. He wanted to invite Neetu too but was extremely shy and conscious to say anything before Rubin. He thought he'd tell Shahana later.

The day finally arrived. It was a day of merriment after a long time…the entire region was, in fact, loosening up since the news of the calling off of the agitation had spread. Four to five years had passed away in anxiety, unsure of how the next moment would be. They had been spent counting losses for many across. Now people were gearing to revive their lives, some trying to rebuild from scratch. Mani too had mixed feelings. Apart from celebrating life once again, he was also going on a secret mission...to close forever, an empty chapter of his life. Maybe he would never look back after today. Maybe he would be able to erase the memories of the gigantic flames forever.

CHAPTER 33

Rubin, Sheila and Mani met Shahana and Neetu in Kurseong. Rubin had booked a vehicle from there to go to Mirik and Soureni. Shahana was wearing a pair of jeans with a long red and white printed top. She had done up her hair neatly in a ponytail. She looked years younger and reminded Mani of the old Shahana he'd met at the bungalow. He smiled at her in adoration and quickly looked at Rubin who could hardly take his eyes off her. But it was Neetu who dazzled everyone with her freshness. She was wearing a long pastel blue dress with beige Roman sandals. She had tied her hair with a printed scarf and looked like a dream. Mani stood mesmerized while Rubin and Sheila looked at each other questioningly.

"She's Neetu, Mani's friend," Shahana said with a smirk. "I brought her along." Mani looked away feeling conscious. Rubin and Shahana smiled at each other knowingly.

Sheila Aunty teased all of them, saying, "Oh! What planning! That means only the driver is available for me today, right?" All of them laughed happily.

They all got on to the jeep and set off for Mirik. Rubin sat in front next to the driver. Sheila, Shahana, and Neetu sat in the middle and

Mani sat alone at the back. Rubin kept looking at Shahana through the rear-view mirror. Shahana was conscious and blushed silently. Sheila and Neetu had already started playing the song game and were making the most of the trip. Mani was soaking in every inch of earth he was crossing. The beautiful hilltops carpeted endlessly with tea gardens, and the infinite range of the Himalayas spreading up to the neighbouring landscape of Nepal. He was totally lost in the scenic beauty. Neetu nudged him once in a while to pass some toffees or wafers. She knew there was something on his mind but was unable to ask. She looked deeply into his eyes with an inquiring expression, but he simply shook his head and smiled lovingly at her.

Mirik was approaching…Mani knew from the dark pine trees that emerged on one side and the heavy mist around them. Mani's heart started beating fast. How well he knew this landscape. He could not act as if he was seeing it all for the first time and squeal in delight like Sheila or Neetu…his heart was too heavy with memories.

"We'll stop at Soureni first…," Rubin said to inform everyone. "I'll get down there. You people can go ahead to the lakeside. I'll join you all later after finishing work."

Mani's heart skipped a beat. Very soon he would be on the road where his yellow cottage stood…he knew the bend. He was dying to tell everyone about himself, he wanted to show them his old school… his cottage, his home, but something restrained him. And before he knew it, the jeep zoomed by. He first shut his eyes with fear, but in a second, craned his neck to see his burnt cottage.

There was, however, nothing there but a dense locality. A whole lot of houses had cropped up and he could hardly make out where his cottage stood. Instead, he saw a long structure like a warehouse painted in green. He turned away, dismayed. Even the debris did not remain now. A piece of his life had indeed been wiped away into oblivion. There was nothing to come back to. It was over. All his hopes died instantly.

The jeep was parked in front of the Soureni post office. Tired of sitting, everyone got down to stretch their limbs and feel the outside air. The women went into a nearby teashop to wash and refresh themselves. Rubin got busy talking to an acquaintance he met. Mani walked around barefoot for some time, feeling the earth of his hometown under him. It felt warm and soothing. He remembered his father going to work to some post office but was not sure if it was the same one. He had a sudden urge to go and ask someone…at least some colleague would know what had happened to the house. He went inside and walked around, taking a good look at all the employees, but remained confused as to whom he'd ask. Thinking it was a pointless attempt, he left the place after a few minutes. He made up his mind to not look back ever now. There was really no point. He was probably getting embroiled in futile sentiments that would take him nowhere. He consciously decided to let everything be and instead make the most of today with his people.

All of them except Rubin left for the lakeside. The women thoroughly enjoyed themselves boating and Mani loved their happy faces. They ate at a popular outlet and chose a dry grassy stretch beside the lake to lie down under the warm sun. Neetu showed her affection unabashedly, pulling at Mani's cheeks and crossing her arm with his, while Mani grew conscious. Shahana looked at him and smiled with a happy gleam in her eyes.

Sheila Aunty teased them saying, "Well, it seems this Tika I'll have more than one new member in my house."

Shahana blushed while Neetu smiled looking at Mani.

Rubin came looking for them in the late afternoon. "Oh my…I went around the whole lake looking for you people. What a cosy hideout you all have chosen!" He lay down on the grass, relaxing.

"Why don't you take *bahini* for a walk around also, now that you've come? She's been guarding me all this while. I have these kids with me right here." She looked at Mani hoping he would get the message and second her.

"Yes, yes…in fact, take a boat ride once more. Sister-*Di* really liked it." Mani added.

Shahana hesitated but before she could say anything, Rubin got up and said, "Let's go, Shahana."

"I'll doze off for a few minutes…don't you kids disappear, got it?" Sheila Aunty said, covering her face with her stole. Mani watched Rubin and Shahana walk away slowly in between the pines. He could see them at a distance, holding hands, and he smiled to himself in contentment. Neetu meanwhile was watching him look at them and took his hands in hers as soon as he smiled.

He came closer to her and smiled at her. Neetu looked at him and said, "Will you believe me if I say something?"

"Of course I will…what is it?" Mani replied, thinking it would be one of her crazy observations yet again.

"I love you," she whispered in his ears.

Mani was totally taken aback. This was something he was least prepared for. He did not know how to handle mush. He stared at her blankly.

"Will you never be able to love me?" She asked imploringly. She mistook his lack of response for rejection.

Mani said nothing but spontaneously kissed her forehead. He knew he could not stay apart from her. After some time, he told her about himself…about every tear he had cried…every night he had spent under the open sky…and every fold and bend of his life as he had experienced it. Tears streamed down Neetu's eyes as she listened intently to his every word, every wound that he opened up for the first time for someone else to see…

At the end of his story, he asked, "Will you still stay with me Neetu, now that you know who I am…never to leave me alone?"

She nodded in between her sobs and kissed Mani's hands locked in hers.

The evening sky was covered in red and orange streaks. All of them got up to return home, refreshed and rejuvenated, and above all, not alone. Rubin asked the driver to stop the jeep once more at the tea stall as they had a long way to go.

"It's getting windy now. Come, let's have a cup of tea before we leave," Rubin said. They all entered the stall. Mani was just about to cross the road and join them when he saw a very familiar face leave the post office.

It was like a bolt from the blue and Mani was shocked to his pores. 'Am I hallucinating? How is it possible?' Mani thought to himself, his steps carrying him spontaneously to follow that face.

The frail man in front of him walked slowly and he was close behind.

Dazed to the hilt, Mani called out, "Sir...Sir..."

The man turned around and Mani couldn't believe his eyes.

"Sir, please may I know your name? Sir, do you work at the post office?"

The man said nothing. He thought probably some ruffian was trying to act smart...it wasn't unusual these days.

"Sir...please listen to me. I need to ask you something." Mani was calling out to him with folded hands.

The man continued walking nonchalantly.

Then Mani suddenly said in desperation, "Sir...do you know Maniraj Khaling, son of Giriraj Khaling?"

The man instantly turned around. In a frail breaking voice, he muttered, "My son...Ahh...yes. He died in the fire. You...are you his friend?"

Mani did not say a word but sobbed profusely as he embraced his father. He was home at last.

A home is not that piece of earth you draw fences around. It is that part of the unfathomable blue sky where your wings can soar across, that haven you call your own.

GLOSSARY

Chapter 1

- *Sala*: An offensive word in Nepali; brother-in-law

- *Harami*: An offensive word in Nepali; sinner

- *Ae*: Slang in Nepali, usually used to call out to someone younger than oneself

- *Hajur*: 'Yes' in Nepali, especially when spoken with respect

- *Kaka*: Paternal Uncle in Nepali; Father's younger brother

- *Pakodas*: Vegetable or Meat coated in seasoned batter and deep-fried

Chapter 2

- *Oye*: Slang in Nepali, usually used to call out to someone younger than oneself

Chapter 3

-*Badi*: Aunt; Father's elder brother's wife in Nepali

- *Kya re*: Slang in Hindi, usually used to call out to someone younger than oneself meaning what's up

- *Keta*: boy in Nepali

- *Kaki*: Aunt in Nepali

- *Chowk*: A marketplace in the middle of the town

Chapter 4

- *Baba*: An expression used to address a child with fondness in Nepali

Chapter 6

- *Bada*: Uncle; Father's elder brother in Nepali

- *Dada*: Elder brother: Nepali, Bengali

- *Kiranti*: A sub-caste of the community; a warrior class inclined to join the army

- *Limbu*: A Nepali sub-caste

Chapter 7

- *Da*: Elder brother in Nepali

Chapter 9

- *Kichu*: An expression used to address a child with fondness

- *Ho*: 'Yes' in Nepali

Chapter 11

- *Kaka*: Uncle in Nepali; Father's younger brother

- *Chhora*: Son in Nepali

Chapter 12

- *Kancha*: Youngest one in Nepali

- *Namaskar*: Indian greeting; aka 'Namaste'

- *Guru Aama*: Way of addressing female teachers in Nepali; literal meaning: 'teacher-mother'

- *Basti*: Small settlement in Nepali/Hindi

- *Chhema*: Aunt; Mother's sister in Nepali

Chapter 14

- *Tika*: A Dussehra ritual of the Nepali community; Applying vermilion on the forehead as a token of affection

- *Puja*: Ceremonial worship; sometimes also referring to the Dussehra festival

Chapter 15

- *Bhai*: Younger brother in Nepali

- *Shaheeds*: Martyrs

- *Pranta Parishad*: One of the first organizations set up with the aim of attaining statehood in the region

- *Yamduts*: Messengers of Lord Yamraj, the Lord of death in Hindu Mythology

Chapter 16

- *Churan*: Tangy sweet balls prepared with tamarind and sugar; usually had as a mouth freshener for better digestion

- *Maato ko balidan ko lagi aaunuhos*: "Come all to sacrifice for your homeland;" a slogan used to arouse the masses to join the movement

- *Buro*: Old man

- *Chhya*: A slang used to express disgust or frustration

Chapter 17

- *Kamaan*: Tea Garden; The tea gardens are the most significant locations in the region

- *Maato*: Mother Earth; Homeland

Chapter 18

- *Angeethi*: An earthen stove used to light a fire

- *Tata*: Elder sister in Nepali

- *Hara Kiri*: Ritual suicide practiced by the warrior class to avoid disgrace in Japan by ripping open their abdomens with a dagger; self-destruction

- *Arre yaar, kaisa?*: "Hey friend…howdy?"; Hindi

Chapter 19

- *Dharna(s)*: Procession, protest: Hindi, Nepali

- *Dhanyawad*: Thank you: Hindi, Nepali

- *Bhadralok*: Gentleman in Bengali

Chapter 20

- *Vidya*: Knowledge; Hindi, Bengali, Nepali

- *Ei to*: "Yeah, just this…" or "Exactly this…;" affirmative expression: Bengali

- *Ei je*: "Here you…"; expression used to call out to someone: Bengali

- *Chakri to*: "It's my job, you see…;" said in the context of its importance; Bengali

Chapter 21

- *Som*: Buddy, friend: Nepali

Chapter 22

- *Bandh*: Closed, general strike; Hindi, Nepali, Bengali

Chapter 23

- *Ek dom*: Ek dum (Hindi), meaning 'at once' spoken with the roundish effect of Bengali pronunciation.

Chapter 24

- *Khada*: A white shawl used as a token of respect; used in various traditions of the region, especially by Buddhists

- *Bahini*: Younger sister; Nepali

- *Daju*: Elder brother; Nepali

Chapter 26

- *Chor*: Thief; Hindi, Nepali, Bengali

- *singharas*: Or Samosas; Hindi, Nepali, Bengali. A savoury Indian snack with a triangular crispy exterior stuffed with spicy potato filling

www.ingramcontent.com/pod-product-compliance
Lightning Source LLC
LaVergne TN
LVHW040001200726
843493LV00005B/1087